THE REALM OF ALBION

By Marcus Pitcaithly

MMXIV

I0680502

"I'll speak a prophecy ere I go:
When priests are more in word than matter;
When brewers mar their malt with water;
When nobles are their tailors' tutors,
No heretics burned, but wenches' suitors,
Then shall the realm of Albion
Come to great confusion...
This prophecy Merlin shall make; for I live before his time."

~ William Shakespeare, *King Lear*

"... his mother, Penarddun, the daughter of Beli..."

~ *Branwen the Daughter of Llyr*,
the only surviving mention of Penarddun

To my beloved wife
Becca

First published by Marcus Pitcaithly, October 2014
© Marcus Pitcaithly 2014
ISBN (print edition): 978-0-9556864-4-3

Preface

This book, and the cycle of which it will be the first volume, had their genesis in my childhood, when I first read Lewis Spence's *Legends and Romances of Spain*. There was something about the story of Amadis, despite its Renaissance Spanish provenance, which felt distinctively Celtic to me, resonating with the Welsh and Irish mythology I loved, in a way which made its ancient British setting feel thoroughly appropriate. Many years later, when I first considered writing a version of the Amadis romance rooted in real history, I ran up against the fact that the story was absolutely incompatible with its supposed setting in the first century C.E.: but I quickly realised that, if one projects it back to the previous century, everything falls into place, El Patin's invasion of Britain directly corresponding to Julius Caesar's in 55-54 B.C.E.

Furthermore, that period surrounding Caesar's invasion was rich in other myths and legends. The Second Branch of the Mabinogi directly ties in to it, which brings in the other three branches, as well as the story of *King Lear*, while the massive *Perceforest* romance, recently translated by Nigel Bryant, also centres around Caesar's invasion.

The Mabinogi connection brought into the story a shadowy character who has long fascinated me: Penarddun, the mother of the Second Branch's central characters. She is only a name in the sources, but the single fleeting mention of her hints at a fascinating untold story. The result is that the cycle became far broader than I originally intended; Amadis barely features in this volume, which focuses principally on my reinterpretation of the Lear / Llyr myth, from Penarddun's point of view.

(It is worth remarking here that I have not consciously set out to deconstruct or respond to Shakespeare's version.

Although I have freely drawn on *King Lear*, I have tried to make this a new retelling of what is after all a legend much older than that monumental play, and to avoid necessarily disappointing paraphrases of its literally inimitable verse.)

Perceforest begins, at first sight absurdly, with an excursion to Britain by Alexander the Great, which seems all the more bizarre when Caesar turns up only a few decades later – but Caesar himself tells us that a real Continental European warlord, the Belgic king Diviciacus, did wield power in Britain within a generation of his arrival. Identifying the romance's "Alexander" with Diviciacus thus became as obvious as identifying El Patin with Caesar. (I have not let that stop me using characters whom *Perceforest*'s author lifted from pre-existing romances about Alexander.)

Linking the romances with real history in this way gave me a vast array of material to work with, even before bringing in the Irish legends set in the same period. Making connections and identifications of this kind, even though I know they are my own invention, feels almost like detective work, as if I am uncovering a true history from flawed sources, rather than creating my own version of a mix of folk legends and other people's fictions. Perhaps this is my historian's training showing itself. In any case, it has made planning and writing these books enormous fun.

<u>A note on names</u>

Many of the sources I have drawn on for this book are non-Celtic and full of inauthentic names. When faced with a name that shows obviously the wrong linguistic roots (Greek, Latin, French, English), I have usually translated it to a Welsh near-equivalent: but where such roots are not immediately apparent, I have generally kept the name as it has come to me. Many characters therefore have names that would not pass a philological investigation: but given that even the genuinely Celtic names are a hodge-podge of ancient Britannic (as filtered through Latin sources) and modern Welsh, which despite their lineal relationship do not look much alike, I hope that the inauthentic names will not stand out too badly.

In these circumstances, I see little point in including a pronunciation guide. The rules of modern Welsh pronunciation are irrelevant to fictional names derived from French and Spanish romances, and hardly seem applicable even to the actual Welsh names used here, given that the language had not yet evolved. Penarddun's name would now be pronounced "Pen-ar-thin", but the pronunciation that looks natural to an English speaker ("Pen-ar-doon") might actually be closer to its Old Welsh origins (though even those are a few centuries after this period). Pronounce names however you like, only bearing in mind that W, when used as a vowel, represents an "oo" sound.

As for place names, I have adopted the following rules: where the modern name derives directly from one which could plausibly have been in use in the pre-Roman period, I have used it. (I have also kept common English prefixes such as "Port", that might be applied to a new town founded now.) Where it does not, I have used the ancient name, if it is known.

Otherwise I have identified the real sites with ones from the romance sources, or invented the most plausible names I can.

CONTENTS

Chapter 1: *The Way to the West*

"Thus to our grief the obsequies performed
Of our too late deceased and dearest queen...
Let us request your grave advice, my lords..."
~ *The True Chronicle History of King Leir*

The Belgic Road, 84 B.C.E.

Penarddun had never travelled more than a day's journey from Dun Belin before she was sent away.

She had never left the lands her father ruled; never slept in a house whose lord or lady was not of her tribe; never been away from her brothers and sister for more than a night.

She was fourteen years old, and a Princess of the Trinovantes. She had always known that she must eventually be married to some allied prince, though she had hoped that his kingdom might be near and the date of the wedding far away – though the children of kings were often married many years earlier than those of lesser houses. But now she suddenly found herself in a wagon, rattling towards the west, wrapped tightly in a wolf-skin cloak, but still shivering, and still not quite able to believe that it was all real.

She had been told nothing of the marriage negotiations. When ambassadors from the west had come, two dark Silurian chiefs with curled hair, enveloping cloaks, and thick accents, her father had spoken vaguely of border arrangements. She had been curious about the men: she had never seen a Silurian before, their far corner of Britain seeming as remote as the stars: but the purpose of their mission had not interested her, until Belin had summoned her into his presence and brusquely informed her that she was to return with them to the west and marry their widowed king.

Of course she had fought it. After the initial shock, she had wept, and begged him to give her a year or two longer, to find somebody nearer home – she had even suggested one or two names. But Belin had shaken his head impatiently, and told her:

"They are princelings of no account, not fit for the eldest daughter of the High King. Every tribe that borders ours, I have already claimed homage from – and beyond them, even as far as the Deepwood and the Severn Sea." He put an arm around her shoulders. "I would not cast you away on such petty men. Llyr ap Bladud is different. He is a High King, like me, a lord of many tribes. The Silures are the most feared warriors in the west: we must be friends with them. Llyr wants a wife, to give him a son: I will not refuse him."

Penarddun stifled her tears; she had long ago learned that there was no arguing with the High King.

"What kind of man is he?" she asked.

"A mighty king," said Belin. "A great warrior in his time. A conqueror."

"In his time?" she said. "Then he is old?"

Belin looked away.

"He has been King of the Silures for many years," he said uncomfortably. "I believe he succeeded his father around the time of the Belgic invasion, a little before I became king here."

"Thirty years ago!" exclaimed Penarddun in horror.

"What does it matter?" snapped Belin. "This is your duty, to your family, your people, and your king. Do you want me to call in the Silures and reject their alliance? The law says I must do that – your choice is your right. Shall I tell them we must be enemies because their king is too old for you?"

She bowed her head.

"No, Father," she said quietly. "I will go."

And so, after a swift round of farewells, and tearful embraces from her brother Imanuentius and sister Fesonas – her youngest brother Nennius had been sent away the year before to be fostered by one of the tetrarchs of the Cantiaci – she was now trundling towards the kingdom of Llyr. Outside the wagon rode the two ambassadors; a small troop of soldiers; Speaker Maddan, the Druid tasked with leading the delegation; and Awel. Penarddun knew little of Awel: a scrawny, wild-haired peasant boy from somewhere upriver, a Cassian perhaps, he had been brought under guard to Dun Belin a few weeks earlier, and placed in the care of the High King's Druids, for reasons nobody would explain to her.

They had already left the Trinovantic lands, and crossed those of the Cassi; they were approaching Ancalitan territory as the sun went down. They had made swift progress for the time of year: though it was bitingly cold, there had been little rain, and the roads were in none too bad a state. Penarddun did not know whether to be thankful or to wish them worse.

Her attendant Sicora rode in the wagon with her; but they had spoken little over the course of this first day. Sicora wanted to speak, to try to comfort the Princess, but did not feel able to press her: and now she had her own reason to be silent. The lands they were entering were those of Sicora's tribe, though she had not been there since infancy: it was the High King's practice to take the children of noble families from the tribes that submitted to him, and bring them up at Dun Belin. They were part hostage, part retainer, part ward – but all Trinovantic. Those who returned home would do so speaking the ruling tribe's dialect, and dressing like them; even if they changed back their clothes and accent, they would bear Trinovantic tattoos on their flesh.

Sicora bit her lip when the wagon driver called back that they were leaving the last Cassian village. Penarddun had always counted her a friend, but they had never spoken before of the older girl's people or her position at Dun Belin; it was simply accepted that that was the way of things. For the first time, she wondered how Sicora must feel; whether it was easier or harder to have been ripped from her people too early to remember. And what of now? Sicora was uprooted for the second time, and in Llyr's country would be twice a foreigner.

Penarddun said nothing, but reached out, and took her friend's hand.

From outside came the driver's voice, muffled by the flaps of the wagon's cowhide cover.

"There's an Ancalitan village ahead. We'll be stopping there for the night."

On learning that they came from Dun Belin, the headman of the village opened his own house to the delegation. He fussed around them, eager to prove his loyalty, and to earn the High King's favour: and he laid on a dinner of venison and wild boar, with a bard to sing them carefully chosen songs of Belin's victories, avoiding any mention of the conquest of the Ancalites.

Few of the travelling party were in any mood for celebration, but they were all hungry, and ate heartily, Awel most of all. There was not much conversation at the table: the Ancalitan chief's attempts to probe into their mission were met with the curtest of answers from Maddan and the two Silures, and neither Penarddun nor Sicora spoke at all.

The bard had just finished an heroic, and entirely inaccurate, lay about the Belgic invasion, and announced:

11

"Now I will tell how King Belin conquered the Cassi, and laid them under tribute." He must have been running out of songs, for that was close to home: the Cassi and Ancalites had been allies against Belin in that war, at least at the beginning of it: but Awel suddenly spoke up.

"We have come from Dun Belin, sir bard," he said. "We all know our own High King's exploits. Sing us a song of Llyr ap Bladud, to whose land we travel."

The Druid glowered furiously at the boy; the bard looked unhappily from one to the other, and then at his own chief, and stammered:

"I – I know no songs of King Llyr, my, my lord."

Belin's guards sniggered to hear Awel named "lord": but Penarddun's curiosity was piqued, and she was thankful to Awel for his boldness.

"If not a song, then tell us a tale," she said loudly. "It is fitting that I should know the high deeds of the man who is to be my husband."

There were some gasps at that. The purpose of their journey had been spoken of only briefly, and in hushed tones; most of the Ancalites knew nothing of it. But while Awel could be slapped down, a princess' wish could not be ignored.

"Ah, now that I recall, there are some verses on King Llyr's doings," said the bard hastily. "There are more on King Bladud and Queen Alaron, however. Perhaps it will be best if I begin with them."

Penarddun inclined her head. The Druid gave a brusque nod; and the bard began.

She had heard snatches of the story of Bladud before, but it had never made an impression: the Silures were a world away, and the history of the tribes she knew was of more importance. But now she heard the whole legend: how, as a young prince, he had desired to study to be a Druid, and had visited many of the holy places of the Western tribes, even travelling over the sea to Gaul and Spain, and beyond them to the land of the Greeks; how he had become disfigured by a terrible disease, and in shame disguised himself, and become a pig-herder in the land of the Dobunni; how the goddess Sulis had cured him, and he had returned home in time to claim the throne in the civil upheavals following his father's death. How he had married Alaron, the priestess of Sulis, and begotten on her a son whom they had boldly named Llyr, in honour of the sea god. How, after his queen's death, he had turned to necromancy in an attempt to win her back, and how at last his magical experiments had left him convinced that he could fly, and he had thrown himself from a cliff.

"It is late now," snapped the Druid. "We travel early tomorrow. The Princess needs her sleep."

Penarddun slept little that night. She lay awake, thinking of Bladud, deranged by love and loss, and wondering how much of his story was true: and what it was in Llyr's own past that they sought to keep from her. She tried whispering of this to Sicora; but she had fallen asleep as soon as she lay down, or pretended to. She had not spoken since they entered Ancalitan territory.

The next morning, as Maddan had promised, they were roused before dawn, and breakfasted on the previous night's leftovers and watered-down ale before setting off once more. Penarddun noticed that Awel winced at the jostling of his pony; he was unused to riding, of course, but he had sat easily enough yesterday. As they trundled out of the village, the Druid rode up to the side of the wagon, and said quietly:

"Lady, it would be as well to be discreet about why we travel west. Not everybody we meet on the road is to be trusted."

13

His voice was stern, and she could hear the threat in it. She knew that, today or tomorrow, they would be entering Belgic lands, held by settlers from the time of the old wars: they acknowledged her father's overlordship, and paid him tribute, but they were still there. Stories about the Belgic invasion were vague as to what agreement they had made with Belin, but some accommodation there clearly was, and the Belgic tribes had done well enough from it.

When they were clear of the village, she put a hand on Sicora's shoulder.

"Thank you," said Sicora quietly. "It wasn't my village, I knew nobody, but it could have been. My father's a headman just like the one last night; maybe that one has a daughter or a son at Dun Belin as well."

That night, they stayed in a Belgic lord's fort, and nobody asked for songs. For several more days they travelled across the Belgic lands, then into the land of the pastoral Dobunni, the latest tribe to submit to Belin: and Maddan announced that they would travel to the shrine of Sulis where Queen Alaron had been priestess. It would honour Llyr if they made sacrifice at his mother's shrine; and the favour of Sulis would be welcome indeed.

"And we can pray to win through the Deepwood," muttered one of the soldiers darkly. The Druid barked at him to be quiet.

Penarddun was glad of the diversion to Sulis' Water. It put off the moment of entering Silurian territory, and she hoped to hear more there about the man who was to be her husband. If he was as old as Father said, it was unlikely that anyone there would remember his mother; but he would be known.

"When should we come to Sulis' Water?" she asked Maddan.

"Tomorrow, my lady, or the day after."

"What lord's house will we stay in tonight?"

"None, lady. The Dobunni have no lords, and have never had a king. Each village has its own headman – some by right of birth, some by election, some by the challenge – and when there is matter to be discussed they or their representatives gather in congress. They do have a Speaker, elected by the headmen to be their representative to other tribes, but he wields no power over them in their villages, nor does any man above the headmen when there is peace. In time of war, the congress of headmen elects a leader, who holds power only until the fighting is done. But that is not often, save when bandits ride out of the Deepwood. The wood and river have mostly kept the Silures away; I believe the last time the Dobunni mustered in numbers worth the counting was in the Belgic invasion. They bent the knee to your lord father without much of a fight; I suppose they will have no more need of war leaders now that they are under his protection."

They made good time, and arrived at Sulis' Water the following afternoon. As they came down the valley towards the springs, they saw many burial mounds: the Dobunni might have no lords, but this had been a sacred place before their tribe had existed, and older peoples had buried their kings and queens as close as they could to the home of the goddess.

The settlement itself was small, a few houses within a simple wooden stockade; it was easy to see that it was not built for defence, but Penarddun had expected it to be built for splendour, towards the glory of the goddess. News of their coming had gone before them, and the chief priestess came out to greet them. She at least was splendid: a tall, white-haired woman with sharp cheekbones and sunken eyes, wearing a robe of mixed dyes in many shades of blue, and with so many golden torques upon her neck and arms that it was a wonder she could move.

A still more imposing, rather younger woman stood beside her: broad-shouldered as a warrior, with sharp grey eyes, a jutting, beaky nose, and dark hair just beginning to grey. She wore a forest-green gown embroidered with the images of beasts and birds, and a gold-and-garnet pendant in the form of a dragon hanging on her breast.

"Welcome to the Waters of Sulis, Penarddun ferch Belin," said the woman in blue. Her voice was soft, but carried a note of command. "I am Glóir, daughter of Locrin and Innogen, adept of the Druidic order and Chief Priestess of this holy shrine."

"And I am Urganda of Avalon, servant of Latis," said the other, inclining her head. Her voice was deeper, richer, and had a touch of secret laughter buried within it, or so Penarddun thought.

Maddan, who had stiffened and clutched at his horse's reins as soon as he saw the woman in green, scowled darkly on hearing her name. Penarddun, who had never heard of either her or her god, could not see why: but she determined to find out.

"My name is Urganda the Unknown, mark me well, and know
me again if you can!"
~ Garci Rodríguez de Montalvo, *Amadis de Gaula*

While Awel and the spearmen were bestowing the
ponies and baggage, Glóir insisted that Penarddun and
Maddan should accompany the priestesses immediately to the
shrine. Sicora, at Penarddun's nod, followed: Maddan looked
disapproving, but did not gainsay his princess. The Druidess
led them down a few worn, ill-hewn steps to a place where the
living rock lay bare: from a cleft in it there issued the warm
spring of Sulis, above which stood a low stone altar with a
rough carving of the goddess. It was all so simple and
unassuming that Penarddun might have overlooked the altar
had she not known it was there: but the pool below was
another matter. Even when the surface was too ruffled to see
through, gold and copper glinted through it: when the wind
died and the water fell calm, she saw a pile of armlets,
necklaces, bent swords, ceremonial helms, brooches, even a
huge beaten bronze shield, lying on the bottom, some of it
seeming only a span or two below the surface.

"Sulis prefers sacrifices of gold to those of blood," said
Glóir. "The shield was dedicated by the last war leader of the
Dobunni, before he went off to fight King Belin."

"The goddess did not bless him, then," remarked
Maddan. "Hardly any rose to join him, and he was swept away
like a buzzing fly."

"She is not a god of war," replied the priestess. "Her province is healing. Evidently she did not approve of his enterprise – or of his asking her for help."

"She is wise," said Maddan gravely, bowing his head. "With so many warlike neighbours south and west, the Dobunni are best under the High King's protection."

"Such warlike neighbours as the Durotriges?" said Urganda with a smile.

"Yes," said Maddan stiffly.

"And the Silures?" she pressed.

"I did not speak of King Llyr," said the Druid. "The Deepwood lies between these lands and his. But yes – it is no secret that Silurians have raided this country in the past; another reason for Dobunni to be grateful for the peace King Belin makes."

"It is, as you say, no secret," said the priestess, inclining her head.

Maddan scowled, but said nothing. Glóir's face remained impassive. Suddenly realising why she had been brought there, Penarddun pulled off the gilt-bronze armlet her father had given her, and said:

"This is my offering to Sulis. May she smile on me, and bless my marriage as she did Queen Alaron's."

She cast the piece into the water: it sank remarkably slowly, considering its weight, and came to rest on top of the shield.

"It is well done," said Glóir. "The goddess will be pleased. Come: I shall lead you to my hall."

The hall of the Priestess of Sulis was somewhat more impressive within than without, but still hardly compared with that of Penarddun's father at Dun Belin. There were offerings ranged along the walls, like those in the pool – including swords and jewels of strange design, unlike any she had ever seen.

"People come here from the far north," said Glóir; "Brigantes and others, even Caledonians. And from the south coast come things brought to these shores by traders from Gaul, Spain, and Ireland. See – that barbed spear comes from Laighinn, the broad shield from Lusitania; and this has come still further." She lifted from a low pedestal a cup to which Penarddun had hardly given a glance, and held it up, so that the sunlight streaming through the open shutters caught it: and the two girls gasped. They had thought it was of dulled metal or polished greenish stone: but the light passed *through* it, refracting into many colours, illuminating the designs along the outside – images of fighting men in heavy mail and high crested helmets, with eagles flying above their heads.

"Glass," said the priestess. "Roman ware, brought from Cadiz. I know of nobody in all these islands who could make such a piece. A Dumnonian chieftain traded one of his strongest bulls for it, and brought it here to ask the goddess to give him a son."

"It is beautiful," was all that Penarddun could think to say. Her father had a few pieces of glass, mostly Gaulish, but they were rough work indeed compared with this.

"It is indeed," said Glóir. "And you will bear it with you to Portskewett. I cannot make it yours – what is given to Sulis remains hers – but it will be a sign of the goddess' blessing, and an answer to your prayers."

"Sulis is good," said Penarddun, bowing her head.

They bedded down that night in the hall, Penarddun sharing a blanket with Sicora: but she could not sleep. At last, she got up, stepped gingerly over the snoring Maddan, and tiptoed to the door. Glóir had posted no guards, but the Druid had ordered two of King Belin's men to keep watch: they jumped when the door opened.

"I am going to the spring to pray," said Penarddun.

"Begging your pardon," said the younger guard – she thought his name was Alban – "but the Druid said…"

"There is only one way down to the spring," said Penarddun. "You can see the stair clearly from here. You'll know if anyone tries to follow me." And before they could think of any objection, she gathered her cloak around her, and hurried off.

The spring had a different kind of beauty by cold moonlight than in the day. The waters looked blue rather than green, and what glinted beneath them could almost be silver; and the shadows of the rocks were deep and black. So deep, indeed, that Penarddun truly believed that she was alone until Urganda spoke.

"You couldn't sleep?" said the priestess. Penarddun started. For a moment she looked wildly about for a weapon; but fear left her when Urganda moved into the light, and let her dark hood slide down, revealing her face.

"No," she admitted.

"It is natural, in a girl soon to be wedded," said the priestess. "And to a stranger. How much do you know about King Llyr?"

Penarddun looked down at her feet, uncertain how much it was proper to say.

"I know that he is the son of King Bladud and Queen Alaron," she said. "That he has been King of the Silures for many years, and is renowned as a warrior. That, that he has lost his first wife, and wishes for a son…"

"And did you ever ask who she was?" said Urganda. "Or what children he does have?"

Penarddun blushed, and said nothing.

"They would have told you little enough anyway," said the priestess gently. "Llyr's first wife was my sister, the last Lady of the Lake."

"I – I am sorry," said Penarddun haltingly.

"For what? You have done me no wrong." Urganda gazed up at the moon, and smoothed her hair. "No doubt you have never heard of the Lady, or the goddess we served. But the name of Latis, and Afallach her spouse, is known all through the West. The Queen of the Standing Waters, and the Lord of the Apple Trees: the gods of Avalon."

"I have not heard of them," Penarddun admitted. "But then, I know little of the gods. I like the old stories, of the great war against the Fomorians – they frightened me when I was little, but I liked them anyway."

"What do you know of the Fomorians?" asked Urganda suddenly. Penarddun was startled.

"They're the sea demons who ruled Britain before the gods came," she said. "My mother told me they were the children of the sea-god and a wicked princess."

"Oh, they have always existed," said Urganda. "The princess' son was the giant Albion. The bards tell us that he led the Fomorians to this island, and made them rulers of it: and he gave it his name. But he was unjust and cruel, and the Dagda struck him down with his club. When the gods came, they drove the Fomorians back to the sea, and changed the land's name from Albion to Britain. But they are not dead, only subdued. The giant sleeps fitfully under the sea. Britain is still also Albion, still belongs as much to the Fomorians as to the gods. They are not wholly evil, any more than the gods are wholly good. Rather they are wild where gods and men are ordered. Albion is the untamed Britain, as tempestuous and unpredictable as the sea. He is there in the Deepwood and the court, and in the hearts of every man and woman. This is the realm of Albion still – forever balanced between law and chaos. Understand that, and you will be ready to be a queen."

Penarddun shivered.

"Where is Avalon, my lady?" she asked, changing the subject.

"It is an island, a great hill rising out of the marshes, in the Durotrigan country," said Urganda. "I am partial because it is my home, but I have never seen anywhere I thought lovelier. Latis is the land; she is the sovereignty of the Durotriges, and who would be king must marry the Lady."

"Kings in the East marry the land as well," said Penarddun.

"In form, yes. But among the Durotriges, the Lady's husband is Penteyrnedd: Prince of Princes. Until their eldest daughter becomes Lady in her turn, and her husband succeeds. In time of peace, the Lady and Penteyrnedd are our highest justices; in time of war, the Penteyrnedd leads the Durotrigan chiefs, while the Lady guards the people. Or so it was, before Llyr came.

"It was in the time of the Belgic invasion. I was a child, and my sister Gogoniant not so old as you are now. My father had gone forth at the head of a host to turn back the invaders, and had fallen: we had barely taken in the news of his death when the Silures landed.

"Yes, landed. Llyr brought ships across the Severn Sea, and fell upon the land. He sailed upriver and attacked Avalon itself. My mother was too overcome by grief and shock to mount a defence: he took the island, and he took my sister. He declared himself Penteyrnedd, and told the surviving Durotrigan chiefs he would burn the sacred groves of Afallach if they did not acknowledge him.

"Oh, he held back the Belgae right enough, until your father made his truce and gave up half the south coast to

22

them; then he sailed back to Portskewett, taking my sister with him. Ever since then, the chiefs and headmen of the Durotriges have paid him tribute, while Avalon has wasted without the Lady. Oh, my mother still ruled it, and I succeeded her, but Gogoniant was the Lady from the moment Llyr dragged her to his bed. I never saw her again; and now she is dead, and cannot return to Avalon."

"I – I am sorry," Penarddun said again. There were tears in her eyes.

"Gogoniant bore Llyr many children, but nearly all died," said Urganda. "Only one survives in Portskewett: I am told her name is Cordelia. She must be a little older than you. Llyr has spread the name of Penteyrnedd throughout the West, claiming his marriage to Gogoniant made him blessed by the gods, chosen to be High King. Tribes who had never heard of the Penteyrnedd before the Belgic war are now full of men who would butcher their mothers to marry this girl. They believe that the Penteyrnedd *is* the High King, and that Cordelia's husband will be Llyr's ordained successor. They will not take kindly to a new wife, or any son she bears. Nor will his other daughters. He has two acknowledged ones, by concubines he took in war; he married them both to kings who bent the knee." Penarddun's head was whirling as she tried to make sense of all of this. Urganda lent in close, and took her face in her hands. She could feel the older woman's breath as she said: "You are going into a pit of vipers; and if your bridegroom is not the most poisonous, he gave the others their fangs."

"What – what should I do?" asked Penarddun, barely audible.

"There is nothing you can do but be prepared," said Urganda. "I did not tell you this that you might run and hide in the Deepwood, but that you might ride to Portskewett with your eyes open, and know what awaits you there."

"A monster."

"A man who came by power monstrously," said Urganda. "Few kings have clean hands; I cannot speak to what manner of man Llyr has grown into. But he is old, and others itch to inherit his power: and some of them will be quite ready to do as he did. Keep your own people about you."

"My people?" said Penarddun miserably. "I have none, save Sicora."

"Then hold her close," said Urganda.

A sudden thought struck Penarddun.

"Come with us!" she said. "You could keep me safe."

Urganda looked at her curiously.

"Come with you?" she said. "And live with you in Llyr's fort? No; even if I could leave Avalon, it would never be permitted. But I shall accompany you to your wedding." She smiled. "That is why I came here. I am not without my informants, and I knew of your journey, most likely before you did. Maddan will not like it, but I have a right to be there. Besides, there are many terrors in the Deepwood, and my guidance will do you more good there than a score of guards."

Penarddun shivered.

"I had forgotten the Deepwood," she said.

"Best forget it still a while longer," said Urganda. "I will see you safely through it, never fear. For you, the danger lies on the other side. But here at Sulis' Water you are safe; you should sleep, while you can."

Penarddun almost laughed. Sleep, after all she had learned? She shook her head.

"I shan't sleep tonight," she said.

"No beautiful lady or maiden within two days' ride of the forest
is safe: Darnant will take them either by force or magic."

~ Perceforest

They departed the next day. Maddan had scowled when
Urganda made known her intention of travelling with them,
but he could not gainsay her: Llyr and his family were her kin,
and Cordelia, as the next Lady, was Avalon's lawful ruler,
making Urganda her deputy. When she declared that she
would ride her own horse, rather than travel in the wagon with
Penarddun and Sicora, it was difficult to tell whether the Druid
was more annoyed at the prospect of her company or relieved
that she would not spend the journey talking to the Princess.
She fell in beside Awel on his pony, and gave the boy an
encouraging smile.

By the time they stopped that night, the green mass of
the Deepwood was visible ahead of them, and they knew they
would enter it on the morrow. The forest straddled the great
river which broadened downstream into the Severn Sea: but on
which bank the border between Dobunni and Silures lay, none
could tell. Even as far afield as Dun Belin, the Deepwood had a
reputation as a haunt of outlaws and murderers, sorcerers and
monsters.

When they trundled onward in the morning,
Penarddun muttered a prayer, and fingered her golden brooch.
It was circular, with two cross-pieces, and rayed edges – a
stylised sun like the one on her father's standard, the emblem
of Belenos. Belin had been named in the sun god's honour, for
the Trinovantes revered him above all other gods.

25

"May Belenos' light pierce the darkness of the Deepwood," she whispered, "and guide us aright."

Then they entered into the shadow of the trees.

Much of the land they had passed through was wooded, and she knew that there was heavy afforestation further north, where less settled tribes had not troubled to clear the ancient woods for farmland. Every tribal centre, every chiefly fort, had sacred groves nearby. The Britons had worshipped trees since time immemorial. But Penarddun had never seen anything as *wild* as the Deepwood. Although a fringe of beech trees clung around the edge of it, they soon gave way to huge and ancient oaks, under which a thick mould of fallen leaves lay in the deep shadow of those yet to fall. The party had already left the Belgic Road behind, and had travelled this last stretch by a much rougher track: but as it entered the forest it dwindled to a dirt pathway scarce wide enough for her wagon, with many a branch hanging in the way. Their progress had slowed to a crawl before they had lost sight of the open country behind them.

"Oaks belong to Taranis, the Thunderer," said Maddan loudly. "He is a dangerous god, but not a malevolent one. His spirit is strong here."

Penarddun was not comforted. Taranis was a god she knew; she had attended sacrifices in his honour in oak groves back East; but this place felt more alien than any she had seen. She would not have been surprised had a dragon like the one on Urganda's pendant appeared from between the trees. Under the wagon cover, seeing only snatches of the shadows through the flaps at front and back, she felt pent in, buried. She had had such feelings before, but only indoors, in low huts or gloomy halls. Woodlands were not like that; they were open, living, free, even if they were not always safe. But the Deepwood cast its shadow upon her mind.

Suddenly, somewhere in front of the wagon, there was a dull thud, followed almost instantly by confused shouts and the whinnying of frightened ponies. Penarddun heard someone exclaim:

"He's dead!"

She glanced at Sicora, and scrambled forward, out through the front flap onto the driver's bench. On the path in front, the riders were milling around in confusion; one of Llyr's ambassadors was slumped over the neck of his mount. His companion took him by the shoulder, and pulled him upright. His head lolled sideways, eyes blankly open. An arrow was sticking in the front of his chest.

"Who's there?" Alban shouted into the green darkness. "Who did this? Show yourselves!"

No reply came – neither word nor arrow.

"The cowards have already fled," said Maddan. "Take your men and clear the brush; if you catch any, bring them back."

"No," said Urganda. "We should push on."

"And let them come at us from behind?" scoffed the Druid. "No. Even if they are already gone, what would we say to King Llyr – that we let one of his representatives be slain by common outlaws and did nothing? We should be after them before they run too far. They obviously fear our numbers or they would have pressed their attack."

"And you think they only noticed our numbers *after* shooting Leil?" said Urganda. "They want to negate our advantage by splitting us up. We must stick together."

"And be picked off one by one if the rats still are lurking in the shadows," retorted Maddan.

"Lady Urganda knows these woods," said Penarddun, startling herself. "I believe we should listen to her."

Maddan inclined his head.

"My lady, I am always ready to take advice," he said. "But you have not been in battle. I have been charged to protect you on the road to Portskewett, and I mean to do so as I see best. Alban, Cadwaladr, Brennus, Drus – go."

The four men named lowered their spears, and rode off between the trees to the right of the path. They had gone very little distance before they were completely invisible; silence fell.

"I hope you have done right," muttered the second Silurian.

"I doubt they'll find anything," said Maddan. "Footpads are cowards; they're probably long gone."

"There are more than ordinary footpads in the Deepwood," said Urganda.

From somewhere amid the trees, there came a scream, cut sickeningly short. Then the man was upon them.

He dropped from a tree branch, straight overhead, onto Maddan's back. The Druid's staff whirled upwards, and cracked against his attacker's head, but the man was unshaken. He already had Maddan's arms pinned above the elbows, and he had jumped knife in hand: he flicked the Druid's beard aside, and cut his throat. The blood was still spraying forth as he flung the body aside, and rounded on the remaining party – which was already one smaller. The moment the attacker had dropped from above, Gruffudd, the remaining Silurian, had kicked his horse into a gallop and disappeared along the road. The remaining soldier, Gurgint, was still fumbling for his sword when the footpad's knife caught him in the chest.

The outlaw was tall and barrel-chested, with a thick black beard flecked with white; his green woollen tunic and cloak, though dirty, looked to be of remarkably high quality, with the worn remains of embroidery around the edges and hems.

"Black Brwhyr, at your service, m'ladies," he said, with a mocking bow. "You may not be aware of it, but you're in the Deepwood. This forest belongs to King Darnant, and nobody passes through it without paying King Darnant's tax."

"If it's gold you want -" Penarddun began, but Brwhyr cut her off.

"Want?" he snapped. "It's gold and more than gold I'll be taking, want or not. I answer to King Darnant, and so will you."

"This wagon won't go off the road," objected the driver.

"Then leave it," said Brwhyr.

"And the treasure inside?" said Urganda suddenly.

"I see a man, a lad, and two strong lasses," said Brwhyr. "You can carry plenty, and if we unhitch those ponies they'll carry more."

Two. He hadn't seen Sicora. But before Penarddun could start to think what advantage could be gained fron this, Urganda said:

"Are you not counting me, then, sir?"

"I was," said Brwhyr, with a crooked grin: and he strode over to the wagon and pulled the front flap aside. "My, my, what a pretty pair. King Darnant will be pleased. Driver – down. Get these ponies unhitched."

"Do as he says," Urganda commanded, seeing the man hesitate. *Is she on his side?* wondered Penarddun frantically. *Did she lead us into this? No, she didn't lead us, there was only one road – but she could have signalled them somehow...*

The driver did as he was told.

"You too," said Brwhyr to Awel. "Be quick."

The boy set to, with nimbler fingers than the older man, and the beasts were soon unhitched; the wagon juddered and lost its balance.

29

"Damn it," muttered Brwhyr, "where are they? Never mind. You two hold those beasts, and don't think of fleeing: you won't get far. Girls – you, down. By the front, so's I can see you *and* the ponies. You, hand down the treasure, the same way."

Penarddun stood up on the driver's bench, and was about to step down when Brwhyr said with a sudden grin:

"Here – let me help you." Before she could object he had caught her around the waist, and was lifting her down, not to the ground but into his arms. "A kiss for payment," he leered, "nothing more – not yet, not till King Darnant's had his -"

Suddenly, his eyes bulged, and he sputtered; his grip loosened, and he fell forwards. Penarddun could not roll away in time, and he landed on top of her; she screamed – and when she realised he was dead weight, no longer moving, she screamed again.

"Come on, you fools!" she heard Urganda say. "Help me roll him off!"

Then the great mass of the footpad shifted, rolled, and finally slid off her to the ground, and Urganda and the wagon-driver were helping her to her feet.

"What – what happened?" she gasped.

"I stabbed him," said Urganda matter-of-factly. "Are you hurt?"

"No... no, I don't think so..."

"Good. Can you ride? There are four mounts here and five of us – Leil's and Maddan's horses ran away – so you'll have to share. We need to be off before his friends turn up."

"But – but the others -"

"May be dead already, and if not we won't help them by blundering about in the bushes and calling the enemy down on us. We don't know how many are out there. The party that

30

attacked us must be small, or Black Brwhyr wouldn't have gone one against so many, but there are more. They don't know we're here yet – Brwhyr must have happened on us by accident."

The prone ruffian twitched. Penarddun jumped.

"He's alive," she said.

"Let him bleed out, or not, as the gods please," said Urganda with a shrug. "He's no more danger to us today with the wound I gave him, and I'll not kill a helpless man. Now, mount up: we need to move fast."

Penarddun shared with Sicora, riding one of the wagon ponies; the driver took the other. The Ancalitan girl was an uncertain horsewoman, though better than Awel, who had never ridden before this journey. The road was uneven, and often overgrown: they could not force their pace: but they made much faster progress than the wagon could have done.

Every time a twig cracked or leaves rustled, Penarddun thought that King Darnant was upon them. She pictured Brwhyr, dead but walking, face purpled, tongue lolling out, lurching towards her with reaching, grasping hands. The day was growing darker, the shadows lengthening, and there was still no sign of the end of the wood. Turning back had never been considered – they had all, in their shocked state, fallen into line with what Urganda commanded, and the priestess was adamant that onwards was the only way. Penarddun's thighs and backside ached from the saddle, her head from weariness and fear; she realised suddenly that she had not eaten since they set out that morning. She felt faint, and swayed: but Sicora held her up.

Urganda had seen.

"I know how it is," she said. "But we must go on."

On they pressed; the light grew dimmer and their bellies emptier. At last it was almost completely dark, but

Urganda would not let them stop: then they saw the torches ahead.

"Look!" whispered Sicora. Penarddun shuddered.

"We should get off the road," said the driver.

"I think not," said Urganda. "We must be near the western edge of the forest by now; Darnant's men wouldn't use torches so near to the forts of the Silures."

"But – but we can't be sure!" exclaimed Penarddun.

"No," said the priestess. "We can't." And she kicked her horse to a canter, and rode straight towards the torches.

"Who's there?" Penarddun heard a voice call out of the darkness ahead.

"Urganda of Avalon!" the priestess declared for half the wood to hear. There was a pause, then an ugly chuckle. Penarddun found that she was struggling to breathe. Then the voice called back:

"Have you the others with you?"

"Who asks it?" demanded Urganda. There was a pause, then more speech, lower, which Penarddun could not hear. *Is she betraying us?* she asked herself yet again. It made no sense, Urganda had saved them, but still she could not but fear...

Then the footsteps came, men tramping along the path, the torches moving. There was nowhere to run, no time to hide – and then, under a torch held high, she saw him.

"*Gruffudd!*" she exclaimed.

If Sicora hadn't caught her, she would have fallen off the pony.

With the Silurian and the priestess were two richly dressed men, their forearms a mass of gold and copper. One was young, slight, and darkly handsome, the other much older, with a heavy belly, red nose, and braided grey beard.

Probably King Llyr, whispered a part of her mind, but at least he was surely not King Darnant.

She became aware that the younger man was speaking.

"… extends his welcome, and his apology for what befell here," he was saying. "I am Euroswydd of Usk, cousin to the High King, and Speaker of the Silures; this is Lord Glevon, Speaker of the Dobunni. Today's outrage will be avenged, you have my word. But come – I have a house nearby. Tonight you will be warm and well-fed, and safe; tomorrow, the High King awaits you."

"Meantime we shall express our darker purpose."
~ Shakespeare, *King Lear*

The low timber-built roundhouse they were led to was warm and softly lit by yellow torchlight; and there was roast pork and mead and baked apples. By the time she had eaten, Penarddun felt she could have slept on hard rock, never mind among the floor rushes: but there was a bed of heaped skins for her and Sicora. She fell asleep almost instantly, and was grateful not to dream.

The next morning, they were roused early, and ate a light and hurried breakfast of bread sops in small ale.

"I have new cloaks for all of you," said Euroswydd; "but we have little other clothing here, nor jewellery. I understand you were forced to abandon your wagon; no doubt Darnant's wolves have scavenged it by now."

"The cup!" Penarddun remembered suddenly. "I brought a glass goblet, Roman ware, from the Lady Glóir."

"Smashed, probably," said Euroswydd. "Or marked for sale in some Cornovian town, north of the Deepwood where no word of your journey has yet been heard. I am sorry."

Penarddun hung her head.

"I had so many gifts," she said. "Now I bring King Llyr nothing."

"Your beauty is gift enough," said Euroswydd gallantly. *That, and my father's soldiers,* she thought glumly.

Fitted out in their new cloaks, they mounted and rode on. Sitting a horse again after yesterday's desperate ride was uncomfortable, but Penarddun gritted her teeth and resolved not to show it.

The sun shone brightly, a welcome change from the shadows of the Deepwood, though the cold air bit at her face and hands. They wound slowly along the road, down to the coast, and along the side of the Severn Sea – the north side, Penarddun reminded herself; they were in Llyr's kingdom now. On the far side, the Dobunnic shore – or was it the Durotrigan? – rose, green and fair, but unattainable; the water might be calm and blue, but was one last barrier between her and home. But this was home now, this land of woods and vales whose Queen she was to be.

After a brief break for a midday meal, they rode on. Euroswydd had spoken of the fort by the sea as if it was no distance at all, but the day was wearing away and there was no sign of it. Indeed, it was only when Penarddun was wondering if they would come there that day that Euroswydd pointed ahead, and declared:

"Portskewett!"

The hillfort was smaller than Dun Belin, but far more visible. It rose from almost flat surroundings, directly above the beach; the outer ditch and fence, Penarddun saw as they came closer, continued almost down to the water's edge. Atop the rise, behind a second fence, sat Llyr's great roundhouse. Within that fort, her bridegroom awaited her.

The gate stood open; the guards, recognising their guides, stood smartly aside to admit them, and they trailed up the winding avenue to the inner gate. As they approached it, Euroswydd swung down from the saddle, while Glevon dismounted rather less gracefully: and they led their mounts in on foot, so that Penarddun was the first to ride into Llyr's courtyard.

An arc of men stood within, waiting. None looked old enough to be King Llyr. Some were only a few years older than herself; the oldest was a long-bearded Druid in white robes. Two were strangely clad, in long tunics with no trousers, sandals rather than boots, and with iron rings on their fingers; one was dark and gaunt and deep-eyed, the other blond and plump, but yet they looked more like each other to Penarddun than like anyone else there.

Then trumpets were sounded, and the door of the hall flung open: and out of it came a procession. A sharply handsome blonde woman and a tall grim-faced man led a young boy with a miniature sword at his belt; a red-haired woman, strongly resembling the first, but more pointed of feature, and a broad-shouldered man with blue whorls tattooed across his square red face, led a smaller boy, who looked around in wonder; and each took their places in front of those already assembled in the courtyard.

Last came a girl of about Sicora's age, slight and pale and fair, with an old man leaning on her arm. He stooped almost double, a staff propping him up on one side and the girl on the other, his yellow-white beard close to brushing the ground; the weight of his cloak, thick black wool trimmed in bearskin, seemed about to bear him down. His eyes were watery, and the red threads of cracked veins were visible on his cheeks. On the front of his purple tunic was embroidered the roiling serpent of the Silures. Penarddun's mouth fell open: she had expected Llyr to be old, but this man looked unlikely to live out the day.

He stopped before her horse, and peered up at her from his lowly position, wheezing as if the short walk had exhausted him... then the gasps turned to a cackle, then a guffaw, as he let go of the girl's arm and stood up, standing as straight as any tree. He was the tallest man present.

"Ha!" he boomed. "Decrepit old Llyr, eh? My legs aren't crumpled yet, nor my loins withered!"

The whole court was laughing; and Penarddun managed a weak smile.

"My lord is ageless as ever," said Euroswydd smoothly. "I present the Princess Penarddun ferch Belin."

"I know who she is," said Llyr. "Aye, and her travelling companion." His eyes lingered for a moment on Urganda; but Penarddun could read nothing in his face. "My lady, I have but lately been informed of what befell you in the Deepwood. I will smoke out this Darnant, never fear; you shall have his head as a wedding gift."

"I, I thank my lord," was all she could say.

"Time enough for thanks when the deed is done," said Llyr. "Euroswydd, present my daughters."

"Yes, sire," said Euroswydd with a bow. "Queen Goneril, King Maglor, and Prince Morgan of the Ordovices; Queen Regan, King Henwyn, and Prince Cunedag of the Cornovii; and the Princess Cordelia of the Silures. May I also present the Princes Pwyll and Perion of the Demetae" – he indicated two young men with curling brown hair, long straight noses, and careless smiles, plainly brothers – "the learned Druid Goll, and the noble Appius Scaliger and Gaius Perillus."

He gestured to the two men in long tunics. Llyr gave a cracked laugh.

"My tame Romans," he said. "Strange creatures, but they have their uses. Every so often a trader from Cadiz or Marseille misses the Dumnonian ports and makes his way up here; it's good to have someone who understands their jabber and can tell me when they try to cheat me."

Penarddun stared, wide-eyed. She had never seen a Roman. Their goods came to Dun Belin, but brought by Gauls, or overland from the ports of the West. In recent years, though, there had been reports of fleeing Spaniards landing on the south coast in little cockle-boats: they brought with them tales of horrifying cruelty, of whole tribes put to the sword, down to the smallest child. The word "Roman" had almost replaced "Belgic" as a bogeyman, a by-word for everything dangerous and frightening. Apart from their slightly odd style of dress, these two men looked no different from any other.

"I bid you all welcome!" exclaimed Llyr. "Tonight, we feast; tomorrow, we marry. I trust my lady can contain herself that long!"

"Are the terms of the marriage set?" asked Urganda sharply. All eyes turned to her: the priestess had spoken out of turn, without giving her name or craving the High King's leave. "The Speaker of the Trinovantes was murdered in the Deepwood," she pointed out. "He came with King Belin's authority to agree terms. What is the Princess' jointure? What are the terms of alliance?"

It was Gruffudd who replied.

"I negotiated the terms with King Belin, together with my late comrade Leil," he said. "The Princess brought no jointure of land, beasts, or slaves – only the gifts which were stolen in the Deepwood, and the promise of three hundred warriors when it should please King Llyr to call for them. The terms of alliance were these: that King Llyr should be sovereign over the Deepwood and all tribes west of the Severn, and in turn shall take no part in wars east of the river or south of the Sea, unless tribes owing him allegiance are first attacked; and that the two High Kings pledge to refrain from all raids on one another's land, and to defend one another's kingdoms against any threat from the Brigantian confederation, or from overseas."

There were some surprised looks. It was clear that the terms favoured Belin more than most had expected: he was left with room to expand his territory, and had spent little enough on the dowry. Either Llyr badly wanted peace in his old age, or he badly wanted three hundred Trinovantic warriors. Penarddun saw Goneril and Maglor exchange glances: the combined forces of the tribes under Silurian rule must run into thousands, but Easterners sworn to Llyr personally might be of value if he did not trust the subject tribes – or their rulers.

"Are these terms acceptable to my lady?" asked Llyr gravely. Penarddun hesitated, then nodded. The High King looked at Urganda, and curled his lip. "And to the Lady of Avalon?" he said mockingly.

"They are not mine to accept, sire," she replied.

"No indeed." He looked back at Penarddun, and beamed. "But come! Get rid of your travelling clothes, I'll have you all dressed anew for the feast tonight. I have other royal guests, but I've kept 'em waiting, as a High King should in his own realm. You'll meet them all tonight." He glanced at Sicora and Awel. "Even your body-slaves will have new clothes."

"This is the Lady Sicora of the Ancalites," said Penarddun. "She attends me, but she is free and nobly born."

"And this is Awel," said the boy. "Awel the orphan, Awel the beggar, poor Awel – just Awel."

The High King cocked an eyebrow.

"Your fool?" he asked.

"I beg pardon, my lord," said Penarddun. "He – he attended the Speaker." More than that, she could not say, for she did not know.

"Then he will now attend us, if that pleases my lady," said Llyr. "He will amuse us. Won't you, fool?"

Awel shrugged.

"Better a King's pet than a Druid's," he said. "At least I know you're not like to sacrifice me."

39

"Not if you please me well," said the High King. "Euroswydd, find this one some patches and a pair of asses' ears. Falyse!" A young woman stepped briskly forward – she was so small that at first Penarddun took her for a child, an impression not abated by her gown cut boyishly short, though the sword at her side told a different tale – and inclined her head. "My lady and her attendant are in your hands. Take good care of them." The little woman bowed, and hurried forward to help Penarddun down from the saddle; then she led her and Sicora to a much smaller roundhouse away to one side of the King's. Two sentries stood guard at the house's door, but they made no move to prevent the women's entry.

When the door was closed, Falyse turned to Penarddun, and said:

"Well, you've met the High King. What do you think?"

"He is... very gracious," said Penarddun, startled. If this woman was a spy, she was hardly subtle. But who would receive her reports? Llyr? Fair Goneril and gloomy Maglor? Sharp-faced Regan and florid Henwyn? Young Cordelia, or the Demetian princes, or the Romans...

"A sight too used to toadies, is what he is," said Falyse. "The man wants standing up to sometimes, but I don't advise you to be the one to do it – not yet, anyway. Queen Gogoniant, now, she could always tell him when he was going wrong, or so they say. Maybe you'll earn that, in time. Or maybe he'll die first, who knows? The man must be all of sixty; Scaliger says that'd be no age for a Roman, but if he's not the oldest man in the West he's surely close to it."

She walked over to a chest that stood against the wall, and threw it open. Silver and gold glinted in the torchlight.

"Cloaks, gowns, brooches, armlets, torques, knives," she said. "All the very finest. Take your pick." Penarddun reached into the chest, and pulled out an armful of clothes, brightly dyed and embroidered. "You too," said Falyse. Sicora gingerly took a gown, as if she expected it to bite, and held it up. It was forest green, with a knotwork pattern worked in yellow along the hems. "Very nice," said Falyse. "Try on as many as you like."

Seeing that the Silurian woman showed no sign of leaving, Penarddun balanced the clothes on the edge of the chest, shrugged off the cloak she was wearing, and pulled her gown over her head; then she picked up a blue lambswool one, and struggled into it. Falyse, unbidden, came forward, and helped her to straighten it out. It was a good fit, once it was on.

"Goes with your eyes," said Falyse appreciatively. "The red cloak, I think, and a serpent armlet – the King'll like that."

"My lord is most generous," said Penarddun. She could not shake off the formality, though a moment before she had been naked in front of the Silurian.

"To some," said Falyse. "Your friend Awel will find him very much so, if he can keep him amused – not so kind if he can't."

"I should have prevented that," said Penarddun. "Awel should have gone back to Dun Belin with Maddan, if, if -"

"Aye, well, 'if' does none of us any good," said Falyse. "Who is he? A boy of your tribe?"

"I don't know," Penarddun admitted. "Of the Cassi, I think, or maybe the Ancalites."

"The Cassi," said Sicora. "He was born to a free peasant woman upriver. She died last winter, and a local Druid took him on as a servant." Penarddun looked at Sicora curiously. She had never noticed the Ancalitan girl speaking with Awel.

"So how did he end up serving the Speaker of the Trinovantes?" asked Falyse.

"I – I don't know that I should say."

Falyse grimaced.

"Listen," she said, "you don't have to trust me. But I think you both need to trust somebody here."

"With our own secrets," said Sicora. "Not with Awel's."

"Quite right," said Falyse. "And is it a secret?"

Sicora blushed.

"He told me freely enough, and never asked me to hide anything," she said. "They thought there was something significant about his birth – a sign of destiny. He was born at dawn on Beltane, and his father had died three months before. I don't know what it's supposed to mean."

"I do," said Falyse, suddenly looking grave. "The Merlin."

"The Merlin?" echoed Penarddun. "What's that?"

"Goll says that, every few generations, the god Mabon takes on human form," said Falyse. "Mabon's vessel is called the Merlin – the Fortress of the Sea, defender of the island of Britain. Goll's been convinced for years that there's a Merlin living; he said all the portents pointed to it. And he's had the King's men looking for a fatherless boy, born at dawn on Beltane."

"Why?" wondered Penarddun. "What do they want with him?"

"If Awel is the Merlin, he carries the power of the god," said Falyse. "He could be the wisest of Druids, the greatest of warriors – such people are dangerous to kings. A wise king would want the Merlin on his side; a fearful one would want him dead."

"Dead?" exclaimed Penarddun.

"But who would dare spill the blood of a god?" said Sicora.

"No doubt Mabon would be angry," said Falyse. "But not all the gods are on the same side. There are some who would find the blood of the Merlin a very pleasing sacrifice."

"Are you saying that Goll and Llyr would kill Awel if they knew who he was?" said Penarddun.

Falyse shook her head.

"No. They want the Merlin alive, under their control. But Darnant of the Deepwood worships dark gods. *He's* been looking for the Merlin, too, and Goll and the High King know it. Llyr's been hunting for a way to draw Darnant out for years; he might think your friend is the perfect bait."

"Who is this Darnant?" demanded Penarddun. "I thought he was just an outlaw."

"That's all he really is," said Falyse. "But he calls himself King and Druid and any number of other things. He comes from the East, somewhere beyond the Belgic lands; fifteen years ago he showed up, and forged the thieves and cutthroats of the Deepwood into one band. Any who wouldn't join him, he burned, in offering to his gods." Penarddun shivered. Human sacrifice was rare in the Trinovantic lands, and most victims were condemned criminals. A kinslayer had been strangled at her mother's funeral; but burning alive was something from old tales. "After that, the Deepwood was his kingdom," Falyse went on. "Only the best armed parties dared to cross it. Last year, Queen Regan and King Henwyn led an expedition there, and killed scores of outlaws, but Darnant and his chief lieutenants escaped. They've been quiet since; but they've grown bold again."

"If Awel is in danger," said Penarddun, "we should warn him."

"Yes," said Falyse. "But not where it might be overheard."

"You would keep this from your King?" wondered Sicora.

"My service is to keep the High King's person safe," replied Falyse. "As I do for you, and the Princess Cordelia. If he

43

is in danger, he will know. For now, the one in danger is your friend."

"Thank you," was all Penarddun could say.

"Thank the Princess," said Falyse with a shrug. "She got me appointed to attend you."

"Will you tell her?" asked Sicora, suddenly apprehensive. Falyse shook her head.

"No," she said. "Not even her – not until she needs to know."

Chapter 5: *The Question*

"But to make trial who was worthy to have the best part of his
kingdom, he went to each of them to ask which of them loved
him most."

~ Geoffrey of Monmouth, *History of the Kings of Britain*

When they were dressed and jewelled, and night had
fallen, Falyse led them to the High King's roundhouse. A great
fire blazed at its centre, with a whole boar on a spit slung
across it; around it were arranged trestle tables and benches,
already laden with food. On the far side of the fire was set a
smaller table, higher than the others, with no inner bench, and
three high-backed chairs replacing the outer one: in the
central chair sat the High King, with Cordelia to his left. When
he saw Penarddun, he rose, and called to her:

"My lady! Your place is reserved."

Falyse led her forward, leaving Sicora standing and
bowed as Llyr took Penarddun's hand; she caught an exchange
of glances between the small Silurian woman and Cordelia. As
Penarddun sat down, Falyse deftly withdrew, and ushered
Sicora to some other part of the hall.

Penarddun looked around, as her eyes got used to the
smoky hall. The King's other daughters were at the adjoining
tables: to one side, Goneril and Maglor sat with Euroswydd,
Goll, one of the Demetian princes, and other folk she did not
recognise; to the other, Regan and Henwyn, with Glevon, the
other Demetian, and more strangers. At Dun Belin, men and
women ate on opposite sides of the feast hall: clearly the
Silures had no such rule, though there were many more men
than women present. She had not seen Urganda. She felt

uncomfortable about being seated above the two queens: she was not Llyr's wife yet.

"Sit," said Llyr. "Grow used to the chair. By my side you will be above kings – and not only our sons-in-law. You'll see some royal grovelling tonight. Glevon!"

The Dobunnic lord got clumsily to his feet, and bowed to the High King as best his belly would allow.

"Sire?"

"Is our Irish guest well bestowed?"

One of the men at Queen Regan's table, a red-haired man with a long moustache, wearing a heavy gold torque and a gold-handled dagger, stood, and bowed, far lower and more showily than Glevon.

"The High King does me honour to ask," he said, speaking Britannic in a thick accent which Penarddun did not recognise.

"Lugaid mac Finnat, High King of Tara," said Llyr quietly. "One of the greatest powers in Ireland, come to make a friend of me." He stood, and returned the Irishman's bow, far more perfunctorily. "It is we who are honoured by your presence, my lord," he called. The Irish king bowed again, and sat down, beaming. Llyr turned to Goneril's table. "And by yours, my lord Aganippus." A burly man with blond moustaches, and an axe-shaped brooch securing his cloak, rose and bowed in the same manner as Lugaid. "King of the Belgic Menapii," Llyr explained. "Only one tribe, and they pay tribute to the Suessiones, but mighty for all that. They even settled an offshoot tribe in Ireland, a couple of hundred years back – who are now subjects of King Lugaid there."

Penarddun considered the two kings, and said nothing. The Menapian was a long way from home. Belgae traded mostly with southern and eastern Britons; their High King had sent many envoys to Dun Belin over the years. Perhaps

Aganippus had even been there himself. What was he doing here? Pushing a claim to sovereignty over his Irish cousins? Many tribes were scattered into different branches, around Britain, Gaul, and Ireland; most had long since lost all connections with their kin over the sea, forging links with their neighbours instead. She could not shake off a vague foreboding that the Menapian's presence boded ill to her father's kingdom. But in that case, why call her attention to it? To taunt her?

Once there was food and drink before them, Llyr grew less talkative, his mouth usually being full. Cordelia talked around him, pointing out people Penarddun did not yet know. She seemed relieved to have a stranger to talk to, and a harmless enough subject to talk about: Penarddun sensed that she was avoiding something else, chattering to keep some hurt at bay.

The fair young man with the squarish face next to Glevon, whom she had taken for one of Lugaid's followers, was the Dobunnic lord's son, Picell; another son, Achlesydd, was acting as cup-bearer. It was a position of unusual honour, as Achlesydd's mother had been a slave. The dark-eyed youth who hovered by Aganippus was his devoted shield-bearer, Denapoll, an Armorican made hostage some years before, who had elected to stay with the King when peace was concluded between their peoples. There were traders and sealords, Dumnonii, Irish, Armoricans, and one man with long braids and a tattoo-covered face whom the Princess identified as Cornal of the Epidii, a Northern slaver who had travelled even further than Aganippus to be there. The High King occasionally stopped eating to pass acid comment on these, in particular remarking that the Epidian would sell his mother for a jug of ale.

"But his wares are good," he added. "The likes of him have to be dealt with."

The meal lasted through the night. The champion's portion was awarded to King Maglor, in respect of a fight in which he had driven raiders away from the sacred isle of Mona – "Cornal's men, probably," muttered Llyr. Henwyn scowled at the award, and looked minded to contest it, but Regan whispered something that made him sit down – no doubt a reminder that the resurgence of Darnant tainted any claim they might have on it.

When every belly was full, and half the hall was falling down drunk, Llyr rose unsteadily to his feet, and slammed his fist on the trestle before him. Instantly, Euroswydd leapt up, and bellowed:

"The High King would have silence!"

The chatter fell to a low murmur; and Penarddun could see the assorted royal guests watching Llyr intently.

"Friends," he said. "Kinsfolk. You have gathered here to see me married; though I know some of you would rather see me buried. Well, you'll not have that satisfaction yet a few years, unless my young wife wears me out!" There were guffaws at that. "The gods have never yet sent me a son," he went on. "And if they do, I know I'm not like to see him grown. But I have three daughters who can wield sword and spear as well as I did in the Belgic wars, any one of them fit to be a Silurian queen!" That provoked cheers; though the daughters themselves were all silent, and looked apprehensive. Llyr's face assumed a stern aspect. "I am not going to lay aside my burden yet," he said, "nor divide my hard-won kingdom into three. But come, my sweet princesses, come before me –" he motioned his daughters forward, and they hastened to rise, Cordelia hurrying round the trestle to stand with her sisters and face him – "and tell me: how much do you love your father?"

Silence fell. Penarddun looked around the hall: everybody appeared as surprised and confused as she felt. Was this some stratagem, or the ramblings of a drunk old man?

"Come, speak," Llyr urged them. "Goneril: you're my eldest. Speak first."

"I hope my lord father does not doubt any of our loves?" said the eldest Queen. "But for myself, I call the gods to witness: you gave me life, and I love you more than life; liberty, light, and life itself, I would sacrifice for you, my King." She spoke loudly and clearly, her head raised: none in all the hall could have missed a word. Llyr smiled.

"You please an old man's soul," he said. "Regan, what have you to say?"

"Why," said Regan, with the same clear inflection as her sister, "I love my lord father above all other creatures; I could know no happiness without the assurance that he loved me in return. What other joy is there? Bring me the woman who says she loves her father more, and I will prove her a liar with the sword my lord gave me."

"You sing sweet as the nightingale," said Llyr. Penarddun bit her lip. Did he mean it? "Cordelia? What can you add to this?"

Cordelia looked up; and Penarddun saw tears glistening in her eyes.

"Nothing," she said.

"Nothing?" echoed the High King, uncomprehending.

"Nothing," she repeated.

"Nothing will come of nothing," said Llyr gravely. "Speak again."

49

"I love my lord with the love a daughter owes a father," said the Princess stiffly. "So much as you have, so much are you worth. I can say no more."

"So young, and so cruel?" gasped the High King. "Well then, you have named your dowry. Nothing! Not a foot of my land will you ever rule, in my life or after it! Your mother's blood has made you proud, Lady of the Lake – but there will never be any Penteyrnedd in the West but Llyr! I *am* the Prince of Princes, by this my sword, and I shall never give it up!" He gripped the hilt of his sword, which he alone wore in that peaceful company, and glowered round at the assembled company, daring anyone to challenge his word.

It was Lugaid of Tara who spoke first.

"My lord," he said, "consider what you say –"

"The High King's word is final," snapped Llyr. "She will have neither lands nor any right of inheritance."

"No bride-price whatever?" pressed the Irish king.

"A chest of gold in thanks to the man who takes her out of my sight," said Llyr. "Nothing more."

At every table, people were now huddling and whispering, keeping fearful eyes on Llyr. Cordelia was openly weeping, nor was she the only one: but in the eyes of her sisters, Penarddun could see a glint of triumph.

Suddenly, from somewhere beyond the fire, the Roman Perillus pushed his way past the drunken warriors and gawping princelings, and stood beside the Princess.

"My lord," he declared, "I may not be able to flatter like a Queen, but I have served you since you first gave me shelter here, and never before spoken against you."

"No," said Llyr. "You left that folly in Spain; if you'd learned wisdom earlier, you'd never have had to leave."

"That is not the lesson I learned in Spain," said Perillus quietly. He turned, and looked around the hall. "Not all of you know my history," he said. "I served on the staff of Titus Didius, Proconsul of Nearer Spain. During the Celtiberian War, great numbers of the poor were dispossessed. They fled to the forests and subsisted any way they could. They became robbers because there was no other way to stay alive – but they wanted nothing more than to live in peace. They sent envoys, offering to submit to Rome: they promised to pay full tribute and send their able-bodied men to fight the rebels, if the Proconsul would only restore their lands and pardon them for what they had done out of pure desperation.

"Didius agreed. He swore to the pardon and the land grant, and the fugitives came out of their forests. There were thousands of them, broken old men and pale-faced women and children thin as reeds: and when they submitted, the Proconsul had every one of them put to death.

"I called that evil. I told Didius to his face that he was an oath-breaker and a murderer. That is why I am here, an outlaw myself, an exile, an enemy of Rome. Perhaps I should have learned to keep silent in the presence of power: but I did not. My lord King, you may give me to whatever god you will, burn me or drown me or bury me alive: but what you are doing tonight is *wrong*."

Llyr's eyes had been narrowing throughout the Roman's speech; on that last word, he suddenly drew his sword, and brought it crashing down on the table in front of him, uttering a furious yell.

"Slave!" he cried. "Wretch! Get out of my sight! Who do you think I am? Didius was too soft-hearted – he should have fed you to the wolves piece by piece! Go: get out of Portskewett. If I see your foul head again after dawn, I'll have it on a spike. Go!"

Penarddun was gripping the arm of her chair so tightly that her fingers stung. It was the only way to keep her hand

51

from trembling. She had never witnessed the likes of this; she could make no sense of what was happening before her, and felt that if she relaxed her hand, she might weep, or vomit over the table before her.

She was aware of Falyse prying her fingers loose, and helping her to her feet.

"Come," hissed the little Silurian woman. "Away. Before you anger him too."

"But – but the feast -" said Penarddun helplessly.

"Do you think anyone will miss you after this? They've other things to be thinking about. You need to sleep; you're to be married tomorrow. Come *on*."

Penarddun let herself be steered to the door, and out into the cold air, the shock of which made her gasp.

"This way," said Falyse. "The Women's House."

"Sicora..." she mumbled.

"Is already there. I sent her ahead before I came for you."

They had to duck low to enter the Women's House. Inside, it was almost completely dark: the fire had burned down to only a few softly glowing embers. Most of the sleeping places were unoccupied, the Princess and ladies being still at the feast; only a few slumbering figures were to be seen – and Sicora, waiting huddled by the dying fire, who jumped up as they came in.

"What's happened?" she hissed urgently.

"Nothing more," said Falyse. "Your lady is safe. Mine... will survive."

"But – what *was* that?" said Penarddun. "Is the High King often... that way?"

"It didn't go as planned," sighed Falyse. "He was three parts drunk – he let it become real."

"Real?" said Sicora sharply. "What was it meant to be? An act?"

"Come – sit down." Falyse led them to the edge of the house, well away from what little light the embers still gave off, and they sat in a huddle on the floor. "The High King always planned to disinherit the Princess," she said. "You've heard this damned word *Penteyrnedd*, haven't you? He's the one who made it mean something, bragging up and down the West that having Gogoniant for a wife made him the gods' chosen ruler, and never thought he was forging a knife for his own back until Cordelia was old enough to have suitors. Gods, how he raged when he realised they were out to replace him! He even thought of marrying her himself to remain Penteyrnedd, but Goll convinced him that would anger the gods. But he daren't let her have a British husband. Those Demetian boys, Picell ap Glevon, even Euroswydd, they all had hopes – they'd promise loyalty for now, of course, but how long do you think that'd last if Llyr looked weak? And sending her overseas would be even worse – it would look like inviting invasion. Now the British princes don't want her, and the others know better than to hope for land or succession."

"You mean she *knew*?" wondered Penarddun. "They planned this together?"

"No," said Falyse. "Llyr planned it with Scaliger. Scaliger told the Queens; they thought they'd wormed a secret out of him. It suited them to be rid of their sister; more power for them when their father dies. They sent me to tell Cordelia – not to ask her, just to present the High King's orders.

"Imagine how that hurt her! But she played her part in duty to her father – played it too well. His rage was more than half real, and all real when Perillus stepped in. Poor honourable Perillus wasn't part of the plot. Now he's truly banished, and all over a mummery."

"So is she to marry one of the kings from over the sea, now?" asked Sicora. "Which one?"

"Whichever will have her," said Falyse. "If the High King's ranting hasn't left them both too scared. She knew that was how this would end – exile and a stranger's bed. She accepted it to preserve the peace of the West; by all the gods, I hope it works. It would be too cruel, if she's endured all this for nothing."

Penarddun shook her head. She still could not make sense of what she had seen; it felt like a bad dream.

"You should sleep," said Sicora. "Lie down." She looked at Falyse. "Will you stay with us?"

"I am sorry," said Falyse. "My Princess will need me. But try to sleep; both of you." She reached out, awkwardly, and touched Penarddun on the shoulder; then she abruptly stood, bowed, and walked away. Penarddun sat, unmoving, until Sicora put her arms around her and gently laid her down. They lay still, together, under one cloak: and at last Penarddun closed her eyes, and the world left her.

Chapter 6: *Two Queens*

"Oh, father Leir, how thou dost wrong thy child!"

~ *King Leir*

Her dreams were full of Llyr, crimson-faced and spitting, and Cordelia weeping silent tears; and she tried to shout at the High King to stop, but had no voice.

She woke with a jerk, moving so violently that she shook Sicora awake. The door stood open, and it was light outside. Penarddun scrambled to sit up.

"It's today," she said. "I must prepare myself..."

"I will prepare you."

Falyse was sitting less than a yard away; she had clearly been watching them sleep.

"But the Princess...?"

"Is attended by her aunt," said Falyse. "She ordered me to see to you. Before last night Urganda would not have spoken to Cordelia, for fear of Llyr's wrath; now, how much more harm can it do?"

Penarddun let Falyse lead her out of the Women's House, Sicora following with the robes the little Silurian had brought; they wound their way to the gates. There a guard would have stopped them: but Falyse said:

"The Queen-to-be is to bathe in the Severn Sea before she dons her wedding robes."

"Alone?" sniffed the guard suspiciously.

"She is not alone. She will be safe with me."

"Darnant's been growing bolder, they say."

"Even Darnant will not raid beneath the walls of Portskewett in broad daylight," scoffed Falyse. "If you doubt my ability to defend her, draw your sword, and see how long you keep your hand."

The man scowled; but he put up his spear, and let them pass.

They followed the path round the outside of the walls, facing the morning sun, and so came at last to the shore. The strand was wide, sandy, and exposed; the ships of Cornal and the foreign kings were beached there, with many lesser boats, and the fort itself looked down from above them. A couple of fishermen looked up from mending nets, and stared at the three women.

"Here?" asked Penarddun apprehensively. Falyse shook her head.

"No," she said. "Further along. Among the rocks, below the cliff."

They followed the shoreline along to the outcrop of rocks. It was still open, to the spray and the cold breeze and prying eyes, but it was more private than the beach.

"Here," said Falyse.

"What must I do?" said Penarddun.

"Go into the water, and ask Mother Severn to bless your marriage. The form of words is up to you. You can keep your gown on if you like, but it'll be a cold walk back up to the fort in wet clothes."

Penarddun smiled weakly.

"I expected more ceremony," she said.

Falyse shrugged.

"Ceremony comes later," she said. "At the wedding, and tomorrow when they mark a Silurian viper on your arm."

Penarddun glanced back along the beach; nobody appeared to be looking their way. She quickly slipped her gown over her head, ran through the surf, and flung herself down flat into the sea: she was not going to give her body time to react to the cold, for otherwise it would take her an age to lower herself in. She gasped with the shock of it, and surfaced spluttering: and, through chattering teeth, she muttered her prayer. Neither Falyse nor Sicora heard it.

She was half-dried, dressed again, and hurrying along the beach still shivering, when she saw a column of men descending the path. The morning sun glinted off helms, shields, spearpoints.

"An expedition?" she wondered. "What's happened? Is it Darnant?"

Falyse shook her head.

"Those aren't the High King's men," she said. "It's the Irish. Lugaid Luaigne is taking his ships and his friendship back to Tara. This comes of last night's folly."

They stopped and waited, while the Irishmen marched down onto the strand; then, when the column halted by Rus' ships, Falyse motioned the other two to follow her, and they hurried up the path. At the gate of the fort, the man who had questioned their exit stood stiffly aside, and allowed them back in; Falyse cocked her head at him, and said:

"The men of Tara have gone, then?"

"Aye," he said. "Lugaid called the High King a madman, for everyone to hear. We shouldn't have let them go."

"Of course not," said Falyse. "A war over a few hot words is just what we need. What of the Gauls?"

The man shrugged.

"They're staying, far as I know," he said. "For tonight, at least – they'll hardly catch the tide now."

Falyse said no more, but swept through, Penarddun and Sicora hurrying behind her, and on to the Women's House.

57

Inside, Urganda and two slaves were dressing Cordelia. There was nobody else there; the two Queens lodged with their husbands, and the other noble ladies who had slept there the night before were all absent, perhaps sent away by the priestess. Falyse dipped her head before them; Penarddun and Sicora hastily followed her example. Cordelia was pale, and her eyes red-rimmed, but she bore herself erect, and wore an air of great calm.

"My lady," said Falyse softly.

"Falyse," said Cordelia. There was no hint of a tremor in her voice now. "I am to be married today. Did you know? King Aganippus has accepted my lord father's terms. Goll has determined the propitious time: my wedding and my lord father's will take place together, at sunset. There will be feasting for his, but not for mine." She turned to Penarddun. "I wish you joy, and many children, my lady."

"And I you, Highness," Penarddun replied.

"The Gauls will feast, and say it is for you," said Urganda.

"And my sisters will drink to my departure," answered Cordelia with a sad smile. "Far more happily than they will drink to the birth of brothers. If you do bear my father's children, Penarddun, tender them well: this is an unhealthy country for an infant."

Penarddun said nothing, but inclined her head.

"Is there news of poor Perillus?" asked Falyse.

"He left the fort last night," said Urganda. "He took little more than the clothes on his back. Nobody has seen or heard of him since."

"And Awel?" said Sicora. "What of Awel?"

Penarddun started. Amid all the confusion and fear since Llyr's extraordinary burst of fury, she had scarcely thought of the Cassian boy.

"He is with the High King," said Urganda. "He has been telling him stories, children's tales from the East. They seem to please him. Llyr has no notion who he is."

"But you do?" pressed Sicora. Urganda smiled.

"I have enough skill to recognise the Merlin," she said. "But have no fear. Mabon will reveal himself in his own time, and I will not take it upon myself to forestall him."

Penarddun blinked. She still could not imagine Awel as an incarnate god: but she knew that the gods moved in strange ways, and that anything was possible to them.

The rest of the day passed with an agonising slowness. Portskewett was full of bustle, slaves and guards and visitors rushing this way and that; beasts and birds being slaughtered and prepared for the night's feasting; but for Penarddun, it seemed as if it was all happening at a great distance. She had nothing to do but remain in the Women's House, while Falyse – and Sicora, acting under the little Silurian's direction – brought her clothes and jewellery. A woollen robe dyed forest green, and a blood-red cloak, replaced her own off-white gown; a slender gold torque, with snakes' heads at the ends, was placed around her neck, and similarly serpentine armlets wound about her forearms. Spirals of woad were painted on her cheeks; and through all she sat, barely moving. She had had a bite of bread on returning from the shore, but no more; yet she noticed no hunger, only a heavy lethargy which descended slowly upon her. Cordelia, after her grim warning, had not spoken to her again, though she often glanced anxiously in her direction; Urganda seemed to be watching her keenly, but likewise said nothing. When she rehearsed her words, it felt as if she was hearing somebody else saying them, a long way off.

"My lady." Sicora was peering into her face. "My lady, the Speaker is outside. It is time to go."

With a jolt, as if awaking suddenly from a deep sleep, Penarddun started to her feet.

"Has the day gone so quickly?" she exclaimed. "Where is Cordelia? What -"

"The Princess has gone ahead with Lady Urganda," said Falyse. "The High King made no provision for her attendance, so her aunt has taken all upon herself. Euroswydd is here to escort you to the sacred grove; I will be behind you."

Then Falyse and Sicora were helping her to her feet, and leading her towards the door. She paused, and shook them off: they took the hint and stepped back. She strode up to the door, and ducked out.

Euroswydd was waiting outside, with a friendly smile, as if none of the previous night's business had happened.

"My lady," he said, proffering his arm. She took it; and he steered her gently towards the gate. After all the busyness of before, the fort seemed all but deserted; only one or two slaves remained – no nobles, and scarcely any guards barring the two at the gate, who snapped to attention as she passed.

They wound around the fort once more, away from the beach this time, inland, to the north, where the grove must stand. She could hear footsteps behind her: Falyse and Sicora, she thought, but did not look round.

"All will be well," said Euroswydd quietly. "His Highness is not a monster. Be brave, but not over bold; love him, and he will love you. Who could not? You look a very goddess."

"I thank you for your kindness, sir," she said flatly.

"No kindness, but truth," he insisted.

They had reached level ground; there were trees ahead, and firelight. As they drew closer, she saw torchbearers flanking the approach to the grove, stood still as stones. As they passed into the light, trumpets blared out, and she saw

Llyr ahead of her in a heavy blue-green gown, a garland of autumn flowers and ears of wheat bound about his brow, the thickest gold torque she had ever seen resting on his shoulders, his eyes glistening almost as if with tears. Goll stood by his side, Glevon a little way away, and others she recognised from the feast the night before were ranged around; Aganippus and Denapoll stood back to one side, Cordelia and Urganda to the other, both almost in the shadows.

"My bride," said Llyr softly. "Welcome."

Euroswydd led her up, and presented her to the High King, who crossed his hands and took hers, right in right, left in left, a dancer's hold. Llyr's face was a hand's breadth from hers; she lowered her eyes.

"Penarddun ferch Belin, Princess of the Trinovantes," said Goll solemnly, "do you come here to be wed to Llyr ap Bladud, High King of the Silures?"

"I do," she whispered.

"And do you both consent freely to be so wed, according to the terms agreed, those terms being known to you both?"

This time they spoke in unison.

"We do."

"Then give me your hands." Llyr dropped her left hand, and held up the right before the Druid; Goll had drawn his knife, whose bronze-gilt blade gleamed redly in the torchlight, and, in one motion, nicked both the King's scarred brown hand and Penarddun's, so that two trickles of blood eased slowly out. "As your blood mingles, be you joined. May Belcnos and Belisama bless this union; may Modron make it fruitful and Mabon make its fruit good." He pulled a length of cloth from the pouch at his belt, and wound it around their hands, binding them together: and it was done. Ordinary folk married without ceremony, but the gods must be seen to bless a royal match.

Llyr leaned slowly, almost clumsily, in, and leant his forehead against hers: when Penarddun raised her face to meet him he kissed her with all the awkward shyness of a boy. But his lips were as rough and wrinkled as his hands, and it was all she could do not to flinch away.

Then people were applauding, and shouting their names, and Penarddun was blinking and trying not to let the world swim out of focus, while Llyr beamed and waved. Goll coughed, and the High King muttered something; and, at a glance from the Druid, Cordelia and Aganippus came forward.

Their ceremony was rushed, full of a sense of uneasiness. Penarddun had wished for her own wedding to be over quickly, but the whole assembly seemed to wish it for this one. The words were all but gabbled; and Goll, perhaps hurrying, cut a little too deep, so that the couple's blood seeped through the cloth he wound their hands in. There were gasps at that: it was surely an ill omen. But at the end of it, Aganippus crushed Cordelia to him, and kissed her with a lover's passion. She looked startled, but after a moment returned his kiss; Penarddun noticed Denapoll frown, but the rest of the Gauls cheered so loud that the Britons felt obliged to join in. Llyr scowled; but she reached up and stroked his cheek, and said:

"This is our night, my lord." *Be brave, but not over bold; love him, and he will love you.*

A goat was dragged forward, bleating, terrified. Goll took it by the back of the head, and raised his knife high.

"Mother Modron," he intoned, "we make this offering to you. Bless the unions of these, your servants."

In a single blow, he struck the goat between the shoulder-blades, sinking the knife almost up to its hilt. The beast thrashed for half a heartbeat, then sank to the ground.

Then the drummers and trumpeters began to play, and the whole assembly to process back up the hill, back to the fort, many dancing and capering rather than walking. Awel appeared from nowhere to lead them, turning a cartwheel out of the grove, then skipping ahead, waving streamers, and loudly singing a bawdy song about a forest nymph and a talking snake. He was wearing a fantastical tattered cloak of many colours, but no ass's ears: perhaps they had not yet been found.

He danced on up the path, and the wedding party followed. The music, though still playing as loudly as ever all around, seemed to recede from Penarddun's hearing as they passed through the gate; the revellers all but carried them into the hall, where a great bed had been prepared by the hearth, a whole bearskin sprawled across it, half a dozen soldiers guarding it. She felt many hands pulling at her gown, and did not resist: but suddenly Llyr barked:

"No."

The fumbling stopped. People froze, confused, and looked up as if fearing another eruption, more banishments. Penarddun realised that the tugging hands had already pulled off her belt, and her gown was hanging open: she was half naked, and did not know whether to cover herself.

"I will not be stripped for all to gaze on," said Llyr. "I am the High King."

"Quite right," exclaimed Awel. "Our eyes would be blinded by the majesty of my lord's member." Some tittered at that, afraid to laugh outright: but Euroswydd was at the King's shoulder, and whispering. Penarddun caught his words:

"Your Highness' potency must be seen, or it will not be believed."

The look Llyr turned upon him was enough to have withered another man, but his Speaker did not so much as blink.

"I am Llyr!" he hissed fiercely. "My potency is *known!* My men will line the bed, and none will look upon me and my bride. I will *not* be spied upon, nor whispered about, and I *will* be obeyed!"

He clambered onto the bed, tugging at the neck of his robe, and held his hand out to Penarddun; she took it, and climbed up beside him onto the pile of furs. The soldiers closed ranks behind them, backs turned, shields raised.

"Th-thank you," said Penarddun in a small voice.

"It was my own dignity I sought to protect, not yours," said Llyr stiffly. "I am old: my hair is grey all over, my belly sags, and I have many scars. I can yet do my duty. I am not accustomed to be gentle; but I will try."

Penarddun bit her lip; and she lay back, and looked up at the rafters. The revellers were shrieking, still in the hall, apparently having turned their attention to the bedding of Aganippus and Cordelia; but they seemed as distant as home.

Chapter 7: *Avalon*

"They rode up and asked them who they served, and they
replied: 'The Lady of the Lake.'"

~ *Perceforest*

Portskewett, 83 B.C.E.

Penarddun swung the wooden sword as hard as she
could: but Falyse ducked under it, and, in one fluid movement,
had a knife at her throat. One of the watching soldiers started
forward, but Llyr waved a hand irritably at him.

"Too slow, again, my Queen," she said with a laugh, as
she lowered the blade.

"Try again," said Llyr, smiling.

The High King had insisted on this training. In Dun
Belin, Penarddun had seldom even been allowed to hold a
sword, much less use one: but among the Silures, all women of
noble birth were trained in the use of arms. Falyse herself was
not high born, but had walked into Llyr's fort one day and
demanded a place among the High King's guards: it had been
granted to her after she overcame half a dozen men in combat.
For all her slightness, she was iron-hard, and lithe and fast as
any wildcat. Where she had come from, none knew – save
perhaps Sicora, now. They had been always in one another's
company almost since Penarddun had come to Portskewett,
and it had not been long after the move to the winter base
before Falyse crawled under Sicora's cloak at night; if the
giggling whispers of other girls who slept in the Women's
House were to be believed, their nights were far more joyous
than the High Queen's, on the rare occasions when Llyr did

not immediately fall asleep. By day, they often slipped away from the fort together – easily achieved at the winter fort, inland and ringed with trees, more noticeable now that they had returned to Portskewett with the spring. Sicora had even begun to move like the Silurian woman, with an easy grace that supplanted her earlier awkwardness.

"I am out of breath, my lord," she said.

"Once more," he urged, though he was wheezing with the effort of watching them.

"I know you can beat her, my lady," added Euroswydd. "Once more."

So they fell back, and once again raised round shield and wooden weapon. This time Falyse attacked first, a lightning-quick series of lunges: Penarddun blocked every one, but was driven back almost to the edge of the ring before she stepped smartly sideways, and began her counter-attack. She knew even as she advanced that she was swinging wildly, with little of the Silurian woman's precision: but she was almost as fast as Falyse, and was gaining by sheer relentlessness. The Silurian stepped back, and back again: then suddenly turned her shield flat, and deflected the next blow upwards instead of back. Penarddun stumbled: Falyse slashed at her leg: and she fell flat on her arse.

Llyr laughed loudly; Penarddun was laughing too, but she felt an odd, sick pain somewhere in her bowels. When she took Falyse's outstretched arm, and tried to get up, she gasped, and staggered, as a fierce jolt shot through her.

"Look to my Queen!" exclaimed Llyr, suddenly on his feet. Sicora was hurrying forward, and Euroswydd striding across the ring; they swam in and out of view as Falyse slipped an arm around her, and began to half-carry her away.

By the time they laid her on a pallet in the Sick House, although she was still wincing, the worst of the pain had faded, and the nausea with it: and she could see Goll clearly when he loomed over her. But though she tried to wave the Druid away, he would not leave.

"Open her gown," he commanded Sicora. "Let me see her." Sicora looked to Penarddun, who shook her head. "Lady, I must examine you," said the Druid impatiently.

"I can open my own gown, thank you," said Penarddun calmly. Trying to still the trembling of her fingers, she unlaced her gown, and pulled it aside. Goll leaned in, and prodded her belly sharply, from first one side, then the other: she gritted her teeth, not knowing what he might do next, but he merely grunted, and stepped away.

"Wait," exclaimed Sicora. "Where are you going? What's wrong with my lady?"

"Nothing is wrong," said the Druid. "The Queen is with child. See her well rested; I must inform the King."

"With child?" gasped Penarddun. "With child!" Her mind raced back over the past few weeks: how long had it been since she bled? She could not remember. In the confusion of moving back to Portskewett from the winter fort, she had lost track of the days – and that had been more than a moon ago. A child! She realised that she was shaking, caught between joy and fear. Childbirth was as dangerous as battle: her mother had died bringing her brother Nennius into the world: and she could not forget Cordelia's warning. She clutched Sicora's arm. "I am to be a mother," she whispered.

Sicora wordlessly embraced her, and Falyse put an arm round them both from the other side. They were still holding her when Llyr burst into the house.

"My love!" he exclaimed. "Are you well? Is my child safe? We must take every care – he will be a king!"

"I am well enough, my lord," said Penarddun, summoning up a smile, "and it is early yet. Perhaps I should not fight any more today, though."

"Fight!" echoed Llyr. "No, never, not till he is born and nursing at the least!" He rounded of Falyse. "You!" he barked. "How could you take so little care of my Queen? She would not have been hurt but for you."

"I obeyed my lord's order to instruct the Queen in the use of arms," said Falyse calmly. "We none of us knew her condition. Now that we do, we shall take every care of her."

"Hrrmm," growled Llyr. He turned back to Penarddun. "I shall have Goll read the signs and learn our child's destiny, and I shall send for the wisest midwives and cunning women in the West to take care of you. Is there anybody you would have me summon from the East, any nurse of your youth?"

"No," said Penarddun. "But when my time comes nearer, it would please me if Urganda were here."

Llyr's brow darkened.

"Urganda of Avalon is no friend of mine," he said.

"I believe her faithful," insisted Penarddun. "I would trust her sooner than a stranger."

"I will think on it," said Llyr curtly. "Now, lie down, my love: you should rest."

"I am quite well," she said, standing. "Have no fear for me." She stood on tiptoe, and planted a light kiss on his lips.

"I will be fearful until I hold a healthy son in my arms," answered Llyr. But he did not try to push her back down, nor make any move to prevent her leaving the Sick House.

His early anxiety, in fact, soon passed; and when Euroswydd suggested that the royal couple should pay a visit to the Waters of Sulis, Llyr was easily persuaded – especially once the Speaker pointed out that the waters would be good for both the High King's aching joints and the Queen's bouts of sickness. It was decided, without any discussion that Penarddun was aware of, that they would travel by sea; the Deepwood had been quiet for many months, but Darnant was still at large, and there was no sense in putting the greatest prize in the West within his grasp.

"Besides," added Euroswydd, "a passage across the Severn Sea may have more value than the savour of the waters. It has been long since the Durotriges saw Your Highness: it would not do for them to forget who is their Penteyrnedd. Let them see your bride with child, and know that the succession is secure."

Llyr nodded; and he said:

"We will travel by way of Avalon. We will show them, it is now the Penteyrnedd who makes the Lady, and not the other way about."

So it was that Penarddun found herself crossing the sea for the first time in her life. In truth, it was a short crossing from Portskewett to the river mouth below Avalon, a matter of a few hours – though they had to leave before dawn to catch the tide; but she had never felt anything the least like the swell and ebb of the waves under her feet, and her stomach had been heaving even before they pushed off from the shore. She spent the first half of the voyage retching, even after she had nothing left to vomit up, and the second half clinging weakly to the side of the ship. Llyr, by that point, had fallen asleep; Sicora was looking not much better than Penarddun felt; but Falyse stood to one side of her and Euroswydd to the other, both clear-faced and bright-eyed, and smilingly told her stories of how much worse these waters could get, which was no comfort whatever.

At last, however, they came to land, and sailed into the calm mouth of the Brue: and far ahead, rearing out of the flat green levels in the distance, they saw the solitary hill of Avalon.

It took them until night to reach it: the road wound this way and that through the levels, avoiding the many patches of marshy ground and open water; and here and there they had to wade through shallow fords, though Penarddun, at least, was on pony-back and clear of the water.

Penarddun was surprised to find that the main complex was by the water's edge, beneath the shadow of the Tor, and not, as she had expected, on top of it: but she was relieved that they should not have to mount that great height in the dark. Night had already completely fallen by the time they reached it. The gate stood open, flanked by warrior Druidesses, and lit by tall braziers; Urganda was awaiting them, torch in hand. By her side stood a girl in a bleached white gown, with a thin torque tipped with dragons' heads about her neck: Penarddun was instantly struck by her resemblance to Cordelia. She was a little taller, and her hair a few shades darker, but it could not be missed – and surely had not been by Llyr.

"Welcome, my lady, and my lords," said Urganda with a bow. "All is prepared; we have roasted four sheep and broached a cask of Gaulish wine."

"You knew of our coming, then?" said Llyr.

"I would be fool indeed if I did not maintain eyes on the coast, after what has happened to Avalon before," said Urganda. "I knew you had put out from Portskewett before you landed."

Euroswydd stepped forward and swept a low, gallant bow before Llyr could say anything.

"We thank the Lady Urganda for her hospitality," he said. "And do I see here the next Lady of the Lake?"

"Not while my niece is alive, sir, and capable of bearing daughters," said Urganda sharply. "But yes: this is my daughter

Gweledydd." The girl in white inclined her head. "Enter, and feast."

The night's meal was less tense than Penarddun had feared. Awel hovered near Llyr, and kept him laughing and distracted; Urganda entertained her courteously and solicitously, while Gweledydd importuned her for stories of the East, and of her journey the year before. Nevertheless, by the end of it, Penarddun was feeling almost choked by fear that some eruption of anger would tear the night apart. She rose abruptly to her feet.

"I would pray in the orchard of Afallach," she said. "Alone, if I may."

Llyr grunted; Euroswydd nodded, and said:

"Of course, the gods must be honoured."

"Take all the time you will," said Urganda. "You are as safe on this Tor as anywhere in Britain."

Penarddun stepped outside, into the blessedly cold air. She did not need shown the way to the orchard: they had seen it from the wetlands below as they approached the Tor before the sun set, and the little complex of houses around Urganda's hall was too small to get lost in. The early blossoms would be closed now against the night air, but she still fancied she could smell the sweetness of the apple trees as she wandered in their direction.

There was no wall or fence between the orchard and the hall, but there was a gate. It stood free, a great wooden frame, always open, marking rather than barring the way; a brazier burned before it, tended by another armed woman – one of the Nine Damsels of Latis. She inclined her head as Penarddun approached, but neither spoke nor made any move to stop her.

Beyond the firelight, the orchard itself was lit only by the moon. It was waxing, and shone brightly, a crisp clean

71

light from a cloudless sky, so that the tops of the trees looked more white than green; even beneath them there was no truly dark shade, for the young leaves and flowers were only beginning to put forth, and the light pierced between the branches to the grass below. Looking into those dappled, shifting shadows, Penarddun saw something move against the wind.

At first she thought it was an animal: but when she looked again, she saw a deeper shadow blotting out the scattered patches of moonlight, too big for anything but a child, unless there were a young bear wandering the orchards.

"Come on out," she said gently. "I won't hurt you."

The little figure moved out into the moonlight, and Penarddun saw him: not a child, but a dwarf. He stood barely higher than her waist on his stout, stunted legs; though his arms were long and looked well muscled. His bristly hair was brindled, brown streaked with red, with paler patches here and there; and the dark blue eyes in his clear, boyish face were deep and sad.

"Why were you hiding?" she asked. "There's no need."

"There is," he said. "*He* must never see me."

"He?" she wondered. "The High King?"

"The High King," he agreed. "Your husband. He must not know I exist."

"But why?" she said, confused. "And why reveal yourself to me?"

"So that you know," he said. "You carry his child. You must know your danger."

"Goneril and Regan will not dare to harm their brother while the High King lives," said Penarddun, with more confidence than she felt. "And if… if anything should befall him… I have friends enough to help me."

"I didn't mean them," said the dwarf. "I meant *him*."

Penarddun blinked.

"Llyr?" she said. "I, I know of... what he has done... the gods know, I fear him – but he would not harm his own child. Least of all a son, and Goll says it will be a son. The stars foretell it. He's wanted a boy all his life."

"He has indeed," said the dwarf bitterly. "And the gods never gave him one. Oh, some of the slaves and prisoners he's raped must have had sons, and many of the babes who died were boys – but he has no living son that he would acknowledge."

"You?" gasped Penarddun. "You're saying *you* are Llyr's son?"

"I am," answered the dwarf. "My name is Ardian ap Llyr ap Bladud, and if I had been born whole I would be Prince of the Silures and you would have been sent to Gaul or the North instead of the West. When Llyr saw what I was, he had it given out that I had been stillborn like so many others, and he ordered that I should be exposed to die. My aunt saved me and brought me here. That is why he must not know I am alive – and why you must."

"Urganda?" said Penarddun.

"Yes," said Ardian. "She has been kind – the only mother I have known. Queen Gogoniant never came here again after he carried her off; perhaps it is best. I don't know if I could have borne seeing her."

Penarddun wanted to say that it could not be true: but she could see Cordelia in every line of Ardian's features. She knew that he spoke the truth.

"I – I am sorry," she whispered.

It was the second time that one of Avalon had surprised her alone to tell her husband's secrets; the second time that she had been reduced to meaningless apology.

Ardian reached out, falteringly, and touched her hand.

"*I* am sorry," he said. "You are no more to blame than I am. But I must be gone; you will be sought soon."

"Of course," said Penarddun distractedly. "I, I thank you... I will say nothing, to anybody. We will not be here long – tomorrow or the day after we leave for the Waters of Sulis."

"Travel safely," said Ardian. "And watch your back."

"Plead with the seas, and reason down the winds,
Yet shalt thou ne'er convince me; I have seen
His foul designs through all a father's fondness."
~ Nahum Tate, *King Lear*

They stayed but a day longer at Avalon, and were two days on the road to the Waters – a leisurely and pleasant journey in the spring sun. Glóir, apprised of their arrival, had brought in food and drink from the lands tributary to the temple, and entertained them well; and they retired to sleep. Pleading the need to purify herself at the springs next morning, Penarddun withdrew to the priestess' house, leaving Llyr in that reserved for male guests.

It was still dark when she woke suddenly, sitting up and gasping. There was shouting outside; Falyse was on her feet, knife in hand, eyeing the door.

The first coherent words to hit their ears were:

"I must see the Lady Glóir!"

Glóir was up by now, tugging on a heavy cloak over the light tunic she slept in; but when she started towards the door, Falyse shook her head.

"Don't go, my lady," she said. "We don't know who's out there."

"A soul in need," answered Glóir gently. "Any assassin could find a thousand easier ways to come at me than by pushing in at the main gate and rousing me from my bed. Besides, I am under the protection of the goddess."

Small good the gods' protection did Avalon when Llyr raided it, thought Penarddun. *Small good it did the Dobunnic warlord who prayed here before going off to fight my father.*

But Glóir commanded her servitors to open the door: and out she swept, Falyse following on her heels, eager to protect her from whatever lay beyond. Penarddun looked to Sicora, who said nothing, but met her eye, stood up, and strode out of the door after them. There was nothing to do but follow.

A young man was slumped on his knees on the ground outside, head down. His hair was fair; he wore a tattered black cloak that had once been of high quality, and a pair of breeks soaked with mud and slime, but neither tunic nor boots. His arms and especially his feet were scratched and bleeding. The night was cool, and he was visibly shivering. A cluster of soldiers, both Llyr's and the temple guards, were gathered behind him, spears and swords levelled at him as if he were some dangerous animal. Hearing the women approach, he looked up, and Penarddun saw that his lip was bloodied and one eye blackened: and she realised that she knew him.

"Picell ap Glevon," said Glóir softly. "You are welcome here at any time: why do you come in the dark of night like a thief?"

"Sanctuary," he said, speaking thickly through his split mouth. "Save me."

The priestess looked to the soldiers.

"This man is no threat," she said. "Let him up; take him to the sacred springs and let him bathe. I will have my women find him clothes. When he is washed and dressed, I will learn his purpose here; he is to be treated well."

The Silurians, uncertain, looked about for Llyr, but did not see him. Penarddun stepped forward.

"Let it be as the priestess of Sulis has decreed," she said. It seemed to her that they still hesitated a moment: but when

Falyse gave an angry jerk of the head, they stood back. One of Glóir's guards pulled Picell roughly to his feet, and steered him along the path towards the springs.

"I will receive him in the hall," said Glóir. "You must be there, and Llyr too: it would be an insult to leave you outside: but it is my protection and that of Sulis that he has sought, and it is I who will hear him and give judgement."

Two of the Silurians were sent to wake the High King, while the women went to array themselves more decently: by the time they assembled in the hall, the dedicatees who slept there had removed themselves, and all the torches had been lit. Three chairs were arrayed to face the door: as royals, Llyr and Penarddun would sit beside the priestess. Llyr was bleareyed and grumbling, constantly asking what was happening.

Picell was brought in by Glóir's guards. Though clean, and decked out in a checked tunic and red woollen cloak that almost fitted him, he was pale and shaky on his feet, and still bore the marks of his injuries.

"Picell!" exclaimed Llyr. "Glevon's boy! What are you doing here?"

"I came to seek the protection of Lady Glóir and the goddess," replied the blond youth.

"Against whom?" said Llyr, his eyes narrowing. Glóir glanced at him; Penarddun caught some slight annoyance on the priestess' normally calm face at the High King's usurpation of her position.

"Against my father."

Llyr spluttered; Glóir's face became grave.

"And why does Lord Glevon threaten the life of his son?" she said.

"I do not know!" exclaimed Picell. "I do not know! I have done him no wrong, none, that I know of; yesterday he was as loving a father as I could wish for, and today he has

77

hunted me across all the lands of the Dobunni! He called me traitor, kinslayer, monster. Some wicked god has made him mad."

"You say that you have done nothing to provoke him?" said the priestess levelly.

"Tchah!" spat Llyr. "I know his *nothing*. The young today, they are impatient to rule their parents' houses and herds, they are godless, impious. What did you do to him, boy? Was your neck itching to put on his torque? Did you see yourself as lord of his homestead?"

"No!" insisted Picell. "I have done nothing!"

"If you have done aught, confess it," said Glóir. "The goddess' protection extends to the guilty as well as to the innocent: but never to those who would deceive her."

Picell placed his hand upon his heart.

"I have never wronged my father," he said. "By Sulis I swear it, and by all the gods, upon my life."

"Then you have nothing to fear if you explain yourself to him," said Llyr. He turned to the priestess. "I say we bind this boy and send him home. Let Glevon deal with him."

"And I say that the protection of Sulis is sacred!" declared Glóir, rising suddenly. "My lord king, you are not in your kingdom: but even if you were, you are below the gods. Picell is safe here from any hasty vengeance, and if he is to be tried it will be before me. The administration of justice belongs to the Druidic order, *my* order. Do not forget it."

"Do not lecture me on your order, woman," barked Llyr. "Both my parents belonged to it." He turned back to Picell. "The gods protect you, boy," he said. "But if the chiefs of the Dobunni lend your father aid, and he comes in arms, I do not see the goddess Sulis raising sword to save you."

Penarddun gaped. She could hardly believe that Llyr had just as good as threatened the priestess.

Glóir resumed her seat.

"The chiefs would never commit such a sacrilege," she said, but Penarddun could hear the doubt in her voice.

"I have no desire to bring my father's vengeance here," said Picell. "I shall leave at dawn. If I can be afforded a horse, I will ride to the south coast, and take ship for Armorica."

"For Armorica?" said Llyr sharply. "Or for the Belgic lands? Why not go to the great Queen of the Menapii for help? You were always sniffing around her when she was here, as if you were good enough for a High King's daughter; now you're perfectly matched – two ungrateful children together. You can enjoy plotting against your fathers."

"For shame!" Penarddun blurted out, before she could stop herself. The whole hall fell silent. Llyr looked at her, open-mouthed, speechless. She blinked, and felt sick as the full enormity of what she had just done rose in her gorge.

"M-my lord," she said, as calmly as she could manage, "you lower yourself to speak so in a holy place. Lord Glevon's case against his son has not yet been heard; all may yet be, ah, resolved…" She felt that she was babbling, and tailed off.

"Resolved?" said Llyr, cocking an eyebrow. "An innocent misunderstanding, is that it? Are all you women's heads turned because he has a pretty face?" There was a menacing pause: then, out of nowhere, he guffawed. "Ha! You're young, and your heart is soft; nobody can blame you for that. You have not seen as much of the world as I have. Let older heads debate this matter; you watch, and learn to be a queen."

Penarddun stepped back, red-faced. Shame and anger fought with fear; at last she spun round and half-stalked, half-stumbled out of the hall, tears streaming down her face.

She ran back to Glóir's house, and threw herself on the floor, weeping. A few moments later, she heard the door open: she looked up to see Falyse and Sicora enter.

"You should have stayed in the hall," she said. "The King will be angry."

"He sent us here," said Falyse. "He told us to protect his son."

"His son?"

"It is only that he fears for you – that you might do something foolish," insisted Sicora. Falyse's curled lip showed what she thought of that, and Penarddun was not minded to disagree.

"Foolish," she repeated bitterly. "Of course, what could he expect of me but folly?"

"Try to sleep," said Sicora gently. "He is in an ill mood because he was called suddenly from his bed. It will be different in the morning. We will keep watch over you."

Penarddun could not deny that she was exhausted. She laid her head down, and closed her eyes: but sleep would not come. Her mind was whirling through what had happened that night, and every creak of the timbers or rustle of the grass outside seemed to echo through her head.

She had no notion how long she had lain there when she heard Glóir speak softly by her ear.

"My lady."

"Yes?" exclaimed Penarddun, sitting up. "What is it?"

"Easy," said the priestess. "It is morning."

"Morning?" Penarddun blinked, confused. It was true that a dim light was creeping round the shutters. Had she slept after all?

"Early, but morning. King Llyr is yet sleeping, and will sleep long: I gave him a strong draught. Picell ap Glevon is readying himself to leave for the coast."

"He is safe, then," said Penarddun, relieved.

"I believe he will be," said Glóir. "He asked me to wake you, that he might give thanks to you for taking his part last night."

"For all the good it did him," muttered Penarddun.

"King Llyr agreed to let him go," said Glóir. "That is something. It might not have happened had you not shamed him."

"Shamed him? I did nothing but enrage him."

"That is not true," insisted the priestess. "Will you see Picell? He will understand if you will not."

Penarddun sighed, and gave a long yawn; then she stood up, and brushed down her crumpled tunic.

"I will bid him farewell," she said, "if that is his wish. But you must be present."

Glóir led her outside. Picell was already present, dressed and armed and wearing a new travelling cloak, with a horse saddled and ready: he had clearly been waiting for her. To her surprise, she saw Euroswydd standing by.

Picell at once fell to his knees, and bowed his head before her.

"My lady," he said. "I do not know how to thank you. To take my part against the rage of the High King... You are truly courageous."

"Truly stupid, some would say," she answered curtly. "I don't believe I did you any good. Get up, and be on your way before my lord husband changes his mind."

Picell looked up, confused.

"I – my lady, I will – I wished only to..."

"Go," she said, more softly. "I wish you nothing but good, but you do yourself none by wasting time. Go."

Blushing, the young man got to his feet, and mounted his horse. At a gesture from Glóir, her guards opened the gates, and he rode out; he glanced back over his shoulder, and met Penarddun's eyes with a hopeful smile. She could not help but return it; and when she felt Euroswydd's hand squeeze her shoulder, she reached up and took it in hers.

"Did I do right?" she whispered. "To defend him?"

"You did well indeed," he assured her. "You showed yourself a true Queen. You spoke bravely and truly, for justice and for mercy; and my lord's heart was moved, I promise you. Nobody's could fail to be."

"Truly?" said Penarddun. "I babbled. Llyr was right, I spoke nonsense."

"Even if that were true," he said, "you still *spoke.* That was what was needed."

"You are kind," said Penarddun with a sigh. "But I'm not sure you're right. In any case, I need more sleep." And she dropped his hand, and went back into the priestess' house.

Glóir's Story

I remember Alaron.

*Of course I never served under her at the Waters of
Sulis. She gave up that life when King Bladud had to go over
the sea again, and left her as Regent in Siluria. But she often
returned here, she and King Bladud both, from the time they
came to give thanks for Prince Llyr's birth, through almost to
the ends of their lives. They held great councils of Druids here,
from all over Britain, with Gauls and Irish attending too – and
the King's two companions from Spain, Saron of New
Carthage and Mago of Cadiz. They were noblemen of
Carthaginian stock, dark of skin and black of hair, who had
studied with King Bladud in Greece, and fled back to Britain
with him to escape the wrath of Rome: they were his closest
counsellors, and said to be as wise as any Druid.*

*The common folk were always glad of their coming,
because anyone with small hope of justice from her own lord
or chief could appeal to Bladud and Alaron. Not as King and
Queen, but as the joint Archdruids of this island. They were
famed for their wisdom and their justice; I never heard any
honest person complain against their decisions.*

If their son was ever like them, he has changed.

*My mother was Irish. She was a free servitor in the
household of King Enna the Generous, whose reign is now all
but forgotten: for Crimthann the Victorious slew him and
slaughtered all his kin, and sold his attendants into slavery,
over the sea in Britain. Mother was bought by a Durotrigan
chieftainess, who made a holy offering of her – dedicated her
to the service of Sulis. It is fortunate that Sulis is a gentle god:
many would rather have had her blood than her labour.*

Queen Alaron was already gone into Siluria by then, her place taken by the Lady Dubricia. She took in my mother, and made her what she had been before, at King Enna's court – a bottler and cupbearer. In Dubricia's kitchens, she met the cook's boy, who would be my father: and very happy they might have been, had she not caught the eye of the Penteyrnedd.

This was the old Penteyrnedd, Urganda's grandfather; his name was Mempricius. His daughter had taken a husband, and they should have been Lady and Penteyrnedd, but he was not yet fallen in age and would not give up the title. When he came to the Waters of Sulis, he looked on my mother, and was filled with lust: and he offered great riches to the shrine if she should be sent to his bed. Dubricia knew about my father: so she told him that my mother had vowed her virginity to the Goddess, and she found a more willing girl for Mempricius. It was not hard to find one who counted it an honour, especially when she was promised a gold arm ring: but she was found bruised and weeping in the morning. She blamed my mother, though there was no reason to it: she would only say, "It should have been you."

But when Mempricius next came that way, my mother was pregnant. He came unexpected, and she could not be hidden from him. He flew into a great rage, saying that either he had been deceived or the goddess had been wronged, and vowing to have her burned and her lover flayed. None of his threats could make her name my father, and Dubricia pretended ignorance: but the cook his master, who had always envied my father my mother's favours, and longed for some of the gold Mempricius scattered to his flatterers, whispered his name in the Penteyrnedd's ear. Mempricius hauled him out of the kitchens, and took him down to the pool: and there he cut him to pieces. He took his tongue first, then his hands, then his

84

member, and he defiled the sacred waters with them before he cut my father's throat. Then he returned for my mother.

Mempricius was twice her size and four times her strength, but that very fact made him complacent. If it crossed his mind that she might twist free of his grasp, he must have expected it to happen at the top of the path, where she might still have hoped to win out of the complex and run off. But she went with him without a word. It was only when they reached the place where the rocks are damp underfoot that she tripped him, and sent him down into the pool where my father's remains were floating; then she took a rock, and waded out into the pool, and smashed his skull. She did not stop hitting until his brain was scattered across the surface of the water.

The Durotriges were told that he had fallen by mischance, and that it was deemed to be a judgement of the Goddess against him for making her pool unclean with human blood. Some of the chiefs would have gone to war, but the Lady of the Lake said them nay. She knew her father well enough, and doubtless guessed that he had earned what had befallen him.

I was born not long after. Dubricia set my mother free, and accepted her into training for the Druidic order, an unheard of honour for a former slave; she did not complete her instruction, dying of a fever when I was eight. But it was always understood that I would follow the same path, base-born though I was. From as far back as I can remember, I learned the tables of the law, the lives and genealogies of the ancient kings, and the hymns of the gods; the secrets of beast and bird, field and stream, sky and sea. Dubricia had always taken a grandmotherly interest in me; and after my mother died, she brought me up as if I were her own. When she herself died, many years later, I was elected to succeed her with no voice raised against me.

The last time that Bladud and Alaron came to the Waters, I was twelve, and I was permitted to attend the great moot of the Druids. I sang the hymns to Mabon and his mother, and to our own Sulis, with the most learned men and women of Britain; I was even called upon to speak in the riddling contest, and answered the riddle posed by Mago of Cadiz. I saw them give justice. They returned two cows to a man whose landlord had seized them because his share of the milk was late; they freed a woman whose husband had sold her to the lord of the neighbouring valley: and I thought: this is true godliness. Justice is what it means to be a Druid. Justice, and the defence of the weak. There will always be tyrants: tyrant kings, I fear tyrant Druids, even tyrant gods. But truth and right are greater than they. Above even Sulis Herself, Justice is my god: and though I am now grown old and weary, I will yet defend it with what strength is left to me.

Chapter 9: *Heir Apparent*

"The king had... no son (therefore was he sorry) his kingdom
to hold."

~ Layamon, *The Chronicle of Britain*

Caersws.

Penarddun knelt by the fire; she had grown too big to
huddle and hug her knees as she would have wished. It had
been an ill journey from Portskewett, lashed by rain and wind
all the way. She had not wanted to travel so near her time: but
Llyr had insisted.

"That is why we must go now," he said. "Would you
make the journey after the child is born? Or have him face a
winter of sea storms before he can crawl? No. He must be born
inland, in the shelter of the woods."

"The King is not wrong," Falyse told her afterwards.
"Portskewett in winter is no place for a newborn."

She supposed they were right: but that did not make
the journey any more pleasant. Crouched in the back of a
waggon, swathed in heavy furs, she had spent it sweating and
cramped, jolted and jarred at every rut in the road, and with a
constantly full bladder. And it was much further than the
previous year, when they had travelled only to Llyr's winter
court at Gray Hill. This time they had crossed the whole of the
Silures' vast tribal lands, to winter with Goneril at the
southernmost fort of the Ordovices. Coming into the warmth
of the hall at Caersws had been but short relief, before she
began shivering again.

She had hoped, foolishly, to meet Urganda at Caersws. The priestess had been sent for before they left Portskewett: but her journey would be far longer than theirs, even if she rode instead of coming by cart. Besides, the only way to avoid the Deepwood would be to come by sea to Portskewett and follow them up the same road they had come by, and none had overtaken them – unless she had skirted the wood to the north, but that was a roundabout route which might add days to the journey. If Llyr had permitted it, she would have begged Urganda to come back with them to Portskewett months before: but he had refused.

"Do you think nobody has given birth west of the Deepwood before you?" he demanded. "We have women who will take care of you, under Goll's direction. They know their business; and if you must have Urganda, she can come when your time is near."

It was near now. How near, Penarddun did not know, could not think. But Urganda was not here.

Others were. She had pushed straight into the hall and flung herself down, not caring for niceties after such a journey: but she became aware that a tall, angular figure was looming over her. She looked blearily up, then sat up sharply when she recognised Queen Goneril.

"There's no need to jump… Mother," she said. "I come only to pay my respects to you and my little brother – or sister."

"It will be a son," Penarddun said defensively, feeling stupid even as she did so. "Goll has seen it in the stars."

"Cherish him well while you have him, then," said Goneril. Penarddun blinked, unsure if she had heard aright – but the threat had barely sunk in when Goneril went on. "He will be sent away for fosterage soon enough. Do you do that in the East? My Morgan has already gone to the Cornovii. At

88

least there he will be with his aunt – and we will foster Cunedag. My sister is bringing him here. My father's idea, to bind the family closer together… by giving us each a hostage. He planned it when they were both yet in the womb. No doubt he has already picked out some favoured ally to bring up your son."

"My brothers were fostered," said Penarddun. "But they visited often."

"Quite," said Goneril. "I'm sure that was a great comfort to your mother. It is a good custom, to be sure – it breeds friendship between tribes and kinship between kings. Maglor and Henwyn were both my father's fosterlings once; and here we are – one happy family."

"Is King Maglor here?" was all Penarddun could think to say.

"No. He is examining the coastal defences. The Irish raiders sometimes like to essay a last attack or two on the verge of winter, thinking they won't be expected. But he will return in a few weeks. We shall all celebrate the Winter Solstice together. But you are tired; I will let you rest." She glided away; Penarddun watched her go, and frowned, wishing she could see past the Ordovician Queen's enigmatic mask. But Goneril was all armour and cool courtesy.

It could not have been long after that Penarddun fell asleep. It was still night when she woke, blinking confusedly and trying to make sense of the noise that had awakened her. The fire had burned low, and had been replenished – the new peat was just starting to catch; somebody had thrown a cloak over her and placed a bundle under her head. People were milling about; the outer door was open and a cold draft was blowing in.

Penarddun rubbed her eyes; and she saw a tall form duck through the door, a red-haired woman with silver torques at neck and wrists – Regan of the Cornovii. Behind her trotted her little son Cunedag, who was to be left here. Penarddun clutched at her belly defensively, and tried not to think of having to send her child away.

Regan swept a low, elaborate bow.

"Hail to the High Queen!" she declared. "And to the future High King." Penarddun could hear the mockery in her voice, but responded coolly:

"Hail, daughter."

It was Regan's turn to blink. But Penarddun was not in a mood to let the Queens intimidate her. She was too tired and sore to put up with their power games.

"Regan!"

Llyr pushed forward from somewhere near the back of the roundhouse before the Cornovian Queen could respond, and wrapped her in an embrace which she stiffly returned.

"How has your journey been? How is young, er, Cunedag? And – who is this?"

The High King had noticed the young man who had followed Regan and Cunedag through the door, ahead of the Queen's attendants. He bowed low.

"Achlesydd ap Glevon, my lord, here to represent my father, who sends his apologies but cannot attend."

"Achlesydd, of course, of course... the slave's boy." Achlesydd's face did not so much as flicker. "Of course he'd have to send you, now that your brother's turned traitor. Well, you'll do, you'll do."

"Greetings, Lord Achlesydd," said Penarddun, inclining her head. He bowed again.

"My lady."

Penarddun turned to Llyr.

"My lord, I feel a little unwell. I was foolish to sleep so near the fire. I will take wine-and-water, and retire."

"Very well, very well; it is late," said Llyr absently. "You may sleep."

Over the next few days, Penarddun often pleaded pains and tiredness to stay out of the way of her stepdaughters. Sicora attended her conscientiously; and, a little to her surprise, she found that Euroswydd too was always on hand to fetch a pillow or offer a drink, and to deflect the queens' probing questions. Goneril and Regan were always solicitous after her health, but she was sure that what they were really fishing for was whether she was strong enough to bear, whether she and the child would survive.

All the time, she itched for Urganda's arrival. She would feel safer if the priestess were there. The days went by, and still there was no news: then, suddenly, she awoke in the night gasping, her clothes drenched, her belly convulsing.

She screamed.

Then Sicora was by her side, squeezing her hand; Falyse was kneeling close by; Euroswydd was there too, chewing his lip nervously. They were in the Women's House; she was not sure how long it had been since she screamed, moments or minutes.

"Where is Urganda?" she asked.

"She is not here," said Sicora gently. "She has not come."

"She said she would come... Where is the King?"

"Sleeping," said Euroswydd. "He drank deep last night; it will be long before he wakes."

"Lie still," Falyse told her. "I will fetch Goll, and Ebren; you're not too close yet." Ebren was Goneril's oldest attendant, a toothless old woman with a face like a dried up currant and a tongue like a whip; she was said to be older than Llyr, but she had birthed more babes than most had ever seen, and while

91

there were those who hated her sharpness and envied her position, none had ever denied her honesty. If Urganda could not be there, Ebren was the next best thing. As for Goll – he was the most senior Druid in Llyr's kingdom, perhaps in Britain. He could not be kept away.

The next few hours were none too rough; the sun was high, and Goneril and Regan had come in, to watch detatchedly, when the true agony began. After that, Penarddun remembered little, only blood and crushing pain, calling out for Urganda and for her dead mother, and Ebren shoving a stick between her teeth; then, at last, it was over. It was near night again: and Goll held up the red squalling thing that had finally made its way out of her, and declared:

"It is a son, whole and well! The High King has a son!"

"Urganda did not come," murmured Penarddun. "She did not come."

"But she did," said Euroswydd. Falyse shot him an angry glance, but not before Penarddun had heard him.

"What? Where is she? Why have I not seen her?"

"She was turned away, on the High King's orders," said the Speaker. "I thought you knew."

"Turned away?" said Penarddun. "Turned away! He promised... He promised... Give me my son."

"He must be presented to the High King," said Goll. "And the court must pay their respects."

"Give me my son!"

But the Druid was already striding out of the door, the baby crooked in his arm, wrapped in a fold of his cloak. Euroswydd followed. Penarddun moaned, and struggled to rise; she fell back, and cursed her weakness. Falyse took her arm.

"No," said Ebren. "She should rest. Goll will bring the child back to her; no harm will be allowed to come to that one."

"She's his mother," snapped Falyse: and she hauled Penarddun to her feet. She staggered, but Sicora caught her: leaning on both of them, she allowed them to half-carry her after Goll, ignoring Ebren's protests.

Entering the Great House, they found Goll on one knee before Llyr, holding up the still bloody baby, who was screaming loudly. Goneril and Regan stood either side of their father, peering curiously at the child; Cunedag stood to one side, blank-faced. Euroswydd had taken up a position next to the boy. Other chiefs and ladies, Ordovician mostly, were ranged around, looking reverently on. Awel sat on the floor at Llyr's feet, playing on a little pipe.

"Behold my son!" Llyr declared. "Behold Bran ap Llyr ap Bladud ap Rhun, Prince of the Silures and of the West! Though we mourn that he has left the Otherworld for this, we rejoice that he is with us, and welcome him into his heritage." He did not seem to have seen Penarddun.

"My lord..." she said. The onlookers were chanting Bran's name, and her head was swimming. She felt her legs ready to crumple beneath her, but Falyse and Sicora held her up.

Llyr looked over at her, and frowned.

"Go back to bed, my dear," he said. "Conserve your strength."

"My lord...!"

But it was no good: the hall was darkening before her. Everything was black. The hubbub and the cry of the child seemed to last many moments after her sight left her, but soon silence descended.

It was dark when she awoke again in the Women's House. Sicora was sitting by her side, rocking Bran back and forth; Ebren crouched by, watching with beady eyes. Everybody else was asleep.

"The child -" exclaimed Penarddun.

"Is well," said Ebren. "Hungry, but well. He's had naught but goat's milk, and I can see your teats are swollen fit to burst there; if you hadn't gone after the Druid you'd not have fainted, and you could have fed him hours ago."

"I am sorry… but they shouldn't have taken him from me. Give him to me."

Sicora gently lifted the little bundle, and passed him to Penarddun: and for the first time she held her child in her arms.

"Bran," she whispered. "The Raven. It's a good name. My Bran."

Two days later, she sat by Llyr's side once again, smiled at his sallies and showed herself to the chiefs; while Sicora stood by and held Bran. This way of things had become normal. She did not dare look on Cunedag, or think of the time when Bran would have to be sent away. She had seven years yet, maybe eight. In the meantime, she would show a happy face to her stepdaughters and the chiefs. She had said nothing of the turning away of Urganda: but she had not forgiven Llyr.

The High King arose, unsteadily. He had been drinking deep, as he commonly did.

"My friends," he said, "I am once more a father. But I have not forgotten my elder children – who have been so hospitable to us all." There were happy murmurs of assent. "Indeed," he went on, "as I grow older, I would spend more time with them, and with my grandsons. My son should see more of my realm – perhaps his realm one day. He should not be confined to Portskewett and Gray Hill, and nor will I." Several of the chiefs shifted uncomfortably, unsure of what was coming next. Goneril and Regan were watching their father intently. Was this planned, like the business with the question? Did they have any idea what was coming next? Llyr had said nothing to Penarddun; nor had Euroswydd reported anything to her, or Falyse overheard anything. Awel no longer spoke to her: it seemed he had aligned himself with Llyr.

"I will not return to the lands of the Silures in the spring."

Dead silence fell. Nobody, Penarddun was sure, had been expecting this. What did he mean?

"I intend to divide my time between the forts of my daughters, and to visit my good kinsmen Pwyll and Perion, and my other vassals among the further tribes," Llyr went on. "Perhaps even to visit Mona where my father learned the Druidic secrets. I am High King of *all* the West, not of one tribe alone. The rule of the Silures will be managed by the chiefs in council; they have rarely met in recent years, but they are wise men, and will do what is best for the tribe, I know. Lord Euroswydd will remain Speaker; he will chair the council of chiefs, and will report to me. To neglect my other kingdoms merely because Siluria is the one I was born to was wrong, and I shall do it no longer."

There was a long, tense pause; then Euroswydd stepped forward, and declared:

"May the gods save the High King!"

The surrounding chiefs obediently echoed the sentiment, but still looked shocked. Llyr sat back next to Penarddun, and sighed.

"Sheep," he muttered. "Bleating sheep. All of them praying for me, while their little minds try to race around what I have just done and why."

"And why have you, my lord?" asked Penarddun. Llyr leant in very close, and put his cracked lips to her ear.

"I will not live to see Bran grown," he whispered. "I am not a fool, I know that. I am old already, and all the West is waiting for me to die."

"My lord is strong," said Penarddun unconvincingly.

"When I die," Llyr went on, ignoring her interjection, "all the princes north of the Severn Sea will look to pick the bones of my kingdom. The Silures must be ready to rule themselves. Ready to resist Maglor and Henwyn, and preserve the throne for Bran."

"But... but a child cannot be King," said Penarddun, bewildered.

"Of course not," said Llyr impatiently. "*You* will be Queen; but Euroswydd and the chiefs will take the labour of ruling off your hands. Without them the other tribes would eat you and Bran alive." He moved back, and snapped his fingers at Falyse. She was at his side instantly.

"My lord?" she said, with a glance to Penarddun.

"I want you to find a wetnurse," he said. "I won't trust one provided by my daughters. Do you know where you could find one?"

"I... believe I do, my lord," she said. "I would have to be gone some days. But..."

"But? But?" snapped Llyr.

"Forgive me, my lord, but Prince Bran is only three days old. Should not the Queen continue to feed him herself a while longer?"

Penarddun laid a hand on the King's sleeve.

"I should prefer it, my lord," she said.

Llyr nodded.

"So should I," he said. "But the choice is not ours. The longer you feed, the longer before you can conceive another."

"Another?" she gasped.

"Another. Bran is strong, but I've seen stronger children die. And I am old. I am capable yet, but who knows how much longer? I mean to put another child in you before the spring comes. So," – and he turned to Falyse once more, "you will find us a wetnurse."

She bowed her head.

"Yes, my lord."

Chapter 10: *Solstice*

"He's entered into mad riot; he's an old man, and now doting."
                                    ~ Wace, *The Story of Brut*

Falyse was gone for half a month, and the weather had worsened by the time she returned. She brought with her a plump, broad-faced woman with wiry black hair and a kindly smile, who carried a baby of her own – a thin little thing with huge eyes, barely half the size Bran had already grown to.

"This is Mefus," she said, "and Mafon. I have known Mefus many years. She will be happy to nurse Bran, and you can trust her as yourself."

Penarddun was about to ask where Mefus came from – what her tribe was – but Falyse had never answered such questions about herself. If she had brought somebody from her past to Caersws, she would have imposed the same secrecy on her.

"I thank you, Mefus," she said, with a gracious smile. "Your daughter is beautiful."

"Thanks, m'lady," said Mefus. "The Prince is a fine handsome lad himself. A big one too, but I've milk enough for him, don't worry."

Llyr accepted Mefus without comment, and she began to suckle Bran. Penarddun had thought she would be expected to hand him over immediately, but Mefus explained that there had to be a transition, for their sake more than his – an easing off for Penarddun and a building up for her. When the High King was told this, he merely grunted,

"As long as it's quick."

It was quick enough, too quick for Penarddun. Her breasts ached in the longer and longer gaps between feeding, and she felt her heart torn when she knew that she had fed Bran for the last time. She made a point of being as much with Mefus as possible, especially when she tended the children; the wetnurse would prattle about anything and nothing, and Penarddun would gaze at Bran and wide-eyed little Mafon, and smile. Everybody about her spoke so seriously when they spoke at all – except Awel, whose jokes were often barbed and encouraged Llyr's cruel humour – that to hear somebody simply chatter was wonderfully refreshing. She wished she could ask Mefus more about herself, but it felt too much like probing into Falyse's secrets, so she said little.

When Bran was sleeping and Llyr did not require her, she took up again her sword training with Falyse. They kept it gentle – Llyr would not be forgiving if she were to be injured – but he himself had said that she ought to be able to defend herself. She knew that Goneril kept in practice; she had once witnessed her fencing with Regan, before the Cornovian Queen had gone home, and since then had seen her at practice with some of her own warriors. From time to time Euroswydd would join in these sessions: though not as fast and lithe as Falyse, he was a competent swordsman, and often kept Penarddun on her back foot. She was suffused with pride when she first managed to land a hit on him.

When the trees were bare, Maglor returned from the coast. Hanging from his saddlebow were the heads of four Irish pirates: his men boasted of a noble victory, but as far as Penarddun could make out they had come too late to save the raided village, found the Irishmen feasting amid the ruins, and slaughtered them before they could sober up. No doubt Goneril's bards would make an heroic tale of this, and Maglor would glower at them and protest modesty while enjoying every line.

The Solstice was drawing near, but it was hard to see how the great feast would differ from the ones held almost nightly. The warriors of Llyr's train had been eating more heartily and drinking more voraciously ever since they came to Caersws, the High King always first among them, and Awel leading the ever filthier songs. Goneril had taken to muttering about empty larders when she heard them carousing, and indeed Penarddun wondered how the fort was supporting them. From everything she had heard, the Ordovician lands were the poorest in the West, producing precious little corn and much scrawnier sheep than those of the Silures. They had gold, of course: perhaps Goneril was buying food in from the Cornovii. Certainly they had seen no shortage of pork, mutton, cheese, roasted tubers, apples, honey-baked pears, rich dark ale, mead, even beef and Gaulish wine, red and white. They ate better here than in Portskewett.

But on the actual night of the Solstice, Goneril's cooks somehow managed to surpass themselves. The biggest boar Penarddun had ever seen was roasted whole, slathered in salted honey; there were more sweetened wheat bannocks and pears stewed in wine than even Llyr's hungry men could eat. The champion's portion went to one of Maglor's men, who displayed six pirate scalps to prove himself worthy; Awel capered about and snatched scraps of food from Llyr's trencher, the High King guffawing every time he nearly caught him.

At last Llyr managed to seize the youth's wrist as he sneaked in to grab a honey cake.

"Ho now, little fool," he said jovially, "have you not had enough?"

"For myself, yes, my lord," said Awel. "This is for poor King Maglor."

"For King Maglor, boy?" said Llyr. "He is not poor; he is rich, and gave us this feast."

"But he is sorely in need of something sweet," said Awel. "He just kissed Queen Goneril, and the sour taste is yet in his mouth!"

Llyr roared with laughter, all the louder when Goneril glowered; Maglor wrinkled his lip but said nothing. Goneril got up, and stalked out of the hall; Penarddun wanted to follow her. But what could she say? She did not know her stepdaughter, and the Ordovician Queen had shown no sign of wanting to be known.

So she sat still through several verses of "The Great Stag's Rutting Time", until she could be reasonably sure of not meeting Goneril, before she excused herself and left the hall. There would be no sleeping in there tonight, or not till the fire burned out. No doubt Goneril had gone to the Women's House; she would walk awhile in the frosty air, clear her head, and then do the same.

There was a small shrine behind the hall to the Three Mothers. It being a holy night, she supposed she should pay her respects before going to bed, and ask them to bless her child. Mefus had long since taken him to the Women's House to bed down; she had held back from the evening's revelry to be better able to mind the little ones, but Penarddun was the High King's wife, and had been expected to dance and drink and feast with him and his retinue. She could not deny that she had been enjoying the evening, until Llyr had grown too loud to tolerate. Awel encouraged him, but she could not be angry with the boy without being angry with herself for it. He had no choice.

The torch on the path to the shrine had gone out, but the moon was shining brightly enough to see her way – and to show a shadow under the eaves of the hall. There was a man leant there, pissing against the wall. One of the guards who had had a little too much mead, no doubt. She hurried past, and reached the shrine; the ground was too cold and hard to kneel on, so she crouched, sitting on her haunches, and bowed her head.

"Triple Mother, true and kind,
Blessings lay on me and mine," she whispered.
"Bless my children and my spouse,
Kine and crops, hearth and house.
Winter morn to summer eve,
Sea to sea and wave to wave…"
"What are you praying for?"

She looked up sharply, almost losing her balance; then gave a relieved sigh as she recognised Euroswydd. She stood up.

"My son's health."

"Have no fear for that; I don't know when I've seen a lustier little lad. Anything else?"

"For my lord to be at peace with his daughters."

"That, yes. That I pray for too. When they fight it is so… wearing."

"Wearing?" she blurted. "I'm afraid every minute -" She bit back the end of the sentence, but Euroswydd completed it for her.

"Of Cordelia happening over again. I know. I work always to keep the peace, but I was elected to do so. You never chose this." He laid a hand on her shoulder; she instinctively drew to him, away from the cold – and a moment later found herself sobbing into his chest, while he made soothing noises and stroked her hair. All this time she had hidden her fears, even from Sicora and Falyse – they knew, of course, but she had not dared let herself weep, or speak ill of Llyr. Now everything tumbled out.

"He terrifies me," she whispered. "Every time I speak I dread what he might do. What he might have done if, if Bran had been a girl…"

"No, no, you are safe," said Euroswydd softly. "We will keep you safe, all of us. We will keep you safe."

She broke away, and looked up into his brown eyes, blinking away the tears: then, impulsively, she leaned in and kissed him. He caught her in his arms, lifting her nearly off her feet, bearing her backwards against the wall, tugging her gown upwards, while she fumbled at the fastening of his breeches.

"Do you want this?" he murmured, not stopping.

"Yes," she breathed. "Yes."

Afterwards, she slipped quietly into the House of the Women, and lay down to sleep, to pleasanter dreams than she had had in a long time. The next day, she half wondered if she had dreamed the encounter, half feared that the whole court knew of it: when she saw Euroswydd, she could not meet his eye: but when the day passed without so much as a hint that anybody knew anything amiss, she began to relax. After that, however, she avoided Euroswydd, and slept every night either beside Llyr or with Mefus and the children.

She thought she was succeeding at acting as if nothing had happened. Days passed, and then weeks. Goneril's complaints grew muted; the winter grew steadily colder, despite the now lengthening days.

Then, one night, nearly a month after the Solstice, Llyr drank himself to sleep early, and Penarddun headed towards the House of the Women. As she passed the deep shadow by the side of the hall, a hand reached out, caught her by the wrist, and drew her into the darkness before she could cry out: and a heartbeat later she was twined around Euroswydd, kissing him greedily, sighing his name.

Afterward he slipped away by the back of the hall, she going the other way. She was about to enter the House of the Women when she paused. Something had moved on the corner of her vision. She looked that way, as surreptitiously as she could. There was a small figure scrambling over the top of the palisade. Even as she looked, it dropped away on the other side: but she had had time to recognise it. It was Awel.

Penarddun frowned. Where was he going? Had he acquired a lover here in these desolate hills? It hardly seemed likely. She did not dare follow him: she had no explanation for Goneril's guards, and no hope of slipping past them both in and out. If Falyse had been to hand she might have asked her to go after the youth, but Falyse was in the Women's House, twined in Sicora's arms. She was half tempted to wait and catch him sneaking back in, but the night was cold and there was no telling how long he might be gone. Better to catch him alone some time the next day – or to have Falyse or Sicora do so; he might speak more readily to them, and she would not have to admit to having seen him herself.

Her hand was on the door of the Women's House: but now she turned, and tiptoed instead back to the main hall, and in. Llyr was lying snoring by the fire; Goneril and Maglor slept against the wall, and a few chiefs, both Ordovician and Silurian, were sprawled around. She crept under the High King's cloak, and nuzzled in against his chest.

"My lord?" she whispered. Llyr did not respond. She prodded him gently in the ribs; he grunted, but did not move or open his eyes. She sighed, and settled down to sleep.

It was still dark, and the fire had not fully burned

down, when the sound of raised voices awoke her. Llyr was groaning and blinking groggily; Maglor and Goneril were on their feet, and many of the warriors about were feeling for their blades.

The door came flying open. It had been violently kicked from the outside, by a man who now ducked through, wielding a torch before him in his left hand and dragging a smaller figure by the neck with his right. A dozen knives were out before they recognised him: it was Rheol, Goneril's gold-bedecked majordomo, his normally equanimous face dark with anger. He hurled his captive to the ground – almost into the fire – and the light fell on the frightened face of Awel. "I caught this little rat climbing in through the palisade," he growled. "He's a spy, selling us to Darnant or the gods know who else."

A clamour of voices arose at once. Penarddun heard more than one name Regan and Henwyn: there was still no love lost between the Ordovices and Cornovii.

"Silence!" roared Llyr. The chiefs were hushed, though they continued to mutter quietly. "This is a nonsense," said the High King. "He has a girl outside the fort somewhere, or he went looking for one. Or else he just wanted to be away from your damned hubbub. Is this a matter to wake your King for? Two kings, by Mabon, and two queens too. Go away, and sleep like an honest soul instead of prowling the walls – you're not a sentry."

"It seems I must do the sentries' work for them, though," sniffed Rheol. It took Penarddun a moment to realise that he had not troubled to add "my lord". Llyr's brow was darkening.

"Do you know to whom you speak, little man?" he said softly.

"Father," Goneril interposed quickly, "Rheol did not think. It is late and we are all tired. I am sure that the boy did not go to any enemy; the matter will wait until the morning. Of course he will have to be punished – for any to leave the fort without leave is a grave matter, and he is unfree – but I am sure..."

"He is *mine!*" snapped Llyr. "Mine to punish or pardon as I like! And this preening jaybird, this jumped-up menial, dares disturb my sleep and then lecture me, without even giving me my proper title?" He stalked up to Rheol, and thrust his face into the majordomo's. "If you ever lay hand on one of my men again," he said, "you'll lose that hand." Rheol held the High King's gaze for several seconds: but when he finally blinked, Llyr punched him in the groin, so hard that he fell writhing to the ground. The chiefs gasped, and even Maglor's eyes widened: but it was only Goneril who dared respond.

"Father," she said quietly, "Awel may be your man, but Rheol is mine. To punish or pardon, as I see fit. And you will not lay hand on him again."

For the first time, Penarddun saw Llyr speechless. He stared so long and uncomprehendingly at his daughter that she thought he might be about to collapse; the only sounds were the sputtering of the fire and the groaning of Rheol. At last, he looked away, and muttered something about needing his sleep. The chiefs dispersed to their beds; Rheol crawled out of the hall, and Awel curled up like a dog at Llyr's feet. Soon the High King was asleep again, and all was still: but Penarddun did not sleep for the rest of that night. The next morning, the High King went hunting, as he often did. There was a light covering of snow on the ground, but the sky was clear and promised a fine day. Euroswydd and Maglor rode with him; Goneril, who normally enjoyed such occasions, pleaded a headache, and lay down in the Women's House.

Penarddun took the first opportunity to corner Awel. She had Falyse and Sicora with her; but after last night there was little point in subtlety. She asked him to walk with them outside the walls; he looked suspicious, but accepted – and as soon as they were beyond the hearing of the guards, she said:

"Where did you go?"

"My lady?" He tried to look innocent.

"Awel," said Sicora gently, "we want to protect you."

"The High King protects me," he said stubbornly.

"As long as he chooses to," said Falyse. "But what if he loses interest? Or what if he becomes the danger? You took a great risk, and you must have known it. Why? If you would tell Llyr, you can tell us; if you wouldn't tell him, then you do need our help."

"I was on the High King's service," said Awel.

"And on his orders?" He said nothing. "No. Against his will?" Still nothing. "So, yes. Don't worry, I know well enough that sometimes Llyr must be crossed to be served – to be saved. But Perillus knew that too, and where is he now?" Awel flinched at the name; Falyse smiled. "Awel," she said, "did you go to see Perillus?"

Penarddun's mouth fell open. Surely the Roman was long since gone into exile, in some Dumnonian trading port or over in Gaul?

"Perillus is gone," said Awel.

"Perillus has never been more than half a day's journey from Llyr's side," said Falyse. "Does he think I didn't know? I guard the High King's person; a bloody poor job it would be if an exiled traitor could lurk around following him for over a year without me knowing about it. I grew up in the Deepwood: if I had that little sense I'd not have survived."

"Perillus has followed the court, and you said nothing?" wondered Penarddun. "Even to me? To Sicora?"

"What I tell Sicora is between us, my lady," said Falyse, without rancour. "But Perillus is no danger to Llyr – he's the best friend he has, if the High King could only see it. The way to keep Llyr safe was to keep Perillus safe, and the way to do that was to say nothing." She turned back to Awel. "But how long have you known?"

"Since the journey up to Caersws," said Awel, dropping all pretence. "He doesn't trust Queen Goneril, and he knew in our isolation up here he wouldn't be able to pick up court gossip as easily as round Portskewett, where every fisherman knows the High King's moods. He wanted a spy inside the fort."

"And he chose someone he barely knows because nobody would suspect it," said Falyse. "If I'd been caught sneaking in or out, or Scaliger, or Euroswydd even, somebody might have thought of Perillus; but nobody'd ever connect him with you. The gods guided his choice."

"But we can't tell the High King this, or Queen Goneril," Penarddun pointed out. "What if they do want an explanation? What should the story be? They won't believe an assignation."

Awel frowned in mock irritation.

"Am I that ugly?" he said.

"I only meant..." Penarddun tailed off. But Falyse said:

"I believe they would. You're clever enough to come up with details, or joke them out of wanting any. It's simple, and that always helps – simpler than the truth, so it sounds truer. It'll do."

They made sure they were talking about something harmless by the time they wound their steps back up to the fort. The sentries parted to let them through, then turned and crossed their spears behind them. Goneril and Rheol came out of the hall: the Queen smiled thinly.

"Seize him," she said.

Two soldiers grabbed Awel by the arms. A great wooden frame had been set up in front of the hall; they dragged the kicking and protesting youth over to it. Falyse's hand dropped to her sword hilt, but Goneril shook her head, and she took the warning: they were surrounded by Ordovicians, loyal to the Queen. Leather straps were produced, and Awel's wrists bound to the corners of the frame: a guard tore off his cloak, then took a knife and slit his tunic up the back, pulling it apart, exposing his curved, weak back and prominent vertebrae.

"The birch rods," said Goneril calmly. Another soldier produced a bundle of thin twigs, like the end of a broom. Rheol held out his hand.

"No!" exclaimed Penarddun. "No, you cannot! The High King forbade it!"

"What High King?" sneered Goneril. "The one who handed over his power to the Silurian chiefs? Do you think they will go to war over a peasant brat who isn't even of their tribe? This is my kingdom. My laws will be obeyed, and those who flout them will be punished." She turned to Rheol. "A hundred should suffice. Do not kill the boy, or cripple him." Rheol bared his teeth. He was a naturally handsome man, but now he looked like a hungry dog eyeing an injured fawn.

"A hundred," he agreed.

The first stroke left a criss-cross of pink marks, and made Awel gasp aloud. At each thereafter, the weals grew bigger, and redder. It was the eighth or ninth blow which broke the skin; at the next, he screamed, and Penarddun wanted to hide her face. But she would not. She was the Queen of the Silures, and would not show herself weak before another tribe. Mefus looked out of the Women's House, perturbed, but Penarddun motioned her back.

By the end, Awel's back looked raw almost from neck to waist, and he was barely conscious. Falyse and Sicora hurried forward, and cut him down; they carried him between them into the Women's House, and laid him on the floor, face down.

"Holy Modron," breathed Mefus.

"Get wine," said Sicora urgently. "There are still a few jars left in the store: bring one, and say Queen Penarddun ordered it."

"I'll go," said Falyse, and hurried out. A few moments later she returned, lugging a great amphora of Belgic that must have cost Queen Goneril dear. Sicora and Mefus dipped rags in it, and washed Awel's wounds, before bandaging them up: he winced and groaned at every touch, but finally heaved a sigh, and fell asleep right where he lay.

It was late by the time the hunt returned. Awel had awakened, and was sitting up, smiling and cooing at Bran and Mafon: but when he heard hoofbeats outside, he struggled to his feet, and began to hobble to the door.

"You sit back down, my lad," said Mefus. "You're not well, and you'll only cause trouble."

"The trouble's already caused," said Falyse. "It is indeed," said Penarddun. "Awel, wait – we will go out together."

And so she stepped out by Awel's side, with Bran gurgling in her arms, and met King Llyr at the gates of Caersws as the sun was dying.

Chapter 11: *Serpent's Tooth*

"But the greatest grief that Leir took, was to see the
unkindness of his daughters."
~ Raphael Holinshed, *The History of England*

Caersws, 82 B.C.E.

The moment Llyr saw the crabbed and stumbling way
Awel was moving, so unlike his usual skipping step, his eyes
narrowed dangerously.

"What has been done to you, boy?" he rumbled: but
before either Awel or Penarddun could speak, Rheol had
stepped forward, smirking.

"I chastised him, sir, by order of the Queen."

Euroswydd reacted before Llyr. Kicking his horse
forward, he leant down and struck the majordomo across the
face, laying him flat in the mud.

"That's a taster," growled Llyr. "I made you a promise,
you little snake, and by Taranis I'll keep it." He reached for the
hilt of his sword.

"You will spill no blood in my fort, sir," said Goneril
sharply. "He spoke the truth: he acted on my orders. I will not
have riot and disobedience here. I have asked you more than
once to check the insolence of your fool and the disorder of
your men; but you will not punish even the grossest faults. I
cannot be safe in my own fort unless I enforce my own
discipline here."

"Am I not your father?" exclaimed Llyr. "Are you not
my daughter? Am I not High King?"

111

"My lord, all I ask for is order," said Goneril exasperatedly. "These characters you surround yourself with shame both me and you. They are not fit company for a man of your age."

"My age?" gasped Llyr. "My age? I am not yet such a dotard that I need to be nursed like a babe! I will keep what company I like!"

"But not in my house," replied Goneril. "If you will keep such men in your train, then keep not so many. Send half of them back to their clans. These numbers cannot be supported here much longer."

"By the Eye of Balor!" roared Llyr. "I am Llyr ap Bladud, High King of the West, and I will not be told what men I may keep about me by any Ordovician wolf-bitch! You are no kin of mine – I have but one daughter!"

"My lord," said Penarddun soothingly, "be patient."

"Patient?" snapped Llyr. "My patience is in not burning this filthy hovel about their ears! Saddle the horses, and load the waggons! We leave this night for Hen Dinas – and may the night-hags tear Caersws in pieces!"

"My lord King," said Maglor, bowing his head with the stiffness of one unaccustomed to it, "I hope you know that I had no knowledge of this."

"You're a liar, or else woman-ruled," said Llyr. "As for you, daughter: may you rot from the inside while you live, and last just long enough to see your son treat you as you have treated your father. I call on the Three Mothers to bear witness to my curse upon you and on all your line. May they perish in flame and the kingdom of the Ordovices with them. Horses, ho!"

"My lord, I beg you -" Maglor began, but Llyr cut him off.

"The only way you will keep me here is if you make a prisoner of me. Do you wish to try it?" Maglor said nothing. "Ha!" barked Llyr. "I thought not. Dumb as a stone when courage is called on. Horses!"

"My lord father is about to embark on a journey," said Goneril crisply. "I would have you all aid him in his preparations. I would have no delay in his leaving Caersws."

After that, servants and soldiers, Silures and Ordovices, all bustled about, making ready for the High King's departure. As they did so, snow began to fall – not the light flurries they had had so far, but heavy flakes coming thick and softly, ever faster, blanketing the hillside in white silence. By the time they were ready to leave it stood a hand's breadth deep, and Penarddun wished that she and Bran were safe indoors and not heading out onto the ill-made hill roads in the darkness. But there was nothing for it but to climb into the waggon with Mefus. At least she had made sure they were provided with plenty of thick pelts – the skin of a bear, two wolves, and several sheep and goats lined the cart; they smelt warm and friendly, and would serve to keep out the cold – if they were able to remain in the waggon all the way to Hen Dinas. If they were forced to disembark... She tried not to think about that.

Sicora, at Falyse's insistence, rode with them; Falyse herself rode outside with the other warriors, though she had dressed warmly, in woollen breeks, double-layered tunic, and fur-lined cloak. They trundled slowly down the hill, and entered the woods; Penarddun had fallen asleep before they stopped for the night, hugging Bran to her breast.

Early the next morning, they went on. The snow had not stopped falling, all through the night, and was falling yet. The trees provided some cover, save here and there where the very weight of it had brought weaker branches crashing down, and they had to be cleared away. But increasingly often, they had to halt while the path ahead was dug clear. Food was doled out in small lumps – they had brought bread and cold meat, but not enough for a journey as long as this now promised to be. At Llyr's insistence, a double ration was sent to Penarddun: she gave most of it to Mefus, who was after all feeding both children. Bran drank greedily, and cried lustily; but Mafon fed only tentatively, and whimpered often.

"She's not well," said Mefus. "She needs to be out of this damn waggon and these furs, but if I take her out there she'll freeze. May the gods get us where we're going soon."

They plodded onwards, getting hungrier and colder with every step. When Falyse visited the waggon, there was frost in her hair and she was shivering; she huddled under some skins with Sicora for a few minutes, and told them what was happening. They had made some progress, but less even than Penarddun had thought; they could not be half way to Hen Dinas. Euroswydd had separated from the main party, the High King sending him to join Goll at Gray Hill – but there was no telling whether he would have made any better progress than they. When Penarddun asked her about the danger of wolves, she said:

"The four-footed kind I don't fear. They don't attack caravans like this unless the travellers are already dead or dying. But hard winters breed desperate men."

"You don't think Darnant would come this far north?" wondered Penarddun.

"He never has before," said Falyse. "There's always a first time, though – but it wasn't Darnant I was thinking of. The more bogged down we get, the more tempting we look to starving peasants and runaway slaves. As long as we keep a sharp lookout, we won't be taken; but there'll be blood on the snow, blood of folk who only wanted food and warm cloaks.

And any who survive will likely run to Darnant and swell his army."

"They'd join that creature?"

Falyse nodded.

"In hard times, you don't have to help the poor to be their hero – just hurt the people who hurt them. Hungry folk don't see Darnant as any worse than the kings and queens – at least, unless they live in the Deepwood."

Mefus shuddered.

"Bloody fools," she spat. "Let 'em join him – they'll soon learn what he is."

Silence fell; Penarddun still did not feel able to ask more.

All that day, and the next, their progress got slower and slower. The snow had finally stopped, and they had left the wooded zone, but their food was all but gone. At last, as the fog cleared on the third afternoon, Hen Dinas rose before them. They had left the Ordovician hills behind them for an undulating plain, from which the heights of Regan's fortress rose abruptly, as if some giant had dropped it there. The fort which sat atop the hill was the largest Penarddun had ever seen. Even Dun Belin or Portskewett could have fitted comfortably inside its palisade; it utterly dwarfed Caersws and Gray Hill. On the journey, Falyse had told them the tale the Cornovii spun about this fortress: how it was built by the Fomorian champion Gogyrfan the Black, and how Corineus Giantslayer had wrestled him for rule of it and broken his body on the hillside.

"Of course," she added, "the South Cornovii say that happened in Cornwall." But whatever the truth of its making, Hen Dinas was a reminder of the might of Henwyn's branch of the tribe. Of all the tribes that had bent the knee to Llyr, they were the richest, the strongest, and the most numerous.

Henwyn's submission had been the High King's greatest victory.

To see the fort was one thing, though, to reach it another. The snow-filled plain still lay before them: the roads might have been broader and more even here than in the hills to the west, but the roads were all but invisible beneath the drifts. The plain was not completely trackless – others had passed that way, hunters perhaps – but more snow had fallen since. It was not until well past dark that they came to the first gate at the foot of the hill.

Llyr came to the waggon, with spare horses. He seemed but little tired by their gruelling journey – he was a little out of breath, but held his head high, and his eyes were gleaming. Awel, riding beside him on a little pony, looked far more worn, barely able to keep upright. Even Falyse had larger bags under her eyes than the High King.

"Come, my lady," he said. "We will greet Regan and Henwyn together. Make ready, you and your women there." "My lord," she said, "Prince Bran is sleeping. He has only just closed his eyes – it would not be good to disturb him, nor to take him out in this cold."

"Very well, very well," said Llyr. "He and the wetnurse can remain in the waggon. It will be late before they reach the fort: the road is steep and winds ever back upon itself. You and I will ride before them."

So Penarddun and Sicora swathed themselves in furs, kissed the slumbering Bran goodbye, and mounted up. Penarddun rode at Llyr's side; Falyse and Sicora, Awel and Scaliger, a junior Druid, and the chiefs of two of the most prominent Silurian clans, behind them. The night, though still, was bitterly cold: and, as Llyr had said, the road was long. Penarddun felt frozen to the bones by the time they reached the main gate, and the Cornovian guards parted to admit them.

Their progress up the hill had been watched, and Regan and Henwyn were awaiting them. Among the nobles attending them, Penarddun recognised Glevon and his son Achlesydd. The younger man smiled and gave a brief bow, but his father avoided her eye, instead chewing his lip and glancing fearfully at Llyr. She wondered what they were doing there: but then, the Cornovii and Dobunni shared a border, and must have much to discuss. Another man wore a heavy travelling cloak with the hood up, obscuring his face: but something about him seemed very familiar.

"Daughter!" exclaimed Llyr. "I am sorry to intrude so. I had not meant to visit you here until Beltane – but your sister's shameful conduct has driven me to it. I could not in honour remain another hour at Caersws."

"Indeed?" said Regan. "I am grieved by it. What did she do to lose your favour?"

"Do?" said Llyr. "I can barely speak of it. Damn her and that nose-in-the-air cupbearer, and damn her streak-of-piss husband! She thinks herself High Queen in the West, as if I were dead and buried!"

Henwyn guffawed.

"What is amusing?" demanded the High King.

"Some might say you buried yourself, Father, when you handed power to Euroswydd and the chiefs," said Regan. "If you have thrown away your authority, why should my sister not exercise hers?"

"I am still alive!" shouted Llyr. "I still rule! I am still Llyr! What do you know of her infamy? You were not there!"

"No – but I was." The hooded man pushed back his cowl, revealing his face. It was Rheol. "I have conveyed the

117

truth to Queen Regan and King Henwyn. They know all that befell at Caersws."

"That man...!" spluttered Llyr. "That man is a liar, a sneak and a snake and a traitor! I have sworn to have his hand!"

"He is my guest, Father, and under my protection as much as you are," said Regan coolly.

"Now I see it," Llyr hissed. "You are all confederate, all of my false children! Well, I will go back to Portskewett, snow or no snow, and when I come back here it will be with an army! If I made one mistake it was forgiving your husband's war against me – I mean to put it right!"

"Be calm, Father," said Regan. "This is no weather for travelling; it is a wonder you lost nobody on the journey from Caersws. You will remain here, until the air is warmer and your head cooler."

"I will remain?" echoed Llyr. "I will remain? Who are you to tell me that? I am not a prisoner, I am your King!"

"I am the King in Hen Dinas," growled Henwyn. There were men moving in the shadows; Penarddun leant back towards Falyse.

"Protect the children," she whispered. Falyse nodded, and backed her horse away: then suddenly swung him round, and ducked out of the gate, disappearing down the hill. One of the guards threw a spear after her; it clattered uselessly on the wooden surface of the road. Llyr gave a wordless roar, and drew his sword: but suddenly half a dozen men surrounded him and Penarddun, levelling long spears at them.

"Put down that sword, Father," said Regan evenly. "It is not needed. You have no enemies here."

"Glevon!" exclaimed Llyr. "Will you stand by and watch this treason?"

"My lord," said the Speaker unhappily, "I had no notion
_"

"He speaks the truth," said Henwyn, with a toothy grin.
"Go on, Glevon – tell the High Queen why you are really
here."

Regan flashed an annoyed glance at her husband: but
Glevon at last raised his eyes to meet Penarddun's.

"The headmen of the Dobunni sent me," he said. "I am
their Speaker, I have to obey their will."

"And their will is to transfer their allegiance from King
Belin to me," crowed Henwyn.

"To negotiate, rather," insisted Glevon, "in case it
should ever be necessary..."

"Treachery everywhere," groaned Llyr. "The very gods
are against me, to give me such unthankful children."

"Place my father and his followers in secure
accommodation," said Regan to her guards. "Then proceed to
the foot of the hill and see that the rest of his train is dispersed,
by whatever means prove needful."

"But my lady," protested Glevon, "they will die in the
snow!"

"Very possibly," answered Regan with a shrug. "That is
not my concern."

"But your baby brother...!"

"My lord father chose to place him in danger when he
left Caersws," said the Queen. "Let his nurse take him back
there if she chooses; I will not hinder her."

Tears started to Penarddun's eyes. From the moment
she had realised they were in danger, her first thought had
been to get Bran away: she had not thought that he might be
safer within Regan's walls than on the cold road.

"Please, my lady," she said. "I beg you – you are a
mother – let my son be brought to Hen Dinas."

"A moment ago you sent Father's sharp-toothed guard-bitch to keep him away from me," retorted Regan. "I've no doubt she'll sell her life to do it. But if I send enough men, I'm sure they'll be able to kill her and bring him back. Shall I do that?" Penarddun hung her head, and did not answer. Llyr was weeping softly. "Take them away," said Regan. They were placed together in a small roundhouse, not far from the central hall of the dun: Llyr, Penarddun, Awel, Sicora, and the Druid, a young man named Dardanon. Scaliger and the chiefs were marched off to another hut.

"The Queen is merciful," remarked Awel bitterly. "It will snow again tonight; she could have refused to imprison us."

Dardanon was muttering prayers, his head bent. Penarddun leant into Llyr's chest, and wept. How long she wept before she at last passed into a troubled sleep, she did not know: nor how many more grey days and cold nights they spent there. They did not count them; indeed, they barely talked after Awel had realised how poorly jokes would serve him. The High King wept daily, and called in his sleep for Gogoniant and Cordelia.

Then, before light one morning, Penarddun awoke suddenly, retching violently. She staggered away from Llyr's side just in time to avoid vomiting over him, instead spattering Awel's shoes and the end of the Druid's cloak. This had happened but little with Bran, but she knew what it meant. She was with child again.

Regan's Story

The concubines' children. That's all we ever were.

Our mothers were not slaves or peasants, they were Llyr's acknowledged consorts, taken to bear royal children – children fit to marry his subject kings. But they were not the Lady; they were not Gogoniant.

I was born to Galaes of the Demetae. Her tribe were my grandfather King Bladud's closest allies, and her parents promised her to my father while Bladud was still alive. After my grandfather died his foolish death, a number of the older chiefs declared my father too inexperienced to rule, while Bladud's fellow Druids wished to keep power in the hands of their order. My father lost no time in having all these enemies butchered, but the troubles of the Silures had emboldened their rivals, the Ordovices and especially the Cornovii. They began to raid the borders. My father raised a force and struck hard wherever they entered Silurian lands; and he called on the Demetae to show their friendship and send his promised bride with an army.

By the time she arrived, the borders were pacified, and my father was bored. Hearing of the Belgic invasions, he decided to take advantage, and mount a great raid across the Severn Sea while the Durotriges and Dobunni were defending their southern flanks. The Demetae had not come for that, and their captains protested – my mother protested: but Llyr let it be known that if they did not aid him, he would turn his anger westwards, and fire their own lands.

That was the raid on which he sacked Avalon, and seized his precious Lady. My mother herself swung a sword in that assault, as she later told me. When they returned to Portskewett, he declared sad-eyed Gogoniant his Queen, and

121

himself Penteyrnedd in right of her. Prince of Princes: nobody west of the Deepwood had ever heard the title before, but the Silures liked it. The younger chiefs who had survived Llyr's accession loved him; he gave them victories and brought home rich booty. They proclaimed him Penteyrnedd and cheered his name, and that of the Lady.

When the Ordovices came again, in greater force, Llyr crushed them; he extorted from them great tribute in gold, young hostages – including Maglor – as fosterlings, and a lady of their royal house, the Princess Nesta. She was the first to give him a child who lived – Goneril. Llyr planned from the first to marry her off to one of her Ordovician cousins and bring the northern kingdom thus under his control; probably I would have been married to Pwyll or Perion if he had not needed to tame Henwyn.

I was born not long after Goneril; our mothers were pregnant at the same time. I am told our father was glad of our births, and cooed and made much of us – until he knew that Gogoniant was pregnant. After that, all his attention was for her: and when she bore a son, he showed him to the chiefs and said "This is your next king". The boy caught a chill, and was dead within a week.

There were others who died. My brother Cherin, my sister Gael, more on Goneril's side. He mourned them, but mourned Gogoniant's children far more. Even the misshapen little dwarf that he himself sent off to be exposed, he wept extravagantly for. It was a sickly time, and when Cordelia was born so thin and frail we none of us expected her to live long. Every day my father seemed to be preparing himself for the worst; he dug his nails into his palms when she cried, and when she failed to cry, until his hands were raw and bleeding. But the days went by, and then the months, and still she lived. When he finally allowed himself to believe it, he was swept away with joy. He had hardly allowed himself to love her for fear of losing her, but after that she was his pet and his darling. He carried her about the realm, and declared that the Lady was born. Men took note of that: they remembered that the Lady's husband would be Penteyrnedd. They knew which daughter was worth the wooing.

Not that Goneril and I needed to wait to be wooed. Our father had fixed our fates from the beginning. When the Ordovices needed a new King, Llyr chose the most pliable of the candidates, and married him to Goneril, as he had always planned. At least I did not have to take Maglor – a dry stick of a man, and a boy-lover into the bargain. How Morgan was ever conceived I do not know.

As I said, I could easily have ended up with Pwyll or Perion, my little Demetian cousins. That was what my father originally wanted, and my mother liked the idea – not that she would have had any say. But the Cornovii took it into their heads to go to war against my father. They had spotted how powerful he was becoming, and wanted to stop him before he ruled the whole West. They failed. There was a great battle, and he brought them to their knees. Then he did something he had never done before: he decided to be merciful. King Henwyn, he pointed out, was his fosterling – taken when the peace was made after their last raids – and like a son to him; and if Henwyn would but bow the knee and pay tribute, he would be welcomed into the family of the High King once more. So I was called for and told I was to marry him.

I had little enough memory of Henwyn from his fostering – a rough boy, who shouted a lot and liked to hit Maglor, was all I remembered. He had not changed much. But I found him refreshing, at first. He did not tiptoe around me because I was a king's daughter. He spoke bluntly, and said many things about my father that I had always thought and not dared voice. I shared in his pleasures of the table and the hunt – and of the bed, where he was unimaginative but vigorous. But my chief joy was not in him, but in escaping from Portskewett and Gray Hill. I was away from the shadow of my father. And if the years have taught me Henwyn's faults, they have not made me forget that escape.

It did not take us long to conceive Cunedag. I did not know it at the time, but like our mothers, Goneril and I were pregnant at the same time. Cunedag was born a little before Morgan, and Henwyn was overjoyed to have a son; and we made the journey to Portskewett to show my father his first grandchild. He was dandling Cordelia on his knee when we came, and when he actually set her down to take Cunedag in his arms, I could have wept – he still had such power over me. But then I asked where my mother was.

"Oh," he said curtly, "she died. A sudden fever, three months ago. I am sorry."

That was all he could find to say. Three months, and no word sent to me. I did not weep there in the face of the court; I wore the mask. I wept later, alone, in the sacred grove, and composed my face again before returning to the fort. If my father suspected, he said nothing; Henwyn was too dull to realise that anything was wrong.

Ah, Henwyn. Always two steps behind me whenever thinking is required. He is an oaf. He has his uses, but I find him less tolerable daily.

Once, he struck me. I do not remember what we had quarrelled over, but I told him that he would never dare strike the daughter of Llyr again. He never has, and the blow itself is long since forgiven: but I cannot forgive him for making me invoke Llyr to protect myself. I will never be beholden thus to my father again.

"The wretched man gan then avise too late
That love is not where most it is professed."
~ Edmund Spenser, *The Faerie Queen*

After a while, they were allowed to move around inside the fort; even called on to dine in the hall, although Llyr refused and the rest felt obliged to follow suit. But they had no word from the outside world. Every now and then Penarddun would overhear some snippet, some complaint about the intransigence of the Silurian chiefs, or some rumour of plots among the Demetae: but then the speakers would notice her, and fall silent. Once, she heard one guard ask another what had become of "the Trinovantian's brat": the other said offhandedly:

"Nobody's heard of him since the night they came here. Most likely the wolves got him."

She had nightmares that night: but she did not allow herself to give up hope. Bran could yet be alive. She prayed daily, to every god she could think of, but chiefly to Sulis and Modron. Sulis was a gentle goddess, and Penarddun had seen only good in those who favoured her; and Modron was a mother, whose son Mabon had been spirited away from her and imprisoned – she would surely look kindly on Bran.

Dardanon prayed too, to a god she knew little of – Ogma, Lord of Eloquence. She asked the Druid once about the gold chains he wore in his ears: and he answered at length about how they symbolised his enthralment to Ogma, chained to the god's golden tongue. He had few other topics of conversation, but any matter that distracted from their

125

situation was welcome to Penarddun. Awel would once have been good for that, but Llyr's despair had infected him, and he was fallen silent. Sicora daily assured her that Falyse would keep Bran safe, but could give her little reason to believe it; while Llyr made less sense by the day, and seemed hardly to know who she was.

It was, Regan took pleasure in informing her, to the good offices of Glevon and his son that they owed their limited liberty. The two Dobunni had pleaded for the prisoners to be shown more kindness, even before they heard of Penarddun's pregnancy, and with renewed fervour thereafter. She tried to thank Glevon, but he avoided her: he still felt so guilty over his tribesmen's plots against her father that he could not look her in the face. When she spoke instead to Achlesydd, he smiled, and bowed his head, saying:

"We did no more than any feeling person would have done. Queen Regan was easily persuaded; she is not cruel, whatever you believe. King Henwyn… has more anger in him, but he is honest."

"I cannot agree with you, sir," said Penarddun, "but I envy you that you can still believe so well of them."

When Beltane came around, it was Achlesydd whom Regan sent to announce that the prisoners would be allowed to attend the celebrations. The great fire would be lit in the sacred groves at the foot of Hen Dinas: for the first time, they were to be permitted to leave the fortress, albeit under guard.

"Is it to you that we owe this courtesy, as well?" Penarddun asked him.

"To my father," replied Achlesydd. "He is a pious man, and would not see anybody denied the chance to honour the gods. May your prayers be answered."

He turned and left before Penarddun could ask what he meant by that.

On the evening itself, Regan sent ten soldiers to fetch them out of their hut. Two to each prisoner, as if any of them was in fit state to fight. The main royal party was already making its way down the path: horns and drums were playing, and hymns to Belenos and Belisama were being rowdily sung. Much had clearly been drunk already. The end of the procession had not yet left the gate, but Regan and Henwyn must be almost at the foot of the hill; the prisoners and their escort joined at the tail of the column. Their dull silence stood in flat contrast to the jollity of the Cornovii.

"The fort's near empty," remarked Awel. "Was Queen Regan afraid we'd escape if she left us here, or that we'd get a good night's sleep?"

Llyr stumbled several times during the descent. The soldiers would not slow for him, so Penarddun took one arm and Dardanon the other; the next time he tripped, they were almost pulled down by his weight, but they managed to hold him up.

When they at last reached the grove, the fire was already lit, and blazing brightly; Regan had slaughtered a sheep by its light, and was holding her bloodied hands aloft. Llyr sniggered like a naughty child.

"Red," he said. "All red."

Mead and ale were passed around; their guards, muttering angrily about not being able to dance, drank greedily, only two or three stopping early to remain sober. After all, what threat were their prisoners?

The night wore on; the fire blazed brighter, the songs and the drumming grew louder, and the dancers began to shed much of their clothing. They remained on the edge of the grove, forgotten. Regan and Henwyn had already disappeared, perhaps returned to the fort. Llyr and at least two of the guards were nodding, almost asleep.

Suddenly, bloody arrows sprouted from the throats of two of the guards. Before they even fell, before anyone could cry out, two more were shot through the chest: and cloaked figures swooped out of the wood, a blur of weapons – one guard was beheaded at a single blow, a second took a long blade under the breastbone as he tried to come behind the dark figure who had swung the sword, two more had their heads dashed into a tree by one man. The two sleepers blinked awake to find they were the only ones living – and knives were levelled at their throats. It had all happened in the blink of an eye: Penarddun was hardly sure yet that she had not lapsed into some horrible dream.

"Come."

One word, hissed out in a low, urgent whisper, but she knew the voice. It was Falyse. Sicora suppressed a squeal of joy, and plunged into the trees after her already disappearing lover; Penarddun and Awel took Llyr's arms, and steered him quickly into the woods behind them. Dardanon looked confused, but followed after, while the captured guards were hustled along at the rear.

Their rescuers were four – one man and three women. They wore hoods, and in the shadow of the trees it was very dark, but Penarddun was certain the man was Perillus. The other two women she did not know.

For perhaps an hour they half-walked, half-ran in silence through the thinning woodland; then Falyse abruptly held up her hand, and they halted.

"We leave them here," she said, gesturing to the guards. "Kneel."

"Have mercy," the younger man begged. "We did only as commanded…"

"I said kneel."

They dropped to their knees. The younger man was weeping, the older twisting his hands and muttering prayers. Perillus took up a fallen branch, and weighed it in his hands: then he swung it so that it struck both of them together on the backs of their skulls. They fell in an instant, moaning, the older twitching slightly.

"They asked mercy..." said Sicora. Falyse shrugged.

"They should live. If we had tied them up they might have frozen or starved before anyone found them. They'll be awake soon enough. We must get on."

"What of Bran?" Penarddun asked.

"He is safe. We will speak later. On."

And on they went, again in silence. When they came at last to the road, there were chariots waiting – old and worn, repaired with rough branches, and pulled by small ponies, but chariots nonetheless. These were guarded by another cloaked and armed woman, older than Falyse's companions.

"Do we go west?" wondered Dardanon.

"South," answered Falyse shortly. "We make for the Deepwood."

Dawn was already breaking; the confused and exhausted Llyr fell asleep as soon as he was loaded into the chariot, and, despite the rattling of its rickety frame as it trundled over the rough ground, Penarddun soon sank into sleep beside him. When she awoke, there were again trees above them, and the road had devolved to a muddy track; and the sun looked to have passed noon. They were still on the move. They were not moving fast: the ponies were strong and dogged but hardly swift, and the chariots were not made to carry so many: but yet they were moving. She felt a fierce pang in her belly, and realised she had eaten nothing since the morsel of the sacrificed sheep allotted to her at Hen Dinas.

"Here." She had said nothing, but Falyse was sitting by her, proffering her bread and a bottle. She took both gratefully, and gulped down first the bread, then a draught of watered wine, thin and sour but welcome. Only when she had finished the loaf and most of the bottle did she speak.

"Bran?" she said.

"Bran is alive and strong," said Falyse. "We will see him soon. Mefus still tends him, as if he were her own." She paused, and looked down. "She lost Mafon," she said. "She was ill before we left Caersws – I don't believe there was ever a chance."

"I am sorry." There was nothing else to say. "But... the Deepwood?"

"It is where I grew up," said Falyse. "Mefus too. We are going to the Forest Hold."

"What is that?"

"When Darnant first came to the Deepwood, there were many woodsmen and their families here. He burned their huts, slaughtered every male he took, and made the women slaves, playthings for himself and his followers. Those who escaped mostly fled to kingdoms beyond the forest, and took what shelter they could, even selling themselves to chiefs and hundred-lords to stay alive and out of his clutches: but a few banded together. They made a camp in the north of the Deepwood, and it became a refuge for survivors of Darnant's wrath. Some of his captives escaped there too. All were welcomed."

"And you..."

"I am of the Forest Hold, yes." More than that, Falyse was not going to say on this subject. "As is Mefus. Cyll and Lysenn I have known all my life." She gestured at her two companions from the rescue. "The night Regan took you prisoner, we chose to return there."

"And the rest of the train...?"

"Went west, mostly – some to Goneril, some to Gray Hill. The two Queens are now calling themselves joint rulers of the West, but the chiefs of the Silures won't have them. Euroswydd leads them, and he still holds for Llyr. The Demetae resist, too – Perion has gone over the sea to Armorica, some say to raise a fleet."

"Why have you stayed, though? Can you not win through to Portskewett? Surely Bran would be safer there than in the Deepwood."

"Maybe," said Falyse with a frown. "If the chiefs can be trusted. But they hardly know that you are alive, you or Llyr. Why should they believe Bran is his son? And if they did... A child cannot be King, but whoever does take the throne, Bran will be a threat to them."

"Euroswydd is loyal," said Penarddun. "He would have kept Bran safe."

"If he could, perhaps," Falyse allowed. "But the chiefs are divided, and the Cornovii are strong, stronger still with Ordovician support. I had to free you and the High King first; so I found Perillus – he's not so good at hiding as he thinks – and we made our plans."

Penarddun sighed.

"Llyr is wandering in his wits," she said. "He takes me for Gogoniant some days, for Cordelia others. Sometimes he rages against the gods, then he'll play with flowers for half a day."

Falyse looked sombre.

"Then I cannot vouch for what will happen if you go to Portskewett," she said. "If Llyr were himself, the chiefs would fall over each other to bow before him, and like nothing better than to follow him into battle as in the old days: but a king without his mind is no king at all. Perhaps you were best to stay in the Deepwood."

"Until when?" wondered Penarddun. "Until he is cured? Until he dies? Until Darnant and Goneril and Regan and every other enemy dies of old age? We must do something."

"And we will," promised Penarddun.

The chariot halted; and the older woman, who was driving, gave a low whistle. To the side of them, what Penarddun had taken for a thick clump of bushes suddenly parted: and the driver wheeled the chariot round, and through the gap. The other followed, and the bushes closed behind them.

They were at the foot of a high stony crag, with trees growing out from it almost horizontally above them: barely any light reached the forest floor, which was all but bare here, just a mass of dead leaves and fallen twigs. A ring of tall, thorny bushes and shrubs surrounded a cluster of low, rounded huts and hide tents, all of it invisible from the outside. Here and there stood women, mostly dressed in skins, their faces smirched and hair greasy, a few with children beside them; one staring, wild-haired man, half naked and grimed all over, sat cross-legged on a tree stump – and then, she saw Mefus.

The wetnurse was holding Bran in her arms. He was twice the age he had been when Penarddun had seen him last, and much grown, but she did not need to ask for any confirmation: she knew her son at once. He yawned, and looked round, with an infant's curiosity as to what the disturbance might be; she was already down from the chariot and running stumblingly towards them, half blinded by tears.

"Bran!" she cried. "Oh, Bran, my boy, my baby!" She caught Mefus and Bran together into her arms, showering kisses on both of them. "I was afraid I'd never see you again!"

Behind her, Sicora hugged Falyse tightly to her; and Llyr rolled over, and snored.

They held a meeting the next day. The wild man seemed more disconnected from reality than Llyr: he spoke to nobody directly, but wailed about the cold and occasionally broke into arguments with his tree stump: but many others spoke feelingly. There were not only victims of Darnant there, but runaways from cruel lords and bad husbands of many tribes; many had been there for years, and they knew the dangers that existed outside the Forest Hold, in all directions. Most were for staying put, at least until they knew for certain whether there would be war between the Silures and Cornovii; Penarddun began to despair of ever persuading them.

Suddenly, Llyr spoke.

"Glevon."

"Yes," said Perillus, surprised. "Glevon helped us. We made contact with him ten days before Beltane, and he arranged for you to be where you were when -"

"No, no," said the King impatiently, shaking his head. "I'm speaking to Glevon. How did you come to be here, old friend?"

He was looking intently at the wild man. The other's eyes darted from side to side; Penarddun peered at him – and realised for the first time who he was.

"How we've fallen, eh?" Llyr went on. "High King and speaker, living in the forest like animals. Is this all there is? Take away the gold and the dyed cloaks, the halls and the hillforts, the roast pork and Gaulish wine – is man a beast of the woods?" He looked round at the assembly, their thin, sunken, blank faces, and sighed. "What kind of a king lets people be brought so low?" he asked. "Every woman here is better than my daughters, and you live like beasts while they

133

act like them. I never knew – nearly forty years a king and I never *saw."* He looked to the wild man again. "Our eyes are open now, though, Glevon: we have Regan to thank for that."

"I must go," said the younger man. His whole demeanour was changed, the mask of madness altogether gone: he was recognisably Picell. "If my father aided you, he is in danger. I must go to him."

Penarddun looked around. Nobody was reacting. Picell's act must have been for her benefit and Llyr's. Falyse answered him, without the slightest flicker of surprise:

"You know the risks, Picell. It is upon your own head."

"How much more have you kept from me?" demanded Penarddun angrily.

"Picell's secret was his to keep," Falyse shot back. "You did not need to know, even that he was here."

"He is a hunted man," retorted Penarddun hotly. "His presence here could endanger Bran."

"We are all hunted," said Falyse. "But Bran's presence here endangers us all. He has more enemies than any of us, but we have kept him safe – because this is a refuge for all who need it."

Penarddun lowered her head.

"I am sorry," she said. How many more times would she have to say that? Falyse looked her in the face, and spoke more softly.

"You have nothing to be sorry for," she said. "You spoke out of love, because you feared for your son. But you must decide soon. The journey to Portskewett lies between Regan's scouts and Darnant's raiders. Do you wish to undertake it? And will you take Bran on that yourney? Whatever choice you make, I will bear you company, and protect you as best I can."

Penarddun looked down at Bran, gurgling sleepily in Mefus' arms.

"We cannot remain here forever," she said. "Nor can I expose my son to the dangers of the road." There were tears in her eyes. "I have only just found him again," she whispered. "I don't want to leave him."

"He is safer here than anywhere," said Mefus gently.

"And if the chiefs do rally to the High King as you hope," Falyse added, "then they will send us an escort, and you will be able to bring him to Portskewett without fear. If you wish to remain here, Perillus and I can take the High King..."

Penarddun gazed at Bran. She longed to stay: but if Llyr was not lucid when he came to Portskewett, Falyse and Perillus would not persuade the chiefs alone. Euroswydd might listen to them, but not the others. But they would listen to her – Euroswydd would make them. She had to be there: and she must leave Bran behind.

Perillus' Story

When I was first sent into Spain, I burned with the desire to serve Rome and win glory.

The Perilli are not an ancient family. We have never been senators, and have not long been knights. Our names are not found in the annals of the city. Indeed, I suspect our origins to have been Etruscan, or even Greek. They say there are Perilli in Crete; maybe one of them was my ancestor. My grandfather's background, before the patronage of the younger Scipio raised him up, is utterly obscure. By Scipio's assistance, he became a tax-farmer, employed to raise the revenues of the Republic from estates in far corners of Italy: and whether honestly or not, he grew rich enough that he became a landowner himself.

But whoever we once were, my father and uncles were born the sons of a Roman knight. They entered politics, though they mostly steered a middle ground between the conservative senators and the radicals, led in those days by the Gracchus brothers. Only my uncle Marcus rejected this caution, and stood with the Gracchi for the rights of the common folk: nobody was surprised when he was knifed in the belly coming home from a tavern one night. Footpads were blamed, but no doubt many of the rich senators who tutted about how lawless the city had become slept easier for his removal.

The Gracchi too paid with their lives for upsetting the social order, Tiberius beaten to death on his way to an assembly, Gaius chased to the Grove of the Furies and forced to fall upon his sword. After that, the plebs were quietened.

My other uncle, Titus, fell in the Cimbrian War, when all Rome was in terror that the savages from the north would sweep through Italy and enslave us. I was then a boy, and thought him and his comrades heroes: I wanted nothing more than to join the legions and fight the German tribes as my uncle had. That war did not last long enough for me to take part in it, but when I was of age I badgered and begged my father to get me an officer's baton. I was a knight's son and it was my due: and the fearful excitement of the Cimbrian War, which we were told had endangered the very existence of the Republic, had created a great spirit of patriotism in my generation, or at least my circle of friends. Its commanders had become legends, and we all longed to meet them, to serve them, to aid them in bringing the light of Rome to new lands, and one day to be like them.

We were largely oblivious to the frenzied debates at home, the attempts to impeach failed generals, and so forth. I didn't follow politics unless a personal story brought them home to me, like my uncle's murder – which happened long before I was born, but was always whispered of. What sides my father took, which generals he spoke out for and which against, I don't think I could tell you now: but he was certainly as close as a man below senatorial rank could get to the heart of the debates, and that was when he forged his alliance with Titus Didius Nepos. Didius, he told me, would go far, and might be able to do as much for our family as Scipio had. When Didius was elected Consul, it looked as if my father had been proven right.

Didius' term of office ended, and he was given a governorship, as was the custom. He received Nearer Spain. The Spaniards and Lusitanians were notoriously difficult peoples to conquer, and after decades of occupation they were still causing trouble for Rome: Didius had great hope of seeing action. I had by this time served about a year in the city garrison, racking up experience, so that Didius was able to *secure my appointment as a narrow-stripe tribune in the legion charged with defending the Spanish provinces: from which he immediately co-opted me onto his own staff. From there it could have been a natural step to the broad stripe, and then a prefecture; I might even have lived to see our family reach the Senate one day.*

We did see action. Within days of our arrival, with the ink scarcely dry on his first proconsular paperwork, Didius marched us to the frontier to inflict what he said would be condign punishment on the rebellious Celtiberians.

The village we destroyed was not large, though it would no doubt seem a city to the Silures. Only a simple palisade defended it, and that was crumbling. There were few men there, most of them old; it was a place of women and children. The Proconsul said that was proof of their guilt: their men were away fighting with the rebels.

I had attended games, but rarely. And it is a very different matter to see death in an amphitheatre from the comfort of the stands, and to mete it out at close quarters, to people who cannot escape but can scream and curse and spit and try feebly to fight back. I remember a woman, about my mother's age, who flew at me with a little knife upraised, nothing more than a fruit knife, I think: I put my sword through her chest and she died with her face a span from mine, still cursing me in her strange language. I remember realising that there were children inside a burning house. I remember the clamour and the blood and the stench of roasting flesh, and vomiting until I had nothing left to bring up when it was done. I remember an old centurion clapping me on the shoulder and saying it was like that after his first battle, but I would get used to it. Battle? This was not battle.

We marched up and down that frontier for months, enduring occasional surprise attacks but brushing most of them off. After these attacks, Didius would hold celebrations for his officers, declaring that we had won victories to be proud of, and our names would be sung of in Rome. His cupbearers were naked slave girls; when he realised that my tastes ran the other way, he added some boys to the mix, but I seldom had the stomach to touch them. Too many looked like Iberians I had killed. I spent most of those parties drinking myself into oblivion. Spanish wine is stronger than Roman, and I took little water with it.

The following year, Publius Crassus was appointed Proconsul of Further Spain. He and Didius were not compatible. Politically, Didius tended to favour the popular party, Crassus the conservatives: but more to the point, Crassus was a frugal and puritanical character, who disapproved of the way Didius lived. But they were forced to work together. Envying Didius' victories, Crassus immediately embarked on a campaign against the Lusitanians, to similarly bloody effect: and when he met with setbacks he sent to Didius for more men.

Didius might have laughed off the request, except that Crassus did him the honour of sending the message by his own son, a youth named Marcus whom he was grooming for the highest office. So instead, he asked Marcus to one of his debauched parties, treated him to wine and whores, and sent him back with a cohort – and me. I served for several months with the Crassi before they sent me back. It was enough time to see how they differed. Publius was cautious, close; Marcus was bolder, and more intelligent with it, and had none of his father's dourness. I lost much coin to him at the tabula and the Bacchus chase: I believe he won fairly, but I also believe that he cheated others, and would have cheated me had I been a strong enough opponent to make it necessary.

It was in Crassus' camp that I made the acquaintance of Appius Scaliger, a merchant from a plebeian family who had settled in Cadiz. He had more sense than I, and never engaged Marcus Crassus in games of strategy, but was happy to wager on games of chance. Gambling helped keep war and blood from my mind. And over our games, he told us tales of his voyages, out into the western ocean, down the shores of Mauretania and up to Gaul, and even Britain. He spoke of Scilly, the green and fertile island where he used to meet with the tin traders of the South Cornovii, as the Carthaginians had before him for hundreds of years.

"If ever the Isles of the Blessed were real," he said, "I could believe that they lay at Scilly. Or Ennor, or Lethowsow, Lyonesse, or what you will: it has more names than Jupiter."

Marcus repeated the stories to his father: I would say that they captured his imagination, but Publius Crassus never had such a thing: I believe it was his son who swayed him, and convinced him that Scilly should be visited; that if Britain had such reserves of tin, let alone the gold and pearls of which rumour spoke, it should be investigated – trade links could be established direct from Rome; perhaps the isles could even one day be conquered.

It was not an easy voyage for those of us who had only ever known the calmer waters between Spain and Italy. The Atlantic is harsh, and Roman galleys are not built for such rolling waves. I was sick most of the way, and was convinced that we were about to sink; but Scaliger laughed and assured me that this was nothing. Certainly we did not sink, but made what he told me was good time, and arrived safely at the island. The sky was grey, and my face no doubt greyer, but I could not say that Scaliger had lied about the island's beauty.

Nothing like the Proconsul's war galley had been seen there, since the days of the Carthaginians at least. When we were sighted, men and women armed themselves and ran to the beach, keen to see the great ship and ready to repulse it if necessary: I believe some of the more warlike ones were disappointed to see Scaliger's friendly face. Be that as it may, they stood back, and let Prince Gandales, their young ruler, welcome us ashore.

By this time I had a few phrases of Celtiberian; the British language is related to it, though closer to Gaulish, which was spoken by many of my father's slaves at home. I understood, therefore, a little of what passed between Scaliger and our hosts, and strove always to understand more – though of course Scaliger was always ready with a translation. Through him, the elder Crassus probed Gandales, seeking information about the size and wealth of Britain, and its preparedness; Marcus would have been more subtle, but Publius asked the questions, and Gandales turned them courteously away, answering as little as possible. That night, the Prince feasted us, and I got drunk on the native mead and went to bed with a British youth – I never knew his name, but I learned later that the way he braided his hair meant he was a Dumnonian of high birth.

We passed a pleasant enough few days before returning to Cadiz, or at least Marcus and I did; but Publius Crassus scowled all the way back, declaring the journey wasted. He had little interest in trade, and had learned nothing useful from a military perspective: and we returned to learn that rebellion had flared up again in the Lusitanian lands, which pushed Britain entirely from his mind. I hope that it has not returned there.

I was sent back to Didius not long after. I missed the company of Marcus Crassus, slippery as he was, and I thought back fondly to Scilly and mead and my Dumnonian boy. Didius had not changed, except that his temper had grown

141

worse. *Failure to bring the Celtiberians to decisive battle had made him bitter, and more violent by the day. I did my best to avoid him, but I was his tribune, and my presence was required almost daily. But I was ever less in his counsel: if he noticed me, it was to bark curt orders at me. I was grateful for it: by this time I did not care for influence, only for spending as little time as possible with the Proconsul.*

Then came the massacre. I knew nothing of it before the fact – I believed we were accepting the fugitives' surrender in good faith. I oversaw the handover of their swords and spears; they were glad to be rid of them, eager to be free of outlawry and enter the peace of Rome.

When I first heard Didius' command, I thought I had misheard. I stood there dumbly, blinking and shaking my head. When he repeated himself, something snapped: and I told him what I later told Llyr, that this was evil, that it would stain his name and the name of Rome.

Didius was as shocked at my defiance as I was at his order. It took him several seconds of spluttering before he managed to order my arrest. I do not pretend to be a great fighter; but the two legionnaires who came forward were not expecting resistance. I caught up a flagon of wine off Didius' map-desk and smashed one in the face; the other I had run through the throat before his sword was more than half drawn, and I was out of the tent and in the saddle before the Proconsul could even shout for help.

I don't know why I rode west. I suppose it was the only way I could get to another Roman province by land: east was the sea, and Rome beyond it; south were the straits; north were Celtiberians who knew my face and had loved ones to avenge. But I do not remember thinking any of this consciously. I simply rode, until the poor horse dropped dead of exhaustion. But by then I was in Crassus' province.

I knew better than to seek the aid of the Crassi. Instead I stripped off my Roman armour, keeping only my legionary cloak to ward off the cold, and walked – mostly by night – across Further Spain. How I found my way to Cadiz, draggled and half starved, I am still unsure; but there I spent my last few coins on a good hot meal, traded my cloak and tunic for cheaper ones that were not legion red, and went to find a skipper who would let me work my passage out of Roman Spain. Scilly was in my mind, and the Dumnonian boy, but I would as soon have taken Gaul or Mauretania, or some port back east so long as it was one where nobody knew me.

As ill luck would have it, I met with Scaliger. He knew me at once, and easily divined that I must be a wanted man. I made extravagant promises of payment, but I had nothing to give him – until his eye lighted on my ring.

In throwing away my armour, spending my coin, divesting myself of my very clothes, I had never thought to rid myself of the gold ring that marked me as a Roman patrician. I had not thought of it as part of my accoutrements: it was part of myself. I did not know whether to curse the folly that could have brought me to my death, or praise my good luck that Scaliger wanted it. He was rich, but still plebeian; this was known in Cadiz, but he traded to many cities where a knight's ring would gain him entry to great houses and high society. And I? I was no longer a knight, or even a Roman. I was ashamed to wear such a thing, and only too glad to trade it for passage to wherever he meant to travel next. And it chanced that Scaliger had a special voyage in mind: he wanted to try whether the hides and gold he bought in Scilly could be had for better value closer to the source, and meant to sail beyond Cornwall, into the unknown: to Portskewett, and the court of the Silurian king.

That is how I came to Llyr's house. I told him my story, fully and frankly, through Scaliger; and he laughed and told me I was a fool, but said he could find use for a Roman if I could learn his language. And so I stayed, and have been in Britain ever since.

Scaliger, of course, returned to Cadiz; but Didius was still trying to track me down, and his agents soon enough followed my trail to that city. My armour had been found; the man who had bartered my cloak was seen in it, brought in, and flogged until he told how he came by it; the innkeeper I had bought my meal from had noticed the ring. It was only a matter of time before Scaliger was taken in for questioning. He told them nothing and was let go, but he knew that the noose was tightening: so, cursing my name, he put to sea with the next tide, and sold his ship to his sailing master for less than half its value when they came to Tintagel, bought a fisherman's coracle, and rowed himself to Portskewett. He dared not trust to Gandales: Scilly lay too close to Roman Spain, somebody would surely come to buy tin, and the prince might think to sell them Scaliger.

If he came with ideas of vengeance in his mind, he did not pursue them. Llyr made us work together, and if he had not, then mere loneliness would have cast us into one another's company – two Romans among those we were taught to call barbarians. I am not sure that I would call him a friend; I don't know that I have had a friend since I left Italy – save one, briefly: Saron of New Carthage, once the comrade of King Bladud. He was an ancient man when I came to Portskewett, and sickly: but he spoke good Greek, so we fell naturally into one another's company. He told me enough to know that the stories of Bladud's travels are not only true, but less than half of the truth. The Britons speak vaguely of studying among the Greeks: but Saron had been Bladud's fellow student under Karneades of Cyrene, at the Academy in Athens, founded by Plato himself. How a British prince came to be so far from home I have never learned: but from Athens Bladud travelled with his friends to Carthage, and thence to Lusitania, where he helped to hold back the tide of Rome, and acquired the disease that would have barred him from the throne if Sulis had not cured it. Saron had become a devout believer in the goddess: he declared that the gods of Carthage had abandoned their people to the edge of the Roman sword, but those of the Britons had been kind to him, and he honoured them for it.

There is so much more I wished to ask of Saron: but I had been in Portskewett a bare month when my only friend died. I had a lover for a while – Cingar, a warrior of Llyr's guard – but he never truly let me into his heart, and he was killed on a boar hunt three winters back. So Scaliger's presence became a comfort, until I made myself a fugitive once more. There is Awel – he is pretty, but I do not know if he cares for me.

It is more than ten years now since I fled from Spain, and I am still running. I am tired, and I want peace: but not at any price. I gave up my Roman citizenship, everything that I was; it has to have been for *something. It has to have been worthwhile.*

"Was ever tale so full of misery?"

~ Tate, *King Lear*

Picell wrapped his ragged grey cloak around him and left that same day. Penarddun remained some days more. The weather was yet uncertain, she told herself; Llyr was improving, and would be better able to speak to the chiefs if they waited; and every day, she played with Bran, rocked him on her knee, hugged him tight.

At last, however, she knew that the time had come to leave. She had grown big, and would not be able to travel with ease or safety if she waited much longer. She went to Falyse, and told her that she must soon go.

"I must take the High King," she said. "But I cannot command any to come with us."

"I will, though," said Falyse. "And Perillus too. I cannot speak for anybody else; but we were best not to travel in too great numbers, in any case."

In the event, they found that Sicora would not be parted from her lover, nor Awel left behind in the camp of women. Falyse might once have tried to argue: but Sicora had been training with sword and knife since they arrived at the Forest Hold, and Falyse accepted that she could defend herself. Penarddun too, despite her growing belly, had done some mild training, though taking care to take no falls or low blows. None other volunteered; Dardanon declared that he meant never to return to the haunts of men, but to make the forest his home that he might commune better with the gods.

146

They went, necessarily, on foot. There were not enough ponies for all to ride, and the chariots would have drawn too much attention: walkers could hide easily and quickly, at least until they left the Deepwood. Llyr, for the most part, allowed himself to be led, although from time to time he would run ahead and slash at the trees with a stick, calling them Goneril, Regan, Maglor, or Henwyn. He had woven himself a crown of ivy and dried grass, and would not take it off, insisting that it was his last mark of kingship.

At Falyse's urging, they travelled mostly by night. The sky was clear and the moon bright, though it was cold for summer. Darnant's people, she said, would be out raiding sheepfolds by moonlight, not prowling the forest, for they would not expect to meet travellers; while Regan's soldiers would be indoors hiding from the outlaws.

They mostly managed to meet nobody. Only once did they hear the clop of horse's hooves: Falyse instantly whispered "Down!". By the time the horseman passed, they were all flat on the ground beneath a thick, thorny bush to the side of the road, breathing in rotten leaves. Something made Penarddun crane upward, and peer through the branches, even though Falyse shook her head warningly.

The horseman was a youth, not above eighteen or twenty, with light curling hair and a fair, delicate face. His forest green tunic and light green breeks were well made, and of richer stuff than the rough black wool of his cloak; a large golden brooch set with garnets adorned his shoulder, a narrow torque sat about his neck, and a long sword lay on his thigh. His horse was a tall and slender dapple-grey. Behind him came two scarred, rough-looking characters in charcoal grey, one clutching a bundle of hunting javelins, the other wielding a vicious-looking axe. As he passed their hiding place, the horseman seemed to pause, and glanced about: but then they passed on.

Not until long after they had disappeared did Falyse finally give a sigh, and sit up.

"Who was that?" whispered Penarddun.

"Cangen," said Falyse. "Darnant's eldest son, and next to him his parents are the gentlest folk on earth. Pray to all the gods we remain out of his sight."

They hurried on; and before long were out of the woods, and travelling through cultivated land, though the fields were neglected.

"Men summoned away to war have little time to farm," said Falyse, "and the ones still here fear to see their crops looted or burned before they can bring them in."

But they were in firmly Silurian territory. It would be bold of Regan and Henwyn to strike this far before war became unavoidable: and they were able to move more openly, and therefore more swiftly.

Coming to a crossroads, they saw two men seated on the ground, one gnawing rat-like on a hunk of cheese, the other swigging from a leather bottle. Both were grimy, ragged, and unkempt, with bristly beards; the elder, the one gnawing the cheese, wore a dirty flaxen bandage over his eyes. Suddenly, Penarddun realised that she knew them. The younger man was Picell, looking even wilder than he had in the Forest Hold; and the other –

"Glevon!" exclaimed Perillus under his breath. "By Jupiter, what have they done to him?"

Llyr was already stalking ahead of them, towards the two shabby figures.

"Another blind man," he declared. "The land is full of them. I was blind once, you know. I saw nothing – nothing; but I can see now."

Glevon started to his feet, dropping the cheese and groping out in front of him with his hands, grasping the air.

"That is the High King's voice!" he croaked. "I know it. My lord – are you alive, or am I dead? Is this the Otherworld? Did I save you, back at Hen Dinas? Was it worth the price?"

"The price?" echoed Perillus. "They took your *eyes*? Was this Regan's doing?"

"Henwyn," groaned Glevon. "With his own hand. There was a fight, I thought him wounded... they say he's dead now... but he didn't stop. He didn't stop."

"What happened?" Perillus turned to Picell.

"I met him, sir, on the road," said Picell, bowing. It took Penarddun a moment to notice that he was disguising his voice – he had affected a Silurian accent, and was slurring his Ss. Did Glevon not know that his travelling companion was his son? "We'd all heard about the High King's escape; then I heard from one of Queen Regan's own guard what happened next. May I speak of it, my lord?"

"You may," said Glevon wearily. "You know it better than I – I mostly remember pain, and their laughter – they *laughed*, Regan and Henwyn, laughed."

"The man said the Speaker was betrayed," Picell went on, still in his assumed accent. "They bound him, mocked him, and the King went to – to do this to him. One of Henwyn's own slaves took up a knife to defend him, but the Queen came behind and stabbed him in the back. Some say Henwyn is dead of the wound the slave gave him, others say dying at least; the guard wouldn't say to the likes of me."

"Henwyn's dead?" exclaimed Penarddun. "What will that do to their plans?"

"The High King's enemies will be ruined!" said Perillus excitedly. "Without the might of the Cornovii, the Ordovices

149

are nothing – they're fierce fighters but can never match the Silures for numbers." But Falyse shook her head.

"Regan is still alive," she reminded them. "I know you Romans don't let women command – it doesn't mean they can't. If the Cornovian chiefs accept her, they'll be as dangerous as ever – and if they don't they'll likely have a civil war, with her able to call half the Silures in on her side."

"Was that Perillus?" asked Glevon. "How many of you are there? Is Llyr still High King?"

"Ask again in a month," said Falyse grimly; but Penarddun answered firmly:

"Yes. And will be while he lives. Sir," she said to Picell, "take this good old man to the Forest Hold; he will be safe there. We must get to Portskewett." Picell inclined his head in thanks for her keeping his secret.

"I will do, m'lady," he said.

"Achlesydd," said Glevon suddenly. "My son Achlesydd, he helped me arrange the High King's rescue... I don't know what became of him... I don't think they knew of his part, but I don't know what they learned, or how... Have you heard anything? Is he safe?"

"I fear we have heard nothing," said Penarddun. "But if he were in danger I am sure you would have learned it on the road by now. May the gods protect him, and you."

"And you also," said Glevon. "And the High King."

The rest of the journey passed without incident: and at last they saw the height and palisade of Portskewett rise before them. When they came to the first gate, the guards were almost ready to turn them away as unwanted beggars: but Falyse shoved her face up to that of the closest sentry, and growled:

"I know you, Emerian ap Cloten, and you know me. And you know your King. This is Llyr ap Bladud ap Rhun, High King in the West, and Penarddun ferch Belin ap Clywel of the Trinovantes, the High Queen. You will admit us, and you will fucking *bow!*"

The sentry goggled, and dropped to his knees, exclaiming "My lord!". Leaving his companion to keep the gate alone, he insisted on escorting them up the approach, and through the inner gate, where he cried out:

"The High King has returned!"

People all around stopped their work, and stared. More came out of almost every building, peering, blinking, whispering to one another; and at last, from the main hall, came Euroswydd, Goll, and several clan chiefs. It took Penarddun an effort of will not to rush into Euroswydd's arms: instead, however, she held up her head, and announced loudly and clearly:

"The High King has returned. He claims the homage of every man here, and your aid against his enemies."

"We are overjoyed to see our lord and lady safe returned," said Goll. "Where is Prince Bran? I trust no harm has befallen him."

"He is safe," said Penarddun. They seemed oddly cool to Llyr's presence.

"Disturbing news has reached us from Hen Dinas," the Druid went on. "It was reported that the High King had lost his reason, and had to be confined. Can my lord assure us that he is well now?"

"I am better than well," said Llyr with a smile. "I am dead, you know. A blind man on the road told me. I hadn't realised, but it makes the best of sense. This is the Otherworld. That is why everything seems wrong. I will get used to it in time."

151

Goll glanced at Euroswydd.

"It seems that the report was true," he said gravely. "My lord Speaker?"

Euroswydd chewed his lip before replying.

"Regrettably," he said, "we cannot allow the High King to resume power." He avoided meeting Penarddun's eye.

"He needs to recover yet," said Penarddun. "He has had a trying time. The council has ruled well, I am sure: it may continue to do so until the High King is well. But we must prepare for -"

"My lady misunderstands," said Goll harshly, cutting her off. "A man deranged cannot be High King, even in name. The council has ruled while we awaited Llyr's return: but now that we know the truth, he must be deposed, and a new king confirmed."

"No!" exclaimed Penarddun. "He will recover – he is already far better than he was! This is just a sickness – it is no different than if he had a bad chill!"

"Shall we put the matter to the chiefs?" asked the Druid. "I believe enough of them are here. Gwenwyn of the Honey Bee Clan?"

"Let the High King be deposed," said the first chief, a bony man with greying red hair and a swirl of tattoos up his right arm.

"Twmyr of the Rocky Hill Clan?"

"Let the High King be deposed," said the second, a stooping, pot-bellied man almost as old as Llyr, with a scar running across his face.

"Twca of the Broad Blade Clan?"

"Let the High King be deposed."

"Iddon of the Green Branch Clan?"

"Let the High King be deposed."

"And Euroswydd of the Sea Foam Clan?" he finished, looking to the Speaker. Euroswydd looked at the ground, and said:

"I do not need to give my voice. The decision has been made."

"It has," agreed Goll with a nod. "We must summon the remaining chiefs before electing a new King – and of course, they can vote only on behalf of the Silures, not for the remainder of the West; in the meantime this council shall continue to rule."

"Then as the wife of Llyr, and mother of Prince Bran and this his second child," declared Penarddun, "I submit myself for election as Queen of the Silures."

"As is your right, of course," said Goll. He turned to a servitor who was standing open-mouthed nearby, openly gawking at the confused Llyr and the stern-faced chiefs. "Show Lord Llyr and his companions to suitable quarters; see that they have all they may require. I will see that guards are posted – for their safety."

"Prisoners," muttered Falyse. "We're prisoners again."

They were invited that night to eat with Euroswydd and the chiefs – even Awel and Sicora were allowed to sit down with them; but Llyr soon grew sleepy, and was taken off to bed. Penarddun had little desire to eat with them after the afternoon's events: but she was hungry, and besides she knew that she needed to win support, to make her case. She tried speaking to Iddon, a grey-haired woman with clear blue eyes and a woodcutter's muscles, but the Green Branch chief was terse and unresponsive; she considered switching her attention to Euroswydd, but he seemed to be avoiding her. She determined to catch him later, alone; and, making her excuses, she left the hall. Falyse and Sicora followed her, but she sent them ahead to await her in their quarters, and stood under the shadow of one of the side huts.

She did not have long to wait. The first to come out for a piss was Twmyr, reeling drunk, but he had not long gone back inside when the Speaker came out.

"Euroswydd."

"My lady," he said, looking up but showing no surprise.

"I understand what you had to do today," she made herself say. "I bear you no ill will for it."

"I thank you," he said, stiffly.

"Euroswydd, please," she said softly. "We are not enemies. Give me your support; make me Queen."

"And?" he said, cocking an eyebrow. "What do I get for it?"

"What happened between us..." she said, and tailed off uncertainly. "It... it cannot happen again. But... I was glad of it. I needed it." She paused. "Euroswydd, I believe this child is yours."

"But never to be acknowledged," he said. "For your sake, mine, and the child's. So what can it mean if it is?"

"I am Llyr's wife," said Penarddun, "and I mean to remain so as long as he lives. But... he cannot live for ever. Euroswydd, if you will give me your support, then I will swear before whatever gods you choose to marry you when Llyr dies."

"And then I will be King?" He sounded interested.

"As my consort – yes."

Euroswydd smiled, a crooked, charming smile.

"Shall we seal the bargain?" he said. "One more time." He reached out, and took Penarddun by the shoulders; she made a token effort to twist away, but let him draw her into her arms. Then, suddenly, he seized her by the hair, and slammed her violently back against the wall. "I have a better

154

idea," he hissed. "You will be Queen, yes, and my wife – but I will be King *now,* and *I* will rule. You will withdraw, and give me your voice in front of the council; you will divorce Llyr; you will marry me and be an obedient wife. And if you refuse, you'll watch your precious friends die one by one – first the Roman, then the fool, then the swordwife, then her lover; and their deaths will not be quick. Well? Which is it to be?" She moaned wordlessly; her eyes were stinging with tears. "Which is it to be?" snarled Euroswydd, tightening his grip.

"I, I will do it," she gasped.

"Very good," said Euroswydd. "Now: shall we seal *this* bargain?" He leaned in as if to kiss her; she wrenched her head away – and he stood back, and let her go. "Go to bed," he said. "The chiefs will be missing me. But you will keep your promise – or I will keep mine."

I suppose I was lucky to be born a Silurian, a lord of the Sea Foam Clan and great-nephew to King Bladud.

My clan had ruled the Silures for over a hundred years. Divine blood runs in our veins – and Fomorian blood too, as old whispers have it; and my grandfather was King, for a little while. Everybody forgets him. They speak as if there was nothing but anarchy between Rhun and Bladud – as if there never was a King Lludd. But Lludd was Rhun's heir. Bladud gave up his claim to the throne when he went to train as a Druid, and that was before he spent eleven years gallivanting in foreign lands. He came back diseased, and herded the sacred pigs at the Waters of Sulis while Lludd tried to keep the kingdom together. When Rhun grew old and weak the clans were at each other's throats, the Cornovii were menacing our borders, and the Druids were trying to gather all power into their own hands; and when he keeled over and died, it was Lludd who took the reins, and kept Siluria from civil war. And what was his thanks? A knife in the back from some Honey Bee clansman with a grudge over a couple of cattle. Then the glorious Bladud came back to save the day, with all his stories of foreign adventures and his miraculous healing, and everybody declared him blessed by the gods, and rushed to bow and scrape and make him King.

I was not yet born then, of course. But my father remembered, and he made sure I knew. He placed me in Llyr's household; it was always his hope that I might marry one of the King's daughters and bring the crown back to our side of the family, where it belonged. But we weren't useful enough to Llyr, not with his ambitions. He wasn't satisfied being king of one tribe: he had to rule the whole West, so he had to make marriages that bound the other tribes to him. One by one I saw my hopes disappear.

Of course, he wasn't blind to my abilities. He got me elected Speaker so that I could manage the chiefs for him, and deal with embassies from Gaul and Ireland and Spain: he never had much patience for the business of government. But he might as happily have appointed a foreigner or a slave if the chiefs would have had them. It didn't matter that I was Euroswydd, that I was his kinsman.

Goneril and Regan were married off. My only hope left lay with Cordelia. I was always fond of her; she saw through the old bastard, like I did – and not many others. But that ridiculous word "Penteyrnedd" had got about, and every lordling in the West wanted to marry her – Maglor and Henwyn would have come wooing if they hadn't been too afraid of their first wives. When Scaliger sowed in Llyr's mind the idea of repudiating her, though, I thought that might be my chance – but no, I had no chance. Llyr might despise me, but he hadn't forgotten that I was close to the throne. As if I'd have moved against him! I'd have been happy to wait for him to die, then face a fair election against Goneril and Regan – even to be just Cordelia's consort. But there I was, too low to be a suitable husband and too high to be a safe one. She had to be sent over the sea.

Even after that, I served him loyally. But I watched him grow more erratic day by day. The banishment of Perillus was the first real sign, but it got worse. Goll and Scaliger noticed it too. We spoke privately about what might have to be done – it was nothing but our duty, to the realm. A tribe needs a capable ruler; much more so a confederation as large as Llyr's. It would have been irresponsible not to plan for the day when he might need to be deposed.

As for the girl – I needed her on my side. I needed to make her understand. She was ready to – anybody could see how Llyr frightened her, and who could blame her? Scaliger helped me to isolate her, seeing that the Avalonian woman was turned away and that she was told Llyr had ordered it; but Llyr did most of the work himself.

I only meant to speak to her of the future, of what might need to happen; I didn't go to the shrine to seduce her. How that happened, I don't know. Some capricious god made it that way; and I was so drunk on her that I forgot to even speak of deposition.

Things happened quickly after that. His idiotic idea to give up most of his power may have opened my way, but it opened his daughters' as well. The moment he announced it, I knew that they would move fast, and I had to as well – for the sake of the Silures, if Maglor and Henwyn were not to parcel up our kingdom between them. The night he quarrelled with Goneril and left Caersws, I rode at once to Gray Hill – with his blessing, remember – to arrange with Goll the governance of the tribe.

For the next five months, I governed the Silures. The chiefs deferred to me, and I was as good as a king. I maintained the peace with Goneril and Regan, though they were champing for war. I kept the Demetian border guarded too: Perion is in Gaul now, trying to win support for an invasion in Llyr's name, while Pwyll musters his men at home. I will have to do something about them: Goll tells me he has a plan. I prevented our trade from being disrupted. I kept the clans in order. I continued the task my grandfather had taken from him, and I loved it.

Then he came back, like Bladud from his pigsty – except that Bladud was young and sane, and Lludd was dead. I am alive. I will not have my rule taken from me by a dribbling dotard and a pack of women. I have worked too hard for it and waited too long. Llyr is unfit to rule, as we long feared he might become. It is only right that he should be deposed. I did not propose it and did not give my voice to it – it was the chiefs' doing, not mine. And it will be their choice to make me King, or not. I know my claim is distant, all but forgotten after Llyr has ruled so long: that is why I need the girl. For some reason she remains attached to the old idiot, but she will soon forget him. I know how to please her; I have shown that before.

The sisters will call it indecent, but who are they to speak? Scaliger has sent me word that Regan married Achlesydd ap Glevon the day after Henwyn was buried. A slave's son! The chiefs will not like that. She has ruined herself in Siluria, if not in Hen Dinas. And she has ruined him among his own people – the Dobunni might have made him Speaker in his father's place, but not now. From what I hear they have broken off all their negotiations for Cornovian protection and gone crawling back to Belin.

I will be King. Nigh sixty years after they murdered my grandfather, I will be King.

"Three Exalted Prisoners of the Island of Britain: Llyr Half-Speech, who was imprisoned by Euroswydd, and the second, Mabon son of Modron…"

~ *The Triads of the Island of Britain*

Penarddun returned to the hut they had been assigned to, flung herself on the ground, and sobbed. It was not long before Sicora awoke, and crawled over to her. She said nothing, but lifted Penarddun's head, and kissed her gently on the brow; then hugged her tight, and held her until she had wept her fill. Only then did she ask if Penarddun wanted to tell her what had happened.

By this time Falyse was awake; Penarddun glanced at her, acknowledging that she had seen her – then poured it all out: even, when Falyse had checked again that the men were still asleep, about her trysts with Euroswydd. At the end, Sicora hugged her again; and Falyse asked:

"What will you do?"

"I have no choice," she replied. "I have to go along with it, to save your lives. Even if we could escape, we have no friends now – our own people would be hunting us. And the best way I can keep Bran safe is to stay away from him."

"I'm afraid you're right," agreed Falyse. "If you can do it."

"I married Llyr," said Penarddun with a grimace. "I have endured these two years. I can endure Euroswydd, as long as I must."

"Maybe he will be killed, if it comes to war," suggested Sicora.

"That might leave us in worse danger than before," Penarddun pointed out. "I would love to have hope of a life after – after *him*, but to have any hope at all we must all first stay alive."

She divorced Llyr in front of Goll and the chiefs the next morning. It took only a simple formal declaration; he was confused, and seemed not to know who she was, but kept asking for Gogoniant. At the same convocation, she withdrew her claim to the throne.

"I spoke foolishly yesterday, in hot blood," she said. "I freely take back my candidacy, and urge you to elect my good kinsman, Euroswydd of the Sea Foam Clan, who has served you so well as Speaker."

Of marriage, she said nothing yet, and Euroswydd did not push her. It would, he must have realised, be unseemly while the election was not yet made; while for her part, she clung to the faint hope that she might yet be spared that fate if he should lose.

The remaining chiefs arrived within days. Invited to attend their deliberations in the hall, Penarddun tried to make the right noises, speaking for Euroswydd with as little conviction as she deemed safe: but as it turned out there was no doubt in their minds. The High King's daughters were mentioned, but all three were dismissed – the news of Regan's marriage to Achlesydd, which came as a shock to her, had greatly angered them. Goll subtly reminded them of Euroswydd's descent from Kng Lludd; and it was not long before Twmyr thumped the table and demanded that they acclaim Euroswydd. In moments every chief was shouting his name. He rose to his feet, smiled graciously, and said:

"My friends, I accept." He turned to Penarddun. "And now I am free to ask that you consent to my marriage with

Queen Penarddun." It took her a moment to realise that he was still addressing the chiefs; only when Twca growled "Aye", followed by Iddon, and then the rest of them, did she realise that she was not being asked. For a moment she considered refusing: in law, no marriage could be compelled: but Euroswydd would not forgive a refusal, and he was now King. She bowed her head.

Euroswydd reached over to her, and took her hand.

"Then here, before you, I pledge myself to her," he said. "We shall make sacrifice later; there is no call for feasting and ceremonial – we have more important matters to concern us."

Penarddun blinked, and swallowed: then she managed to say:

"And I pledge myself to Lord Euroswydd."

Goll called on the gods to bless the match – and there, in a few dozen words, hands clasped across a trestle table in Llyr's hall, it was done. They were married.

The meeting continued almost as if nothing had changed. Penarddun wanted desperately to excuse herself – she felt ready to vomit – but could hardly be seen to run out as soon as the marriage was done: she must wait a little while.

Iddon asked if Euroswydd meant to claim the homage of the other Western tribes, and he answered calmly, saying:

"They are at liberty not to accept me as High King: but I am King of the Silures, and they will accept *that*, or learn that our doughtiness did not depend on Llyr."

"And do you think they will?" she pressed.

"Goneril and Regan might find me easier to accept than each other," he pointed out. "That's if the Cornovii don't kick out Regan and her slave-born husband – but whether they do or not, they'll never consent to be ruled by Ordovician hill folk they outnumber five to one. As for the Demetae, they are fishermen, not warriors."

"But if Perion brings back aid from Gaul..." said Gwenwyn doubtfully.

"He'll set every other British tribe against him," finished Euroswydd confidently. "But in any case, I have already set a plan in motion to neutralise the Demetae. Goll, call in the renegade."

Goll stood, and went to the back of the hall, where a deerskin hanging obscured an area used for storage.

"Hafgan, come forth," he said.

From behind the hanging, there stepped a tall, broad-shouldered man in Druidic robes, much patched and mended. His hair, which hung halfway down his back, was pure white, but his pale face was unlined – so far as could be discerned beneath the tattoo of two fighting snakes which covered its left side from temple to jaw. His intense dark blue eyes glared out from under thick, lowering brows; he carried a heavy hardwood staff carved with much Ogham lettering and images of dragons and strange beasts; there were no fewer than four daggers in his belt.

Twca leapt to his feet.

"You let a stranger overhear our council? And he is *armed?*"

"I never go without my knives," said Hafgan with a perfunctory bow. "They bind me to my god."

"And which god is that?" demanded Iddon.

"Arawn," he answered. "The Death Lord."

"What is this man here for?" said Gwenwyn.

"Arawn is a god much feared among the Demetae," said Goll. "A little while ago, Prince Pwyll accidentally desecrated his sacred grove – he chased a stag into it while hunting. He abased himself and made sacrifice, and the Demetae hope that the god was appeased, but -"

"He is not," Hafgan interrupted. "I am the instrument of his wrath. The blasphemer will be destroyed."

"You intend to murder Pwyll?" said Iddon. She sounded more curious than condemnatory.

"I intend to challenge him," said the white-haired Druid. "To fight him at Arawn's Ford, in Arawn's name, upon Midsummer Eve: and to offer his blood to the god. Only so will Arawn truly be appeased. He will die at the first blow. The first blood is sacred; the second defiles."

"But Midsummer is past," Iddon pointed out.

"The day must be right," said Hafgan. "Otherwise Arawn will not be satisfied."

"But if we must wait nearly a year -"

"*Pwyll* must wait nearly a year," Euroswydd interjected impatiently. "A year of near seclusion, preparing himself for the sacred combat. A year in which he will have the threat of death and the god's displeasure hanging over his head. A year in which he will be forbidden to go into battle, and no Demetian will follow him if he tries."

A grin spread across Twmyr's scarred face.

"It's brilliant."

"It is the will of the god, no more," said Hafgan. "It is as it must be."

At last Penarddun managed to excuse herself, and ran to the Women's House. Falyse and Sicora had been allowed to take up residence there; the three men remained yet under closer watch. She told them what had happened; there were no words to comfort her, but merely being with them was something.

The afternoon wore agonisingly away. When at last Euroswydd did come to bring Penarddun back to the hall for dinner, she let herself be led as if in a dream; she sat beside

164

him through the evening, toying with her food and barely speaking, but drinking as much as she could keep down. At the end of it, Euroswydd ordered hangings put up before their bed.

"It serves no purpose to see us bedded," he said, "as the Queen is already with child." For that, at least, Penarddun was thankful.

When the chiefs and the servitors had respectfully withdrawn, Euroswydd sat beside her, and caressed her hair.

"You know that I mean no harm to you," he said softly. "Not unless you force me to it. I threatened only because I had to; because I could not see you lead my tribe to destruction. We need not lie together tonight. In time, we will, and you will give me children – our own, acknowledged children." He stroked her belly. "This will be Llyr's, whatever is the truth of it – but I will be as a father to it, and to Bran, when you bring him back from wherever you have hidden him. I won't ask you to do so yet. You should – he will be safer here – but I won't ask it. Not until you trust me." He kissed her lightly on the shoulder, then the neck. "Trust me," he whispered. "Believe me. I love you; and you love me. I can wait for you to realise it." She did not respond. He sighed deeply. "They will be listening out there in the hall," he said. "But they can be disappointed for one night. Let us sleep." And he drew her down into his arms, and closed his eyes. He slept soon; it was long before Penarddun could do the same.

Many days and nights passed much the same way. Euroswydd continued always gentle, never raising his voice or making an open threat. News from outside remained confused: all the surrounding tribes sent angry denials of Euroswydd's High Kingship, but the threats that accompanied them were vague, and Euroswydd's best intelligence was that nobody was yet moving an army. Hafgan made his challenge, and the Demetian forces melted away as predicted; Prince Pwyll had reportedly vowed to eat no flesh and know no woman until he had proven himself clean of blasphemy in the fight. Perion returned from Gaul with lukewarm promises of aid in Llyr's name, but no men; and when the Gauls learned that Llyr was deposed, they would surely abandon those promises. Of Bran, Penarddun had no news: she did not dare communicate with the Forest Hold.

In the autumn, when Bran would have just passed his first year, her daughter was born. Perhaps she was seeing what she wanted to see, but in her eyes the girl resembled Llyr more than Euroswydd. Goll slaughtered a lamb in thanksgiving: but this time the naming was left to Penarddun. It would not have been proper for Euroswydd to name another man's child: so it was she who stood before the chiefs, and said:

"Her name is Branwen. Branwen ferch Llyr ap Bladud, the White Raven, Princess of the Silures and of the West."

Euroswydd frowned for only a moment; Goll's mouth dropped open, but he said nothing. A moment later, Twca cried out:

"Branwen! Hail the White Raven!"

"Branwen! Branwen!"

The chant went round the hall; and Euroswydd smiled down at the child. Penarddun shivered – but she could see no malice in his look. There was every appearance of true warmth in his eyes.

He believes she is his. Rightly or wrongly, may the gods grant that he keeps believing that.

"And when he came to the Ford, a knight arose and spake thus… 'do all of you stand aside and leave the fight to be between them.'"

~ *Pwyll Prince of Dyfed*

Gray Hill, 81 B.C.E.

Winter had come and gone, and the peace had held. Formally, Euroswydd was not recognised as King of the Silures by any of the surrounding tribes – but nor did any make a move against him. There had been much traffic to and fro between the Ordovician and Cornovian courts, but little had come of it; while the Demetae had been left hanging by the long preparation for the prince's duel.

Llyr, Awel, and Perillus had been left at Portskewett through the winter, still under guard; but Penarddun had been allowed to bring Falyse and Sicora with her. Euroswydd remained affable, and loving to Branwen, showing barely a flicker of the side Penarddun had seen when he made her divorce Llyr. He had found a nurse for Branwen from among his clan, although he allowed Penarddun to nurse her herself for many months. Though smaller than Bran at her age, the child was healthy and happy, and was by now sleeping through the night.

Come spring, Euroswydd made an announcement.

"I intend to make a tour of the West," he said. "We cannot continue forever in this state of peace that is not peace, with war hanging over our heads. My Queen and I shall visit each of the neighbour tribes, show our trust and goodwill, and reach agreement with my good kinsfolk."

Penarddun was taken by surprise: it seemed a dangerous plan in such a tense situation, and she had little desire to return to Hen Dinas after her last experience there. She pleaded the need to remain with Branwen, but Euroswydd answered:

"My enemies say that you are my prisoner. I must needs show you off, as a free woman. Branwen will be well cared for here."

"No," said Penarddun. "If we mean to demonstrate our trust, what better means than by bringing her? She will not leave my side." She had been separated from one child: it would not happen again.

So it was that they rode out from Gray Hill to Hen Dinas, whose towering slopes looked yet more forbidding under the glow of the spring sun; and were there greeted by Regan, wearing a poisonous smile, and Achlesydd, who was now all adorned with gold, though he did not call himself a king.

"Welcome, Mother," said Regan sweetly. "And must I call Lord Euroswydd Father now?"

"The former High King's indisposition grieves us all," said Euroswydd. "But it was you yourself, lady, who first had cause to place him under guard."

"Indeed, yes," agreed Regan. "I would not dispute that my father was unfit to rule. But that does not make you High King."

"No," said Euroswydd. "The chiefs of the Silurian clans made me their king, by due election. High Kingship over the other tribes I have not claimed."

"And will not claim, or have not claimed *yet?*" said Regan sharply. Euroswydd did not answer.

"Come," said Achlesydd, "we are not enemies here. Our interests are as one; we shall discuss them further at dinner."

Beef and pork and ale and mead were plentiful that night: and Regan laid out to Euroswydd – never speaking directly to Penarddun – the basis of alliance.

"We both share the menace of the Deepwood on our borders," she said. "And yet we cannot march against Darnant and the other outlaws while Goneril is plotting against us in the mountains and Perion over the sea. I hear he has returned again to Gaul: perhaps this year he will bring back ships. But to do what? To restore Llyr? That's a dream. I fear the Demetae mean to ally with Goneril."

"But why should they do that?" asked Euroswydd.

"Because neither tribe alone is a match for the Silures, but together they are... if they can keep the Cornovii out of the fight. Because Goneril is the eldest. Because I was the one who imprisoned Father, which they call impiety."

"And because Maglor is a king and I am a Dobunnic chiefling's slave-born get," added Achlesydd.

"And could they keep the Cornovii out?" asked Euroswydd.

"My son Cunedag is a hostage," said Regan. "A fosterling in name, but a hostage nonetheless. I have Morgan here: that keeps us neutral. There have been... disturbances in the border region; but there will be no war between Ordovices and Cornovii. No matter how much you hope for it."

"I desire no such thing," said Euroswydd, a little too quickly. "I want peace for all the West."

"Peace under one High King, as it was before?" said Regan. "Those days are past."

"And the Demetae?" pressed Euroswydd. "What if it came to war with them?"

"Hen Dinas is a long way from Carn Goch," said Regan, "and a long way from the sea. We fear no Gaulish fleets here. I understand Pwyll is tied up in this matter of blasphemy – don't think I didn't see your hand in that, my lord, and admire it too. If the Demetae must be brought down before you can move against Darnant, we will lend you men: five hundred spears, let us say, so long as we are not at war ourselves when the call comes. But against the Ordovices we will do nothing, unless they invade us first."

They did not stay long at Hen Dinas: it would, after all, have been impolitic to celebrate Beltane there. They did not have far to travel to Goneril's court: she had remained at the winter fort of Caersws, sending Maglor to the coast. No doubt she meant to stay close to the borders and keep an eye on the Cornovii and Silures. Without snowdrifts, it was an entirely different journey, and the landscape barely recognisable as the same: but still Penarddun shuddered at the memory of when she had last gone by this road.

Along the way, Euroswydd declared his satisfaction at the neutrality of Regan.

"What she means, of course, is that she daren't leave her own territory for fear of the chiefs," he expounded airily. "Did you see how some of her nobles looked at Achlesydd? Not that I blame them."

"I could almost feel sorry for Achlesydd," said Penarddun later to Falyse and Sicora. "To be so despised, merely for his birth..."

"It's not for that," said Falyse, and spat. "It's because he betrayed his father."

"We don't know that," said Penarddun. "He helped Glevon, remember? He knew beforehand that we were escaping, so why not betray all of us?"

"That's what I've been puzzling since it happened," admitted Falyse. "But I see it now. He *wanted* us to escape. As long as Regan held Llyr, she had more power than any prince in the West, and she didn't need the likes of Achlesydd – but at the same time Euroswydd had a perfect excuse to attack the Cornovii in Llyr's name, maybe even with Goneril's support. With Llyr gone, Regan was undermined, and forced to lean on Achlesydd – and then he served up Glevon to make her sweet. Meanwhile we brought Llyr home to Portskewett and forced Euroswydd's hand – he had to make himself King, and alienate Llyr's allies and the subject tribes. Henwyn's death... maybe that was just luck, and maybe not. Either way, he's turned a subject queen into the independent ruler of one of the largest tribes in Britain, and made himself her husband."

Penarddun gasped.

"If half of that is true, he's a monster," she said. Falyse shrugged.

"Nobody rises so far so fast with clean hands," she said, with a dark glance in the direction of Euroswydd.

Like her sister, Goneril welcomed them in person, and feasted them richly. Cunedag ate with them at the feast – a marked contrast to the near invisibility of Morgan at Hen Dinas.

"How is my dear sister?" she asked solicitously. "And her husband?"

"They arc both well, and friendly disposed towards you," answered Euroswydd.

"I am glad to hear it," she said. "And to hear of her reconciliation with you, lady – I know you suffered much at her hands, but I trust you understand that it was for the best, in the light of my poor father's madness."

"Of course," said Penarddun, summoning up a pleasant smile. "There is no rancour in my heart."

"That is good," smiled Goneril. "Bitterness is such a terrible thing. But anyone can see you have none – you are looking so fresh. And little Branwen is beautiful – she is your image."

"I will be blunt," said Euroswydd. "I crave peace and friendship, such as there has long been between the Silures and Ordovices. Shall we have it?"

"And why should we not?" asked Goneril innocently.

"Because you might think to dispute my claim to the throne that was your father's. So might others. Perion of the Demetae -"

"I have nothing to do with Perion's comings and goings," said Goneril. "If you think he means to advance any claim of mine, you are mistaken. Most likely he's seeking a kingdom for himself in Gaul – they say he's married an Armorican princess."

"I had not heard that," admitted Euroswydd. "Of which tribe?"

"The Venelli, or the Veneti, the reports are confused. In one version, she's not Armorican at all, but Belgic. Perhaps being a mere co-prince is constricting him."

"Perhaps," said Euroswydd. "And what of yourself? Would you be willing to renounce any claim to the rule of the Silures?"

Goneril laughed.

"My dear cousin," she said, "you might choke on a fishbone tomorrow or die next week of a cold. Who would rule the Silures then? No, I will never renounce my claim: but you have been duly elected, and while you are alive and accepted by the chiefs, who am I to contest it? Rule in peace."

"And if the Demetae do revolt, or the Gauls invade?" pressed Euroswydd.

"We will send aid," said Goneril. "Two hundred bowmen, if we are not at war ourselves. You cannot in reason ask more than that."

Penarddun expected that they would move on again with as much speed as before: but Euroswydd preferred to remain at Caersws until Beltane was past.

"That way we will see who visits here, from south and east," he said; "and we will come to Carn Goch in time to witness Pwyll's Midsummer duel."

There were, in the event, no visitors from the south identifiable as Demetian envoys; though from Hen Dinas there came a few, always with some legitimate business that was discussed in front of the Silures. But they were there long enough for the rumours about Perion's marriage to become slightly more concrete – and far more confusing. He had married, it seemed, either Princess Elisena of the Veneti – a tribe of Armorican merchants and pirates with brine in the blood – or a Menapian, a sister of Aganippus. Or both. Or he was bringing one or the other back as Pwyll's bride, except, of course, that Pwyll could not marry before the duel was fought. And Pwyll himself was rumoured to be under some kind of spell, the work of a malicious Druidess.

The summer was waxing when they at last set out to ride south: by which time, Penarddun was again with child.

Falyse offered to procure drugs which would end it, though it could not be done without great danger: but Penarddun answered:

"Euroswydd needs an heir. If I don't give him one, and he looks for another wife, Bran and Branwen lose their last safeguard."

At Carn Goch, unlike Hen Dinas and Caersws, they did not seem to be expected. Nevertheless, food was hastily prepared, and Perion greeted them in person – and introduced them to his wives. Elisena of the Veneti, a dark-haired, slender beauty who wore her gown short and man's breeks beneath it, and Tungra of the Menapii, a softer, fairer woman with a warm smile and a marked resemblance to Aganippus, were *both* married to Perion – and both heavily pregnant: both children must have been conceived when he travelled to Gaul the previous year. Euroswydd smiled and greeted both women warmly: but Penarddun could see the moment of fear that came before the smile. By taking royal wives from multiple tribes, Perion was acting like Llyr, or her own father – like a High King.

"I meant to collect one bride for myself and one for Pwyll," said Perion, "but how was I to choose between these two? There will be more princesses left when Pwyll is free to marry."

If, of course, he lived to be free to marry. If Pwyll were to be killed in the duel now, Perion might well be recognised as sole Prince of the Demetae. Goll's and Euroswydd's plan could lead to a brother-in-law of Cordelia, with a fleet at his call, ruling alone on their western frontier. In all their fear of Goneril and Regan, they had forgotten the youngest daughter, far away in the Belgic lands. Euroswydd must be cursing his own folly now.

Pwyll himself declined to see them. His refusal was delivered by the Druidess, Rhiannon – a very tall woman with green eyes and a mass of auburn hair, who carried a longsword and had the image of a prancing horse embroidered on the front of her gown. Perion and his wives seemed a little afraid of her, and Penarddun could not blame them. But she said that the Prince had now gone into complete isolation, seeing only her until the day of the duel.

When at last the Summer Solstice came, the entire court rode out to Arawn's Ford. Pwyll wore a boiled leather cuirass, a short cloak, and a wooden buckler, but no helm. He looked thin and drawn. The warriors of the Demetian side ranged the bank, their helms gleaming, brightly painted shields before them. From the other side came Hafgan, alone, in a coat of scale armour, with an iron-and-leather cap on his head, and strode into the water. He wore no shield, but instead carried his staff in his left hand, and a drawn longsword in his right.

"Let none interfere," declared Pwyll. "We fight for the honour of the god."

Euroswydd was biting his lip. After planning this meeting, he now had to hope that his champion was defeated, or see Perion's power multiplied.

Pwyll stepped down from his chariot, and advanced into the waters of the ford, drawing his sword. Hafgan attacked first, swinging both sword and staff in a scissoring movement at the Prince's neck; but Pwyll ducked back, so that the Druid missed entirely, and stumbled with a great splash into deeper water, up to his thighs. But Pwyll was now too far away to deal a killer blow, and when he lunged downwards Hafgan easily parried his attempt – and he was forced to step into the deeper part himself, giving up the advantage of ground to come within range. He was shorter than the Druid, and the water came higher on him.

He struck, and Hafgan parried again, in a cross-handed motion; Pwyll slid his sword away, and evaded the Druid's counter-attack, causing Hafgan to stagger again – and the Prince brought his sword down. Hafgan met it with his staff, but the wood was cleft in two; and the blade came down, glancing off the side of his helm, slicing off half his ear, and bit deep into his collar-bone. He slumped to his knees, with a look of stunned surprise. The water was up to his chest now. Blood was swirling in the flood, and more was bubbling from his mouth.

"Finish me," he croaked. "Finish me."

Pwyll shook his head.

"The first blood is sacred," he said. "The second blow defiles."

Hafgan groaned, and fell forward into the water. Pwyll reached down, and held him under; when the bubbles ceased, he dragged the half-floating corpse to the bank, to cheers from his tribesmen, and a relieved smiled from Euroswydd. There he cut off Hafgan's head, and held it aloft by the long white hair.

"The Prince is proven clean of blasphemy," declared Rhiannon. "The god has claimed the blood of his accuser. All honour to Arawn! All honour to Pwyll!"

"All honour to Arawn! All honour to Pwyll!" chorused the Demetae.

"All honour to Arawn," declared Pwyll solemnly, "and to the Lady Rhiannon, whom I take here as my wife."

They returned to Portskewett with the Princes' goodwill, though with no promises of men. Euroswydd remained dissatisfied and distrustful, muttering darkly that the Demetae might have lessons to learn yet, but happy at least that the sisters would not combine against him: still less so if Perion was allied to Cordelia, whom neither would wish to see return to Britain.

"The one element of which I still know nothing", he said to Penarddun, "is your father. What will Belin do? To whom will he send the promised men, if he sends them at all?"

"I do not know," replied Penarddun. "We have had no word from the East in months – who knows how much my father has heard of what has happened here? He will have enough to concern him in his own kingdom."

Belin's Story

I have not long left. If one of my kin can keep what I have built, then I have lived long enough: but I greatly fear that it will fall.

There are not many now who remember the Belgic invasion. It was a different time. The Trinovantes were a small tribe, though a rich one, lucky that the sliver of land we were crammed into between the broad Thames and the plains of the Iceni horse-lords was temperate and fertile. West and south-west of us, the Cassi, Bibroci, and Ancalites all ruled powerful kingdoms.

Then everything changed.

There had been raids on the coasts for many years. Sometimes the raiders would stay for weeks and burn whole hundreds – but they always returned to the other side of the Channel by the end of the summer. Cheulf's invasion was different. It was no raid: it was a migration.

Cheulf was not Belgic by birth, but a mercenary from east of the Rhine, who had risen high in the service of one of the Belgic kings. When his master died – I do not say at Cheulf's hand – he seized his throne, and his queen, and set about seeking to expand his kingdom. But the other Belgic princes banded together, and he was defeated. That was when he determined to lead his newly acquired subjects across the sea, and found a new kingdom for himself in the fertile southlands of Britain.

His intelligence was good, his strategy better. He split his fleet into four parts, and landed simultaneously in the lands of the Cantiaci, the Cassi, the Ancalites, and the Bibroci; his commanders wasted no time in raiding coastal settlements, but rushed against the main forts of those tribes, and took them by surprise. Only the Cantiaci recovered from the blow, because they had the best warning system, and because they are ruled not by one king but by a tetrarchy: the senior Tetrarch was killed, but by then the other three already knew of the invasion and were mustering men from the river valleys, well away from the coast.

The Cantiaci, therefore, rallied, and drove the Belgae from their territories. But the other tribes were routed. Some were taken resisting, and enslaved to the Belgae; many more fled across the Thames. A few submitted and were able to keep their homes, but Cheulf could never have allowed many to do so, for he needed land to settle his own tribesmen on.

The scattered tribes now begged their neighbours for help. In the west, the Dobunni and Durotriges retreated to their hillforts and waited to defend themselves; to the north, the skin-clad Corieltauvi and the fierce Iceni shrugged – what were the quarrels of the south to them? But we Trinovantes had not the luxury of ignoring the invasion. It was into our land that the refugees were pouring, ever more, ever hungrier. We had long traded with the Belgae, and made alliances with them: my mother, Morina, was a Belgic princess. The defeated tribes now begged that we find a way to appease Cheulf, make the peace that they could not – or else that we go to war.

My father chose war. And my father died.

Cheulf sent his head home. That was a good gesture. The head of a king was a worthy trophy, something he could have shown to guests and boasted of for years, but he chose instead to return it – and with it, a message. He promised not to advance north of Thames, if I would not come south of it. He had what he wanted, and more than that: now he was ready to rest content, and what is more to lend his voice to my election as king in my father's place, young as I was, if I would lend my influence to keep the three dispossessed tribes from *reprisals. I promised. Peace was made; the three tribes were too wearied to do more than feebly protest, and the Trinovantes wanted nothing more. Cheulf was left as lord of the south coast, and I as King in my father's lands.*

The years passed. The peace was uneasy, but it held. The survivors south of the Thames adjusted to Belgic rule, while the exiles slowly abandoned hope of regaining their former lands. Cheulf grew old, while I grew up. I took wives and fosterlings from neighbouring tribes, and sired a son of my own, Imanuentius.

Cheulf had become a fact of life: we hardly thought of him as mortal: but one day he choked on a piece of gristle, and died. He had spent his reign eliminating any and every rival, with the result that there was not one prince or chief in the Belgic lands of the stature to succeed him. The Belgae at once began to tear themselves apart as petty warlords vied for his throne: and the exiles north of Thames began again to hope for return, and revenge.

They spoke also of revenge on me. Dependent on Trinovantic aid when they first came north, they were filled with resentment, of that and of our survival while their own kingdoms were all but gone: and they muttered darkly of my Belgic blood, some even declaring that I had been secretly on Cheulf's side from the start, and had engineered the death of my own father to make myself king. I had spies in their lands, but none could learn who led the discontented.

I chose not to wait. The Ancalites were already mounting raids into Trinovantic territory: so I summoned my warband and marched into theirs. I laid waste enough villages to teach them a lesson, then moved against the Bibroci, and did the same. Everywhere I took noble hostages, the younger the better. They would make companions for Imanuentius –

and for Penarddun, who was born to my favourite, Icenian wife while I was on this campaign.

The Cassi were different: they were prepared. That was where the man behind all those plots was lurking: my own brother-in-law, Imanuentius' uncle, a princeling whom I had thought far away in the West, training to be a Druid. But here he was, arraying his forces against me: Darnant!

The war was bloody and vicious. The Cassi and their allies loved Darnant, who had prophesied victory to them in the name of the war goddess, the Mor-Rigan. He paraded a priestess in a red robe, attended by tame crows, who he said was the goddess' incarnation. When warriors of mine fell alive into their hands, she would cut their throats and observe the spatter of the blood, and predict great victories from the patterns it made; others were given the Triple Death, strangled, stabbed, and drowned at the same time, in offering to the grim goddess.

The Cassi were swept up in a wave of religious fervour against me. I had to resort to terror. I burned village after village, and tortured those I caught for any information about Darnant: but even in the utmost pain they lied to me. Only when I had utterly laid waste the lands of the Cassi did news of him finally cease – until the rumours started to come out of the west, of a King in the Deepwood who robbed and raped passing travellers, and paid homage to dark gods.

Thus I made myself master of the Ancalites, the Bibroci, and the Cassi – not only north of Thames but in those parts where they survived south of it. For those on the south bank had never followed Darnant: to them, I was not the enemy, but a distraction from the true cause. When I offered them my lordship, they leapt at the chance to have a lord born in Britain, and not one of the hated heirs of Cheulf. I even managed to win the allegiance of many Belgic chiefs and *headmen, who preferred stable rule to that of their own squabbling princes.*

The kingdom of Cheulf never recovered, but remains a fractured mess of little fiefs: while my lands stretch from the east coast to the west since the Dobunni bent the knee. At a glance one should say I have heirs enough. Little Vellaunos, my youngest, is still a child, but Imanuentius is wise and well liked by the chiefs. He has been fool enough to take a low-born wife, but that can be amended. My second son Nennius has come home from his fostering full of charm, and deadly with a long sword, equally important qualities in a king. My brother Cassamus is capable and loyal, ready either to support one of my sons or to take the rule on himself if the chiefs will have neither.

I have not made Cheulf's mistake, but still I fear his fate. There are still enough among the subject tribes who resent my rule – to the point that they might even be ready to ally themselves with Belgae against the Trinovantes. If that were to happen, who knows what might follow?

The Belgae in Britain are divided, but may unite again; their cousins in Gaul are a mighty power. There are two folk of ambition among them. One is the Princess Lydore of the Suessiones. Their numbers in Britain are tiny, but her uncle is High King of the Belgae across the sea, and she is said to be shrewd and fearless. The other is a Caletic lordling called Clarvorus ap Penuchel. He recently got himself elected as Prince of the continental Caleti as well as those in Britain, and had the audacity to seek the hand of my daughter Fesonas. I refused him – his tribe is insignificant, and Fesonas is young yet – but he may be dangerous. I have warned my sons against them both. I have done all I can to make the Trinovantes great: but will my work outlive me?

182

"Didst thou hear't, or did th' inspiring gods
Whisper to me alone? Old Lear shall be
A king again."

~ Tate, *King Lear*

Portskewett, 79 B.C.E.

The peace held longer than anyone had hoped or feared. There were raids, every summer – not ordinary lawlessness, but probing, as Goneril, Regan, and Perion felt along Euroswydd's border for weaknesses, while he pushed back to warn them off: but they never flared into open war.

Penarddun bore twin sons, Nisien and Efnisien: Euroswydd doted on them, and grew kinder to her, fussing around, always concerned for her health and theirs. She was relieved to find herself able to love them; though her heart still ached for Bran. Branwen's nurse undertook to care for them too: Sicora shared drynursing duties, and watched the Silurian woman.

Euroswydd disapproved when Penarddun resumed her combat training with Falyse, but did not forbid it: it was Silurian custom for noblewomen to be made proficient with sword and spear, and he would not go against it.

The twins were not the only royal boys born in the West. The Demetae had now no fewer than three young princes. Tungra, whose own mother had come from east of the Rhine, had given her son the outlandish Germanic name of Florestan; his half-brother was named Amadis, and their cousin, the Druidess' Rhiannon's son, Pryderi: though the latter was reported to be sickly and not expected to live.

Two winters had passed since the duel at Arawn's Ford when the news came from the East that Belin ap Clywel was dead. Penarddun was surprised to find that she had tears for him. It was nearly five years now since she had left Dun Belin, sold by him to Llyr's envoys like a cow: but of a sudden she found herself desperately missing Dun Belin, and her brothers and sister. It was for home, more than for her father, that she was weeping, perhaps – but either way, she wept: though not for long.

When the news arrived, Euroswydd was away. He had ridden west to investigate fresh disturbances on the Demetian border: Gwenwyn the Honey Bee was losing cattle to rustlers, and had demanded aid. The next morning, they saw the ships.

They were Venetic craft – there was no mistaking the rig. Though smaller than the longboats of the Irish raiders, or of the Belgae, they carried more sail: the Veneti built for speed and manoeuvrability. But they had crept up the Severn Sea like pirates, under cover of night. Garinter of the Veneti had raided the Belgic coast and the Dumnonian ports before, but had never come so far north, nor had any ever thought that sea-raiders would dare attack Portskewett – yet here they were: and though Twca's son Taginos had been left to command Euroswydd's guards, as Queen, Penarddun was the ultimate authority.

"Shall we prepare to defend the fort?" asked Taginos worriedly, looking to her for leadership.

"The beach," she replied. "They have not landed yet. We may prevent them – or be there to greet them if they come in peace. To stay here would be to give enemies an easy landing, and to insult them if they are friends. I will do neither.

Assemble archers and slingers with all speed – and Falyse: bring me my armour."

"You, my lady?" Taginos stared, uncomprehending.

"I," she replied. "Be they friend or foe, I will not hide from them: I am a Queen." Falyse smiled proudly at her, and hurried to fetch the armour.

When she was fully arrayed, Penarddun went out and spoke to Taginos' men.

"Be swift, and be sure-sighted," she said. "Do nothing without my command, but be ready to loose as one."

She led them down to the beach. The fisherfolk and net-menders had scattered, leaving only the lookouts from the fort; the Venetic ships were now close in, so that the men on board could be seen clearly – and they were armed for war, every one in helm and shield. They looked to be in hailing distance: she signalled to Taginos, and he called out to them.

"Why do you come here?" he shouted. "What do you mean towards the Silures and their King?"

There was a pause: then a figure mounted the prow of the foremost vessel. It was a woman, slight of build, but armed in scale-mail, targe, and light helm. Her hair was pale blonde, and her cloak white: and painted on her shield was a roiling, writhing serpent – the viper of the Silures.

"We mean nothing but friendship to the Silures," she replied, "and to their true King, Llyr ap Bladud, if yet he lives. As for the usurper Euroswydd, if he will lay aside his stolen title and surrender, his life will be spared, as will those of all his followers."

Taginos' jaw dropped.

"Who are you to speak thus of our King?" he demanded.

"I am Cordelia ferch Llyr, Lady of the Lake, and Queen of the Menapii," the woman replied: and she pulled off her

186

helmet. The ship was close enough now to shore that she would have made an easy target – but also close enough to let her be recognised. There was hardly anybody on that shore who did not know Cordelia by sight, nor was there any doubt that this was she.

Taginos raised his hand to give the signal, and looked to Penarddun for confirmation: but she said, loudly and clearly, for the sailors as well as her own people to hear:

"Lower your weapns! We will receive Queen Cordelia in peace."

Taginos looked stunned: but his men did as ordered. Cordelia shouted her thanks, and the Venetic ships moved in, men jumping down into the surf to draw them up onto the shore. There were four boatloads of twenty warriors each – enough to outnumber the garrison of Portskewett, but not to have taken it had it been closed against their coming. But Penarddun strode down to the strand where Cordelia was disembarking, and knelt before her, waves lapping around her knees: and she said:

"My lady, I welcome you home. This only I ask before I surrender Portskewett into your hands: that you guarantee the safety of all my children."

Cordelia smiled gently.

"Of course," she said. "I swear it by the Three Mothers, and call these present and all the gods of Britain and Gaul to witness."

Penarddun bowed her head.

"Then the fort is yours," she said. Cordelia took her by the arm, and lifted her from the water – then drew her into an embrace, kissing her warmly. Disengaging, she turned to the Veneti.

"Queen Penarddun is my good and honest friend," she said. "Neither she, her children, her servants, nor any bearing her allegiance is to be harmed."

They proceeded up to the fort side by side: and as they went, Penarddun told Cordelia what had befallen in the past four years – including how Llyr and Awel, though allowed to move about the fort, remained prisoners at Portskewett. Perillus had been granted liberty the year before, upon condition that if he should ever leave Silurian territory, he might not return there. Now he lived somewhere on the edge of the Deepwood – but visited often; she believed that he and Awel had become lovers.

When she spoke of her long separation from Bran, Cordelia squeezed her hand; when she spoke of Llyr, she blinked back tears. When they came at last to the fort, while Goll sputtered and gasped in impotent astonishment at the sight of them, she took Cordelia straight to her father's hut. Awel was leaning against the wall outside, playing despondently with a cup-and-ball: at the sight of them he stared, then flung himself on the ground.

"My lady!" he exclaimed. "My lord the King – I beg your pardon, my lord your father – he, he is resting – he has not been himself..."

"His self was taken from him," said Cordelia. "He will be Llyr again." She turned to her men. "Wait without," she said. "I will go in with my lady stepmother and this good fellow."

They entered the hut. Within, Llyr was lying on a pallet, his eyes closed, his brow damp; Perillus knelt by his side, clasping his hand.

"He grows worse," he said. "Not the fever – it is light, and will pass soon, but his mind... Lady Cordelia!" He jumped to his feet.

"Hush," she said. "Is it safe to wake him?"

"I do not know, lady," said Perillus. "I cannot say... how long he has left."

Llyr's eyes fluttered open.

"What is this place?" he murmured. He struggled to prop himself up, but failed, and fell backwards; Perillus caught his head and held it up. "I know these people," muttered Llyr. "Think, man, think – you have been here before. This is not the Otherworld, these are not demons and ghosts, they live." He looked from Awel, to Penarddun, to Cordelia. "No," he said. "No, no, that is not possible. She is gone." He sighed deeply. "I thought... that I was getting better," he said. "Seeing what was truly there; but I am not. I can see my daughter – my one true child, whom I sent away, whom I shall never see again – my Cordelia!"

At that, Cordelia fell to her knees by the bed, weeping indeed; she seized his limp hand, and showered it with kisses.

"It is I, Father," she murmured. "I am here; and I will see your wrongs righted."

When Llyr had lapsed back into sleep, Penarddun led Cordelia to the hall, calling on Perillus to attend them there while Awel watched over the former King. Falyse attended too, while Sicora remained with the nurse and children: Cordelia brought two of her own captains, and a female attendant named Arante, but all others were turned forth.

"I spoke warily before Taginos," she said when the doors were closed. "Do you know which of your people here are to be trusted?"

"All serve Euroswydd," said Penarddun. "I trust none but Falyse, Sicora, Awel, and Perillus."

"That is ill," said Cordelia. "Do you believe Euroswydd will fight?"

189

"Sooner than give up his throne, yes. He is on the Demetian border at the moment -"

"I know," said Cordelia. "By now, Garinter has landed at the mouth of the Tywi with his main fleet, and support from Gandales of Scilly, to join with Pwyll and Perion. They have been my allies from the start – Perion urged me to come sooner; but I would not plunge the West into war."

"Forgive me, lady, but what has changed?" asked Falyse.

"War has come, with or without me," answered Cordelia. "My sisters have made a secret pact against Euroswydd. They mean to invade Siluria and claim joint rulership of the West."

"Where do you have this information from?" wondered Perillus.

"From Appius Scaliger," said Cordelia. "He has been in fear ever since he went over that one day they would cease to find him useful. What decided him was when the steward Rheol's head was flung over the walls of Caersws one night. He is certain that Regan and Achlesydd were behind it, warning Goneril off – and that he will be next if they ever suspect he has played them against one another. He says he has not. He is lying; but he thought me his best hope of mercy."

"What of King Aganippus?" asked Penarddun. "Does he not accompany you?"

"He had other duties," said Cordelia. "He accompanies the Belgic High King Diviciacus to the east of Britain. War brews there too. Clarvorus of the Caleti plots to unite the British Belgae against Diviciacus, invade Gaul and make himself High King on both sides of the Channel. Your Trinovantic kin are in danger from him: if they are wise, they will join with Diviciacus."

190

"Is there then no High King in the East since my father's death?" said Penarddun with a frown.

"The Trinovantes chose your eldest brother," said Cordelia, "but the Belgae do not recognise him. The upriver tribes are restless too. But there is nothing we can do, save pray for his good success and ours."

"You are right," Penarddun admitted. "But it grieves me to think of my brothers and sister in such distress."

"Diviciacus will aid them if they let him," said Cordelia. "He is a good man, a great warrior, and a fine king. But if Euroswydd will not give up the throne, we must move against him before he seeks to join Goneril and Regan – for the force they mass against him will surely now be turned on us. How many men has he?"

"A few score charioteers only," said Penarddun. "He went to chase off rustlers, not to fight a war. But if he has wind of your landing, he will send runners to the chiefs – they all voted for deposition."

Cordelia sighed.

"I cannot say that they were wrong to do so," she confessed. "Poor Father: he has brought much of his ill fortune on himself. But Euroswydd had no right to imprison him and his people, nor to force this marriage upon you." She took Penarddun's hand. "Nor was it any true election," she said. "I know that he forced you to withdraw, and neither I nor my sisters were considered. We had a right to be. So did my brother." Penarddun gaped; Cordelia smiled. "Not Bran – no infant can be King – but I have learned much since I left these shores. Urganda has visited our court more than once: and I have met Ardian."

"But the law says -"

191

"The law says that only a whole man may be King," said Cordelia. "Ardian has all his limbs – they merely happen to be a little smaller than other folk's."

"Forgive me," said Penarddun. "We had heard nothing here of Urganda travelling to Gaul."

"She has," said Cordelia; "and she has brought back with her the next Lady of the Lake. I named my daughter Urganda, in my aunt's honour; and she is in Avalon now, where she belongs. My mother should never have been taken thence: my father blasphemed in that."

"Then – would you settle in Avalon?" asked Falyse. "Rather than be Queen here, or in Gaul?"

"If I could first see the West at peace," said Cordelia. "But that is not possible yet. Now we must take what force we safely can and go at once against Euroswydd. If Garinter and the Demetae take him from the other side, he will be in a trap, and may yet be compelled to surrender before my sisters know we have landed. We shall divide our people – take half the Veneti west, and leave the other forty here, doing the same with the Silurian garrison. Perillus, will you accept command of Portskewett, in the name of King Llyr?"

"Gladly," answered Perillus, bowing.

Penarddun sent Falyse to call in Taginos: but a few minutes later, she returned to report that he was not to be found.

"Run to Euroswydd, no doubt," she said, and spat. "Now we have no choice: we must ride today."

"My Veneti can run all night if need be," said Cordelia. "Ready your chariots, and we will leave as soon as may be."

And so they rode out from Portskewett, chanting a hymn to the Mor-Rigan, to bring down the King of the Silures. West they rode, towards the Demetian lands, and the spring breeze blew in their faces so that their hair streamed behind them. And as the sun was sinking, they met with Euroswydd.

He gave them no greeting nor chance to negotiate. The moment he laid eyes on Cordelia, he screamed, a long, wordless cry of anguished wrath. He turned on Penarddun.

"I spared you! I made you my Queen – my *wife!* How can you do this to me?"

"When you so generously didn't murder me?" she spat back. "Me or my friends whose lives you threatened? 'First the Roman, then the fool, then the swordwife, then her lover'!"

"Have you hated me all this time?" asked Euroswydd. His voice had sunk to a hoarse croak, and his face was ashen: he truly seemed stricken at the thought.

"I do not hate you," said Penarddun coldly. "I despise you."

Euroswydd's eyes bulged: and suddenly he was yelling: "On! Fall on! Kill, kill, kill, kill them all!"

Some of his charioteers whipped their horses forward, but more hung back. Those who did charge were easily picked off by archers at a wave of Cordelia's hand, their numbers not enough to bear through.

"We'll not fight the Lady of the Lake," shouted Gwenwyn.

"The Lady!" called another. "Lady! Lady!"

More took up the shout. Euroswydd scowled.

"Are you all turned coward?" he demanded. "I am your King!"

"You may still surrender," said Cordelia, "and your life will be spared."

"It is more than you deserve," added Penarddun.

"I will never surrender to a pack of Gaulish pirates," snarled Euroswydd. "I will see you dead, *Lady of the Lake* – and as for you, you traitorous bitch, I will flay you alive!"

He whipped up his horses: Taginos, who was standing by his chariot, leapt and scrabbled, and barely managed to haul himself onto it as Euroswydd gained speed, almost being dragged behind him.

"Let him go," said Cordelia calmly.

"But if he goes to Goneril..." said Penarddun doubtfully.

"Goneril and Regan were massing to attack Euroswydd when he was a king – they'll not make friends with him when he's a lone runaway. He has nowhere to go. He should have given himself up." Cordelia turned to the charioteers. "You are all Silures, my true and well beloved people," she said. "My tribe are my children. Enemies gather in the north, who threaten your homes and your families: will you join with me against them?"

"Hail to the Lady!" shouted Gwenwyn. "Queen Cordelia, Lady of the Lake!"

> "What more despite could devilish beasts devise,
> Than joy their father's woeful days to see?"
> ~ John Higgins, *The Mirror for Magistrates*

They made camp by the road that night, all together, Silures and Veneti: Cordelia dined and drank with Gwenwyn, and he readily agreed to go on the next day and meet with Garinter and the Demetian brothers. He and his warriors seemed somehow under the spell of Llyr's youngest daughter: though Penarddun felt uneasy, and slept with her knife in her hand that night. But no treachery occurred.

Cordelia had sent runners ahead to alert her allies of their approach: and early the next morning, not long after striking camp, they met with the Demetae and Veneti. Penarddun gasped when she saw the size of their combined host: Garinter had emptied his fleet onto the shore, and rank upon rank of his long-braided Armoricans with their light spears and slings stood alongside the Demetian archers and charioteers. Pwyll, Rhiannon, and Perion rode in gilded chariots pulled by fine horses from Spain, far taller and smoother of coat than the ponies of their warriors; the Druidess had armoured herself, and had painted on her broad shield the same horse whose image had been embroidered on her gown when Penarddun saw her last. There were wings on her gleaming bronze-gilt helm, and the sword at her side was as long as her husband's.

"The Ordovices moved from Caersws yesterday," Perion told them. "They will join with the Cornovii today."

"Then we will meet them," said Cordelia. "Riders will take them an offer of parley: I am here to make peace, not war."

So the riders were dispatched: and the army began to move northeast. They had an unimpeded march, and made camp in northern Silurian territory that night: in the dark watches, the runners returned, bringing the enemy's agreement to meet. Cordelia sent to have Penarddun awakened.

"I would have you by my side when we parley," she said.

They met the four foes on an open moor. The two armies had advanced almost to within sight of one another, but the meeting place was out of bowshot of either. Each rode in a separate chariot, with their driver lashed to the reins beside them – Goneril and Maglor in green, with winged helms and gilded axes at their belts, Regan and Achlesydd in blackberry purple, with silver torques and square bucklers intricatedly embossed. The men had limed their hair into warrior spikes, while the women's was tightly braided. Behind them came standard-bearers, holding aloft banners embroidered with the totems of their tribes: the grinning severed head of the Ordovices, and the red fox of the Cornovii. Goneril spoke first.

"So, you have come back, sister," she said with a sneer. "You stayed in Gaul long enough. Have you grown tired of your husband, or he of you?"

"I have come to restore peace to the West," said Cordelia.

"If that is all you want, you can have it easily," said Goneril. "You have already rid us of the main obstacle to it – the usurper Euroswydd. For that you have our gratitude, I promise. Lead your army off this field, instruct the Silurian

196

chiefs to accept the joint rule of myself and Regan, and go home to Gaul. The West will be at peace."

"For how long?" demanded Cordelia. "How long before you two turn on one another as you turned on Euroswydd?"

"Do you think so little of your sisters?" retorted Goneril. "Besides, what business is it of yours to guess the future? Leave, and you will have created peace now. If we break it as you expect, you can always invade again, since that is apparently how you resolve family problems."

Cordelia shook her head.

"I think of you as you have shown yourselves," she said. "I will not abandon Father to your care, still less Queen Penarddun and her children."

"Euroswydd's brats," spat Regan.

"Innocents, and two of them our own sib," Cordelia corrected her. "But innocents still, if they were no kin to us."

"So if we let you take them home, you would leave?" said Maglor. His wife glared at him – but Penarddun could not help thinking it an intelligent question. He was trying to trap Cordelia, to force her into an appearance of hypocrisy. But he failed.

"These are my terms," answered Cordelia, evenly, but loud enough for all to hear. "The High Kingship is ended, unless all tribes agree to choose one of their number as High King or Queen, who may not pass on the title unless the agreement is renewed by all tribes' consent. The tribes of the West will be allies, but not co-subjects. The monarchy of the Silures will be put to a free election, in which not only the chiefs but the headmen and women of the largest villages will vote – say, four from each clan. They will be given the chance to choose between Llyr and all his adult children – including our brother Ardian."

197

"You lie," exclaimed Regan. "Ardian is dead – he died before you were born."

"Ardian is alive, in Avalon," said Cordelia calmly. "I have met him: and if you call me liar again, sister, you will rue it. Any Silurian clan chief who wishes may also stand; and all who do will swear to Mabon and Modron that, if they are elected, they wil take no vengeance on the losers; and that if they are not they will honour the winner. All will guarantee the safety of Queen Penarddun, her servants, and her children. If these conditions are met, and I am not elected Queen, then I will return to Gaul, I swear by the Three Mothers. One more thing only – should she so choose, Queen Penarddun also will have the right to seek election as Queen of the Silures."

Regan scoffed aloud at that, and spat on the ground.

"Never!" she said. "You would let Euroswydd's bed-slave pollute our father's throne?"

"You let Euroswydd himself sit in it for two years," said Cordelia mildly. Regan scowled.

"I will not submit my rights to the vote of peasant headmen," she snapped.

"Nor I," said Goneril. "I am Father's firstborn; you are an exile whose home lies over the sea, and you have no rights in Britain."

Cordelia's face was grave: and for the first time she let her tone become harsh as she said:

"Then you have chosen war?"

"Aye," said Goneril, and Regan echoed her: then their drivers turned their chariots and headed back towards their own lines. Maglor and Achlesydd had nothing to add, but followed their wives. The standard-bearers turned and marched away.

Cordelia shook her head sadly.

"So be it," she murmured. She turned to Penarddun. "I would not have you fight," she said. "But the decision is yours. What experience have you?"

"I have fought," said Penarddun. "And I have seen blood and death, more than I cared to. But I have never been in battle. I do not wish to hamper you: but nor do I wish to sit uselessly and do nothing."

"And you will not," promised Cordelia. She looked to the princes. "My lords, I think it as well to place the Silures who have joined us in the centre, under my own command, with Veneti to the right and Demetae to the left," she said. "But we will require a rearguard. I propose that Queen Penarddun should command it, with the assistance of Gaius Perillus and Falyse."

Penarddun's eyes widened. She had not thought of command, and the notion frightened her. Garinter was curling his lip: but Pwyll and Perion were nodding, and Perillus – who had attended on foot – smiled, and said:

"I would be proud to serve under Queen Penarddun. She has been our commander in times as trying as any battle, and she has done well."

"I accept," she said. "And I thank you all."

The rearguard remained behind a row of spaced stakes, with gaps wide enough for a single rider but too narrow for a chariot, as the main army advanced. Though they had the high ground, the moor below was rocky and uneven, and the curving slope opposite partially hid the approaching enemy.

Penarddun forced herself to watch, Falyse squeezing her hand, as the chariots of both sides gathered speed, and the javelins started to fly. She saw a Cornovian chief, big as an ox, scream as Garinter's spear was driven into his stomach; Gwenwyn tumbled, and was crushed beneath Twmyr's wheels.

The chariots milled around like ants; the infantry behind them hung back, letting the nobles have their day and enjoy their heroics. Only when enough had died to prove the skill of the survivors would the main bodies of the two armies advance. Chariot fighters took great pride in being able to throw javelins accurately when both they and their targets were travelling at speed: some would even climb up onto the rim or out onto the horse-pole to make themselves more vulnerable and the shots more impressive.

At last the armies were moving forward, between the still racing chariots, in columns with shields locked and spears out. They clashed with a terrible cacophony of iron and bone: and soon Penarddun could not tell who was who, which side was which – she could see only confusion across all the plain below. She looked anxiously to Perillus: but he too was frowning, staring down at the carnage, trying to make sense of it.

At last, it became clear that their people were falling back.

"Should we go to their aid?" asked Falyse. Penarddun had no answer; but Perillus said:

"No. We should only impede their retreat and crush them between ourselves and the enemy if we advanced now. We must make ready to harrass the foe when they come closer, and cover our people's retreat up the hill."

"Prepare, then," said Penarddun, relieved. "Draw our men to the right, and be ready to attack when the enemy comes below us." Her orders were passed on: and the pony-riders and the slingers moved forward, through the stakes, and into position for an attack. She herself mounted a hill pony, a strong and resilient beast, and took her long cavalry sword in hand.

It was not long before the first of the enemy came within their range: Regan in her chariot was leading a snaking column of Cornovian spearmen, harrassing and driving back the Veneti. Penarddun looked to Perillus, and he nodded.

"Now!" she cried: and they surged down the slope. Her pony was swift and sure-footed, and she led the charge, her blood pounding through her; she could hear herself whoop as she brandished her sword, urging her people on. The Mor-Rigan was with her; she felt like a god of battle.

She aimed straight for Regan. She had not forgotten the months of captivity at Hen Dinas, nor Glevon with his eyes torn out.

The Cornovii saw the new assault too late, and were struggling to turn their spears when the riders fell upon them, cutting through them like a scythe through grass. Regan was shouting to her charioteer, who tried to turn the chariot, but her own men were impeding her as they fell back from the slope, while in front of her the Veneti had halted their retreat and were regathering.

Penarddun cut down a Cornovian, a young man, perhaps in his first battle: she saw him fall, and the pain and fear in his pale blue eyes – then another, and another – she was within striking distance now – she drew her mount up, and lunged. Regan tried to parry with one of her javelins, and deflected the sword's point up, but not far enough: it struck her in the shoulder. A look of utter shock came over her face, to be replaced by one of fury and hatred when her eyes met Penarddun's. She lashed out sideways with the javelin: Penarddun, expecting a direct thrust, raised her sword, but the edge of the spear caught her on the side of her head below her helmet.

The world faded. She lost her grip on the reins; something hit her, again, and she slipped from the saddle. She never felt herself hit the ground.

"Those you look favourably upon, you quickly raise to great power, and as soon as you turn away your face, you quickly reduce them from something to nothing."

~ Wace, *Brut*

She awoke in shadow; as her eyes got used to the light, she realised that she was still outdoors, in the shade of a spreading oak, the sun sinking in the west. Falyse was kneeling by her; Perillus stood a little way off, his hands bound before him. Goneril, Regan, Maglor, and Achlesydd sat in an arc facing them, three on camp-stools and Regan on a more elaborate chair: she was bandaged and her arm bound up where Penarddun had wounded her, and she leaned into the back of the chair for support. There was an ugly gash across her temple, that Penarddun had not given her; a sheen of sweat lay on her face, and her hand was twitching, while her eyes darted anxiously from side to side. Behind each of them stood shield-bearers, tall men with long moustaches; armed guards stood to either side. Further back, there were tents and huts, and people moving around, some carrying bodies, others chests of weapons. She was in the camp of the enemy.

Maglor had taken a spear-thrust to the hand, but seemed little concerned by it. He and Goneril were stony-faced, while Regan scowled through her obvious pain; Achlesydd wore an expression of faint amusement.

"You are alive, then," said Maglor.

"Worse luck to you," Regan added.

"Cordelia...?" said Penarddun faintly.

"Lives," replied Maglor curtly. "For the moment. There are many dead to be honoured; a sacrifice will no doubt be required, and a Queen's blood might please the gods."

Penarddun sat up, and winced as the wound at the side of her head smarted.

"My blood, too?" she said with a grimace.

"Perhaps," said Maglor. "Or perhaps not."

"When we take Portskewett, which will be soon," said Goneril, "we will have three of your children in our power. Three, but not the one who matters – not my father's son."

"Nor will you ever have him," said Penarddun. Maglor raised his eyebrows.

"Would you sacrifice three children to save one?" he said. "Tell us where Bran is to be found – alive or dead – and you may take your other children and go to the East or to Gaul, and be troubled by us no more."

Penarddun sighed deeply. She had no way of knowing if Bran was even alive; she had not seen him since he was a babe in arms. Branwen and Nisien and Efnisien were alive and precious and could be saved, and were at Portskewett: and they would be in her enemies' power by tomorrow. Bran, wherever he was, was certainly further away than the others – she could buy time, at least; perhaps time to find some way to save him.

"He is in the Deepwood," she said. "I do not know where; but I... I may be able to find out. I will say no more until I know my other children are safe."

"Thank you," said Maglor with a smile. "I did not think you would co-operate so quickly. Now, to other business." He turned to the Cornovian shield-bearers. "Seize him," he said.

They moved instantly, wrestling Achlesydd's arms behind his back while a third guard moved forward, punched him in the gut, and pulled off his sword-belt, throwing it aside. Goneril and Regan were both on their feet, shouting, demanding explanation, Goneril angrily, Regan wildly, looking close to collapse; Maglor looked on unperturbed.

"You know the reason already, dear wife," he said, his voice dripping honeyed poison. "It was your plot as well as his. The slave you used as go-between has confessed – it took long torture, but she broke. I was to die in Portskewett so that you could marry this slave's whelp, I and Queen Regan too. I understand the need for murder – we both command too great loyalty to be safely divorced. But your taste, that I confess baffles me."

Regan's fevered face was contorted with rage.

"You lie!" she shouted. "Achlesydd would never betray me!" She wheeled on Goneril. "You did this – you – you bewitched him – you would destroy us both!"

"You think I would incriminate myself to hurt you?" snapped Goneril. "You always were stupid."

Regan leapt forward: and, before Maglor or anyone else could stop her, her knife was in her hand, and she was upon her sister, stabbing again and again and again. By the time she was hauled off by the Ordovician guards, gasping, her eyes so dilated as to appear black, the wound in her shoulder had burst, and she was covered in Goneril's blood and her own; Goneril lay in a pool of gore, gasping out her life. Penarddun stared, scarcely comprehending; even Maglor looked stunned. And Achlesydd – Achlesydd was *laughing*.

"She should have died to please the gods," muttered Maglor. "They have been cheated of her blood – unless Taranis will accept such as seeps into the roots of his oak. But they will have yours, Achlesydd." He clapped his hands, and a round-bellied Ordovician strode forward, bearing a carnyx almost as tall as himself, its mouth fashioned like the head of a wild boar. "Sound the signal," he ordered. The fat man raised the horn to his lips, and blew threegreat blasts: then there was silence.

All waited: the world seemed to hold its breath. Achlesydd smiled.

"Whatever you're expecting, it looks like it's not coming," he said. "Did you think that Arawn would arise from the earth to claim me?"

But the soldiers and servitors were drawing apart, clearing a path through the camp: and along it stronde a man, armoured in boiled leather, with a wooden targe in his right hand, an axe in his left, and with a cloth tied across his face below his eyes. Even Achlesydd's swagger was drained from him; and his face was pale as he asked:

"Who are you?"

"Justice," said the masked figure.

"Release him," ordered Maglor. Achlesydd's captors dropped his arms, and stepped back: he stood up, stretching, grunting. "Arm yourself," Maglor told him, "and quickly. You must fight."

"Must I, indeed?" said Achlesydd. "I am wounded and winded and weary; I have been in battle all day. What kind of fight is that?"

"Justice will be served, and the death of the loser dedicated to Ogma," said Maglor. "If the gods favour you, then you will be victorious."

"Very well," said Achlesydd. "Bring me my arms."

He was still wearing his coat of mail from the battle; the Cornovian warriors hastened to bring him a helm, an oval shield four times the size of his challenger's targe, and a long sword. He turned it over in his hand a couple of times.

"Hacked half to hell," he said. "Good: I know it can stand use. If you'd given me a new one I'd have expected it to break in my hands."

The tramp of marching feet was heard: and, looking round, Penarddun saw guards leading the bound Cordelia up to the oak. She gasped when she saw her sister dead on the ground; but Maglor coolly inclined his head towards her.

"Greetings, sister," he said. "As you can see, the gods are not slow to judge the wicked."

"But what – what – *Goneril?*" she stammered.

"She meant to take him from me," murmured Regan, "with her black magic. I had to do it, I had to. She would have taken Achlesydd and my kingdom. I am the Queen, I am the Queen." She was talking to herself, not to them.

"Gag her," snapped Maglor, his mask of calm slipping. A burly Ordovician seized Regan by the hair, and thrust a dirty rag into her mouth. "Now," the Ordovician King went on, collecting himself somewhat, "we were about to have a duel. May the gods guard the innocent party, and guide his blade to the heart of the guilty one. Fight!"

Achlesydd had been standing languidly, holding his sword casually, but sprang into action almost before the word was out of Maglor's mouth. He swung the sword down in a great sweeping arc; the masked man caught it on his targe with a juddering clang, and swung his axe at Achlesydd's neck. The Dobunnic warrior ducked in front of it, throwing his whole body forward, and collided with his opponent; dropping his shield, he caught the other around the chest, and flung himself sideways, trying to bear him to the ground. The masked man held his footing, and beat on Achlesydd's back with the butt of his axe; but at last Achlesydd succeeded in pulling him down, and they rolled on the ground, clasped together, Achlesydd stabbing blindly with his sword.

As yet he had done no more than scratch his opponent. He stabbed down again: the masked man rolled aside, and the sword struck a rock – and snapped. Maglor smirked;

Achlesydd cursed, and flung the useless hilt away. He was on top now: he seized his enemy by both wrists, and forced his arms apart, crawling forwards to kneel on them. His enemy brought his own knee up into the small of Achlesydd's back, but he did not flinch. He drove the masked man's axe-hand against the rock, and struck it, smashing it, again, and again, until the battered, bloody fingers parted, and let the axe drop.

Achlesydd reached down, and picked it up.

"Now," he said, "let us see Justice unmasked."

He lifted his free hand to the other's face, and tore off the cloth. It was Picell.

Only a flicker of surprise crossed Achlesydd's face – only a moment of hesitation: but it was enough. In that moment, Picell seized the broken-off sword blade from where it had fallen, and struck upwards, driving it into his brother's side. Achlesydd's mouth fell open; he dropped the axe, and sat back, sliding off Picell's body.

"It… is just," he gasped. "Ogma has his due."

He fell back upon the ground. Picell sat up, reached forward, tenderly, and closed his eyes. Regan was weeping silently; Penarddun and Cordelia stared in horror.

"It is done," said Maglor evenly. "Good sister Cordelia, you will be free to go, on condition that you first swear that no reprisals will be taken against me or my tribe – or the Cornovii if they agree to peace. What to do with Queen Regan, if her mind returns when her fever breaks, must be her chiefs' decision – but I have friends among them, any one of whom would make a fine king, and would I believe be amenable to peace between our four tribes. I will make no claim on the Silurian throne – that died with my wife – nor on the High Kingship: the Ordovices are too small a tribe to maintain it. What say you? And you, Queen Penarddun? Will you have peace?"

"My children?" said Penarddun dazedly. "Including Bran?"

"Are safe from me, as long as you and they do no harm to me and mine," said Maglor. "I threatened before because I had a part to play before these traitors – and a point to make. I would have been quite ready to execute every threat if you had made it necessary. I will obviously require hostages until the peace is agreed, but I believe that I can take them from the families of the chiefs: that will guarantee that any mischief you do will have no support. King Garinter and the Lady Rhiannon I will hold until peace is assured; the Demetian princes escaped the battlefield, but will do nothing while I hold those two. What do you say?"

"I... would have peace," said Cordelia slowly. "It is all I have longed for, why I came back from Gaul... But first, I would see my sister accorded proper funeral rites. With an animal sacrifice – a horse will be suitable; enough human blood has been spilled."

That night, Regan's fever raged more fiercely than ever; she was reported to be raving and unable to stand. She did not attend Goneril's hurried funeral the next day, and only grew worse thereafter. Maglor had sent messengers to Pwyll and Perion to confirm the truce; when they returned on the third day, he permitted Cordelia, Penarddun, Perillus, and Falyse to leave, Picell going with them.

As soon as they were safely out of the camp, Picell approached Penarddun.

"Your son is well, my lady," he said quietly. "I have come from the Forest Hold not six days ago; he is strong and happy."

Penarddun tried to speak, but found herself choked with tears; she leaned up and kissed Picell on the cheek. After that, however, they rode in near silence back to Portskewett. She had a thousand questions about Bran but did not know how to begin asking; and everything else remained in doubt. There was yet no certainty what the Cornovii would do, and whether Regan would recover; peace was far from secure.

Maglor might easily have kept them in chains: between the captured and the dead, he had removed half the Silurian ruling caste and nearly all his rivals: but he realised that, though he could take the High Kingship, he would never command loyalty sufficient to keep it. It was to that fact – the mere accident that the Ordovices had not the numbers to crush Silurian resistance, as the Cornovii might have done with such advantages – that they owed their freedom and probably their lives.

They were met at the fort by Sicora, who ran out to greet them. The tears on her face were of joy: but her hair was disordered and her cheeks raked, as one in mourning. Falyse leapt down from her chariot and hurried to her, sweeping her into her arms and covering her with kisses: when at last she broke free from her lover's arms, she looked up in a kind of fearful wonder at Cordelia.

"My lady," she said, "we had heard you were taken, and hanged from a tree!"

"I was taken," said Cordelia. "But I am free now, and alive as you see. There is much to tell. Is my father well?"

"Lady…" said Sicora, looking down. "The High King… the news broke him. He thought you gone…"

"What has happened?" asked Falyse gently.

"The High King is dead."

"It was accorded, that Cordeilla should also go… to take
possession of the land."

~ Holinshed, *History of England*

Llyr was buried with all the ceremony that the hard-hit
Silures could muster. Penarddun gave what comfort she could
to Cordelia, but to her his death was like a weight lifted. The
customary rejoicing at a soul's entry into the Otherworld, with
toasts to his new life there, for once did not ring hollow to her.
He might once have been her protector, but that was long ago.
She would protect herself now, and her children.

When it was done, and the surviving chiefs
foregathered, most were eager to elect Cordelia Queen and
prepare for defence: they placed little trust in Maglor and
none in the Cornovii. But Cordelia answered:

"Maglor let us go when he had no need to. He has no
more stomach for war. The Cornovii are without a leader, at
least while Regan's sickness lasts; and they lost many chiefs in
the battle. Moreover, I have vowed that all with a claim on this
throne shall have the right to contest it, and they will."

"I do not desire it," said Penarddun. "Not when you are
here to claim it. You have my support."

"But there remains Ardian – and Regan," said Cordelia.
"And you good chiefs yourselves – both those before us, and
those yet to take up their titles in unheaded clans. And I have
other responsibilities. My husband's tribe is with King
Diviciacus in the East; my mother's heritage lies in Avalon,
where I have sent my daughter. I will do my duty by the
Silures if elected; but for now, we must wait, Wait until we

have all our chiefs assembled. Wait until the Cornovii have made plain their intentions. And wait until I have learned the mind of my brother Ardian in this matter."

She gave permission for preparations to begin for defence, but not for any attack; nor would she hear any word more of queenship.

Within days, news came that Regan had died; it was said that Achlesydd had poisoned the dressing of her wound as part of his plot with Goneril, though others blamed Maglor. She had named Cunedag as her heir, but he was far too young; the Cornovii had elected instead an elderly and childless kinsman of Henwyn's, presumably in the hope that he would live until Cunedag came of age and die early enough to leave his path clear. The new King at once sent messengers assuring Cordelia and the Silurian chiefs of his friendship and peaceful intentions: and Cordelia called Penarddun to her.

"The time has come to travel to the Deepwood," she said, "and to bring home Prince Bran. I would bring back all who dwell in the Forest Hold: but I understand that some of the women there are escaped slaves. Their masters would apply for their return, and as I am not yet Queen I would be bound to the decisions of Goll and the chiefs. But they will have their freedom yet, I will see to that."

The tears started to Penarddun's eyes.

"Thank you, my lady," she said. "Thank you! I will leave at once -"

"I am coming with you," said Cordelia. "I will bring my Menapian attendants and selected Veneti – that way we will be a force great enough to scare off Darnant, without showing the way to any Silures who may be kin to those who have enemies there. We will set off tomorrow."

Half a dozen Venetic slingers were detailed to make sure they were not followed. The fewer Britons knew where the Forest Hold lay, the safer those dwelling there would be.

The day was bright and warm – only a little cooler even after they entered the shadow of the Deepwood – and they had an easy journey of it. Penarddun's mind was full of Bran: he would be nearly four years old by now. Would he have any memory of her? Would he accept her? How would he and the other children take to one another? She tried not to think of these things – not to let hope get the better of her – but she could not suppress either her excitement or her fears.

About an hour after they entered under the trees, Falyse held up her hand.

"The Gauls halt here," she said. "The greater our numbers, the more risk of alerting Darnant. We might be enough to fight him off, but we must not show him where the Hold lies."

None argued: and their little group got down from their chariots and went on unaccompanied, until they reached their halting place, which still looked no different from any other part of the forest. Falyse gave a series of bird-calls: the bushes parted, and they were admitted to the Forest Hold.

Penarddun looked urgently around – there were children, yes, a few, none the right age – where was Mefus? Then she saw her, peering out of one of the low huts. She was thinner and her hair was streaked with grey, but she had still the same motherly smile.

"Mefus!" she cried. "Mefus!"

Mefus gaped.

"My lady!" she exclaimed. "Bran, lad, come out – your mother's here!"

A few moments later, a tousled pale-blond head poked out from behind Mefus' skirts. The boy's big grey eyes blinked in confusion, and Penarddun's became clouded with tears as she realised he was looking at the four women with no notion of which Mefus meant. She moved forward, tentatively, afraid to scare him, and reached out.

"Bran?" she said, her voice trembling. "I – I'm your mother."

"Go to her, child," said Mefus gently, prodding him forward: and he suddenly broke into a stumbling run, rushing towards her, arms outstretched. She dropped to her knees, and caught him, sweeping him into a tight embrace – he was hugging back so hard she could scarcely breathe, and both of them were weeping.

"Bran," she sobbed. "Oh, my Bran – I'm so sorry, so sorry I haven't been with you. I'm here now, my love. I'll never leave you again."

The Forest Hold was by this time home to a vegetable patch, a few goats, and a number of pigeons: the people there looked less hungry than they had: and Lysenn, who had become a sort of leader there, proposed killing some of the pigeons to honour their guests. Cordelia, however, would not hear of it. She had brought bread, cheese, salt pork, and dried beef, which they disbursed among the people of the Forest Hold. The bread was almost fresh, and oven-baked – it was more welcome even than the meat to people who had dwelt for months or years in the forest and tasted little but wild food. But more welcome yet were the flagons of beer that Perillus and Picell had carried.

"So is King Aganippus in the East, with Diviciacus?" asked Lysenn as they ate.

"He is," said Cordelia, surprised. "You have heard of events there?"

"A little," said Lysenn. "No doubt you know more. I know of the Trinovantic prince's marriage, and the troubles it's caused; and the war with Clarvorus."

"Marriage?" exclaimed Penarddun. "What news is this?"

"You don't know?" said Lysenn, surprised. "Your brother's married a peasant girl, and turned down Clarvorus' daughter, or sister some say. Said he'd only ever have one Queen. One of your own tribe, even! That's why the chiefs made your uncle Cassamus King instead of him."

"Cassamus is King?" said Penarddun. "We had heard nothing! What of the war?"

Lysenn shrugged.

"Most seem sure there'll be war between Clarvorus and your uncle, but I don't know if it's started. Clarvorus has his own problems with Queen Lydore, and she's got Diviciacus at her back – the Belgae must be too busy fighting each other to have ought to do with the Trinovantes. If your uncle's wise he'll make a friend of Diviciacus, but I've heard nothing about that." The conversation moved on.

When they had eaten, Cordelia made to rise: but Penarddun laid a hand on her arm.

"I must speak with Mefus first," she said. She turned to the nurse. "Mefus," she said, "I haven't been a mother to Bran; you have. The gods know I would have it otherwise, but the choice was taken away from me. I won't be parted from him

215

again – but nor should you be unless you will it freely. I have no right to come here and take him away from you. I would have you come back with us to Portskewett, if you will: but if you would keep him in the Hold, say the word, and I will stay here with you."

Mefus smiled gently.

"May the Three Mothers bless you, my lady," she said. "Of course I'll come with you."

"Thank you," said Penarddun, the tears starting to her eyes again. "Thank you."

She nodded to Cordelia, who stood, and announced loudly:

"My friends and I return to Portskewett this afternoon. I know that not all of you are free to leave the wood; I mean to change that when I am Queen, so that you may come, go, or stay as you will – Darnant and his clan will be rooted out, as they should have been long ago, had it not suited my father to have the Deepwood as a barrier between his lands and those east of Severn. But I am not Queen yet.

"Nevertheless, I can offer some protection. If you have no enemies outside the wood, or none with a claim of law upon you; if it is but hunger and uncertainty that keep you here, and the fear of Darnant; then I will house you and feed you, give work to those who are capable of it and care for those who are not. Any who wish will be welcome to come with me."

There was silence. At last, after what seemed an age, a young girl stepped forward: she could no have been more than twelve or thirteen.

"I will come," she said. "Please."

After that, more came forward – a shaggy-haired boy who turned out to be the girl's younger brother; two old women, one hobbling but sharp and bright-eyed yet, the other vague and three parts blind; a woodswoman, kin to Mefus, who had grown up in the shade of the trees but had lost her family to Darnant's arrows. And with these companions, the strange little party wound its way back to the Gauls, Penarddun carrying Bran in her arms.

She was still desperately worried about what would fall when Bran met the other children, whom he had never seen. But he had never been an only child – though Mefus had nursed him, all children in the Forest Hold were in the care of all adults. People came and went there: some of the family he had known had arrived but days before, others had long since struck out to seek a new life among other tribes far beyond the Deepwood's bounds. Leaving them behind was not, while he had Mefus, so great a wrench as leaving the forest itself, the only home he remembered; and meeting his siblings aroused no envy nor confusion – rather a friendly and phlegmatic interest, just as if they had been new children brought to the Hold. On their part, Branwen conceived an instant, fierce attachment to her elder brother; while the twins were too young to remember long that there had been a time without Bran.

The weeks passed, and they grew closer; and Penarddun spent every moment she could with them, with all four. It was wearisome, and she was glad of Mefus' aid: but the weight of danger and the pain of parting had been lifted from them, and she could not help but be wrapped up in delight. So much so, that she scarce noticed the passing of time, with no further word from Avalon or the East: until one day Cordelia called the chiefs together.

Many were new faces, chiefs who had succeeded by whatever law their clans employed since the war had claimed their predecessors; others were chosen spokespeople there in place of chiefs still held captive by Maglor. They assembled quickly, coming to Portskewett in a matter of days – no doubt many thought that they had been summoned to elect a monarch. Cordelia greeted them in the hall, standing: she would not sit on Llyr's chair until she was Queen.

"My lords and ladies," she said, "my friends. I have said since I came to this land that I must travel to Avalon – to pay my dues to the gods as Lady of the Lake, and my respects to my aunt who has governed there; to see my little daughter, who will be Lady after me; and to learn of my brother Ardian whether or no he means to contest this election. I hope also to learn there news of my husband, King Aganippus. I will return to you: but this can be no fleeting visit. I need to spend time with my child – and I have no way of knowing whether the war in the East has yet touched Avalon. I must make contact if I can with my husband and the High King Diviciacus. I shall therefore be gone from Silurian lands for weeks, perhaps months.

"I am not yet Queen. Nor am I Speaker, nor empowered to appoint one. These last months it has pleased you to follow my lead: but now it is imperative that a Speaker is chosen, to govern the Silures by your consent until the tribe has a ruler, and to mediate thereafter between you, that ruler, and the other tribes.

"If she is willing, I should be happy to nominate my stepmother Queen Penarddun as Speaker."

The chiefs looked startled; Twca growled, but said nothing. None of them dared bring up her marriage to Euroswydd, for all had supported him under less pressure than she. A female Speaker was a rarity, but that was not an objection they cared to make in front of Cordelia. After a strained silence, Penarddun stepped forward.

"I thank you, my lady," she said. "If the good chiefs will have me, I am willing to serve as Speaker until the election of a new Queen or King: but then I will lay down the responsibility, and let another be Speaker. I am not a Silurian born, and I have no desire for power."

Iddon was the first to answer.

"Let her be Speaker, then," she said gruffly.

"I'll say aye to that," said Gwenwyn's daughter Adsiltia. Her own succession to the chiefship of the Honey Bees had caused some comment, on account of her youth. At twenty, she was some months older than Penarddun and no younger than Cordelia: but she had not lived through a lifetime's toil and woe in the last five years.

After that, the rest soon assented, even Twca grunting a grudging yes, and Goll inclining his grey head.

"So be it," said Cordelia. "The rod and chain of the Speaker were lost when Euroswydd fled – new insignia will have to be made. But you are all witnesses to Queen Penarddun's appointment, and therefore to her authority: and, lest another sign of it be needed, let her wear the torque of the King. For she was Queen of the Silures, though a consort, and marked with the sacred viper: and as Speaker she is the highest authority of the tribe, until a monarch is chosen." And, with a flourish, she produced from the bag at her belt the heavy gold torque of Llyr, with its serpent-headed ends. The chiefs gasped: but none gainsaid her when she stepped up to Penarddun, and placed it around her neck. The metal was icy cold, and the weight of it, made for a broad-shouldered man, pushed down upon her; nor did it fit well about her slender neck. But if it forced her to stand rigidly, and to move with slow deliberation, she could feel the regal dignity that this lent to her bearing.

"My lady," she whispered, "you honour me beyond words."

The chiefs bowed their heads: and Cordelia herself, stepping back, bowed lowest of all.

"...there had been a great gathering of forty maidens of the forest... All the maidens had a mortal hatred of Darnant's clan."

~ *Perceforest*

Portskewett, 78 B.C.E.

Picell, Awel, and more than half of Cordelia's Gauls accompanied her across the Severn Sea: but even without them, Penarddun could at last feel safe in Portskewett. There were no more border skirmishes; the Irish and Epidian pirates did not come far enough south that year even to touch Silurian territory; and Darnant seemed to have fallen quiet.

Only dribs and drabs of news came back, of the wars in the East and the North. The latter meant little to Penarddun – the wranglings of the Epidii and Caledones had but small effect upon Portskewett – but she pounced on every morsel from the East, only to find them a contradictory mass of nonsense. One week her uncle was dead and Clarvorus had conquered the Trinovantes, the next, Cassamus had married Lydore and declared himself Highest of High Kings over all the Britons. Diviciacus was about to march west; no, he had returned to Gaul; no, he had been slain; no, he had never come to Britain.

In this way, untouched by the wars but ever starved of true news, the summer waned and autumn passed, and a quiet winter at Gray Hill followed. Few disputes were brought as high as the Speaker; the chiefs were content to govern their clans, and a tour she made in the autumn found the clans largely content with them. She had time to spend with the children, to watch Bran and Branwen grow closer, Nisien and Efnisien more quarrelsome. The twins were an undeniable handful, but she remembered Nennius being just as boisterous when he was their age: she wondered if Bran had been, and ached at the thought of the years she had missed.

"He was always a good boy," Mefus told her. "But we can't all be alike, or it would be a dull world. You should have seen Falyse when she was little! Littler, anyway. Some are just made that way. Most likely they'll get all their naughtiness out now, and grow up quiet."

At Falyse's insistence, she took up again her training with sword and buckler, and with knife, spear, and bow. She had no plans ever to be in battle again: but she had her children, and, as Speaker, the tribe, to defend. It would be as well to be ready, in case danger ever came to them.

When Imbolc had been celebrated and the earliest spring flowers were appearing, she brought them back to Portskewett: and a few weeks later, when all was green again, she determined to travel to the Forest Hold.

"Lysenn seems to have a knack for learning truth," she remarked to Falyse. "She may well have heard news from the East that has not come this far, or has been lost amid the welter of lies and misrememberings."

So a small party prepared to set out: Penarddun, Falyse, Sicora, Perillus, and a knot of Gauls. Goll tried to insist on accompanying them, declaring that his place as senior Druid was by the Speaker's side: but Penarddun would not have it, and he was left grumbling at the fort.

They parted from the Gauls at the same place as before, though they had little fear: the road was clear, the day was bright, and the last complaint of the outlaws had been many months before. Besides, all four went armoured. They found their way to the Hold – Penarddun was sure it had been somewhere else the last time, but Falyse led them straight to the entrance and gave the signal: and they were, once more, admitted.

Lysenn embraced them all, and they once again distributed bread, salt meat, mead and ale: then they talked. She was eager to hear of Mefus and of Bran, and almost childlike herself in her pleasure at the little stories they had to tell of him and the other children; and when at last there came a lull in this conversation, they turned to darker matters, and asked of news from the East.

But as it turned out, she had heard little more than they of the war. There had been a great battle before the frosts thawed, she could tell them that, but no two accounts agreed as to its outcome. Most spoke of a dead king: but whether it was Cassamus or Clarvorus or Diviciacus, or some other, who had fallen, she could not say.

"Not Aganippus of the Menapii?" said Perillus gravely. Lysenn shook her head.

"He has not been named, not in any story I've heard. But one peddler insisted that *all* the kings had fallen, and both armies been wiped out. The gods grant that it is not so." Penarddun shivered.

"You have not been troubled by Darnant?" asked Sicora. Lysenn spat on the ground.

"That one and his brood are always trouble," she said. "But he has not yet found us, and we have picked off many of his people – foolish recruits, no commanders, but at least we have kept their numbers down." She paused, and cast her eyes at the ground as if embarrassed, before looking to Penarddun. "There is... one thing I must tell you," she said, reluctantly. "Your former husband... he has joined with Darnant."

"Euroswydd?" said Penarddun. Lysenn nodded.

"And Taginos ap Twca. We first saw them in the snow-time; there are both Sea Foam and Broad Blade clanswomen here, and both were recognised. They seem to be deep in his councils. I am sorry."

"Do not be," said Penarddun. "It only confirms everything I have thought of him. When Queen Cordelia moves against them, he will perish with the rest. The world will be well rid of him."

"Unless she negotiates a pardon," said Lysenn.

"No," said Falyse firmly. "For the lesser ones, perhaps: but there will be no pardon for Darnant or his lieutenants."

"There had better not be," said Lysenn. "He and the crow-priestess and their double-damned son, they are not human. Last Samhain they took a captive to the Black Rock Fountain – just a boy, ten or eleven, taken from one of the villages on the Cornovian edge of the wood – and put a sword in his hand; Darnant carved him up and called it a fight."

"Why?" gasped Penarddun.

"Sacred combat," said Lysenn. "Darnant calls himself a king, and believes he gains the Mor-Rigan's favour by defending his crown in battle. It was a sacrifice – a mockery of sacrifice and of all that's holy, if anything is in this world, but a sacrifice in Darnant's mind. He goes often to the Fountain; he grows more superstitious as he gets older, fears that another King of the Deepwood will come and pour out *his* blood to the goddess. So she must be appeased."

"This is what they all believe?" wondered Falyse.

"The crow-woman has a hold over them," said Lysenn. "And they are all afraid – Darnant of age and losing his power, the rest of Darnant and Cangen, or of facing justice. He knows he might be betrayed for a pardon, so he makes sure each one has a murder to his name. The greater their fear, the more they kill; the more they kill, the greater their fear. There will be more blood in the Fountain come Beltane. Most likely they have their victim already – it's only, what, two days now?"

Falyse grimaced.

"The Fountain was the ancient place of challenge," she said. "It marked the meeting point of three tribes – Dobunni, Cornovii, Silures. Kings duelled there, and challengers fought kings, and blood spilt was dedicated to the gods of the water – but helpless victims were never sacrificed there before Darnant."

"How can his wife allow this?" wondered Penarddun. "She is a Druid, and this is blasphemy."

"Blasphemy is what doesn't suit priests," said Lysenn with a shrug. "This suits her very well. It keeps Darnant feared, and her too."

Sicora steered the conversation to happier matters: but a shadow hung over the mood of all of them, and did not lift.

When at last they prepared to leave, it was with a muted sadness.

"I'll come a little way with you," said Lysenn. "Best to see you safely on your way."

"Will you be safe going back alone?" asked Penarddun. Lysenn nodded.

"I go armed," she said. "Shortsword and dagger. And I know these woods better than anyone. But if you would prefer it, I'll bring a companion."

Cyll volunteered; and they set off through the parted bushes. The sun was low, and a chill settling over the forest, by the time they joined with the Gauls and bade the two forest women farewell; and it was in dull quiet that they headed back towards Portskewett.

They were on the edge of the woods when they heard a cry behind them. It was wordless, anguished, animal: but the voice was human – a woman –

"Cyll," said Falyse.

A moment later, the forest woman was stumbling along the path towards them. Her gait was changed to a sort of hobbling lurch, and her face was grey; her cloak was gone, and there was a great dark blotch of blood on her tunic.

"Cyll!" exclaimed Penarddun, running to her. "What has happened? How badly are you hurt?" She caught the older woman by the arm, and Cyll half collapsed onto her; there was blood on her back as well, Penarddun felt, sticky and warm.

"Lysenn," she gasped. "Lysenn."

"Here – lie down," said Penarddun, helping her gently to the ground, and kneeling by her. The grass by the roadside was soft, and there was a convenient tree trunk to rest against.

"You're safe now – no need to run further." She turned to Sicora. "See if any of the Gauls knows anything about tending wounds," she said, wishing that Mefus were there, or even Goll. "What happened? Slowly – don't exert yourself."

Cyll was wheezing painfully; she tried to raise her hand, but it fell back by her side.

"They have her," she managed to say. "Alive... they thought me dead... they wanted Lysenn."

"Slowly," said Penarddun, smoothing her hair. She became aware of Falyse standing over her.

"We'll need to cut that tunic open," said Falyse. "So we can see the wound, and treat it. Don't be afraid." She looked to Penarddun. "Are you able to do it?"

"Yes," said Penarddun, though she was far from certain that she could do anything more. She drew her knife. She could see no tear or hole, no point of entry, on the front of Cyll's tunic, so she inserted the point carefully under the collar and began to cut.

"I'm dying," said Cyll. "Wanted her... alive... sac... sacrifice. Beltane." She sighed, and closed her eyes. Her breathing was growing shallower.

Falyse slammed her fist into her palm.

"Two days," she said. "If he goes to the Fountain at dawn, a day and two nights from now. The Fountain's on the other side of the Deepwood – hours from here. We've scarcely time to get back to Portskewett and muster warriors, and if we did we'd have to get to the Fountain without alerting Darnant."

"We can't let Lysenn die!" exclaimed Sicora.

"And we won't," said Penarddun. "We go to the Hold. Now. The Gauls together with the rest of us. Two can take Cyll

227

back to Portskewett by chariot, have her treated, and tell the folk there what's afoot. I mean to be at the Black Rock Fountain two dawns from now, and to rescue Lysenn."

The news of what had happened shook the women of the Hold: but as one they pledged themselves to follow Penarddun and to see Lysenn to safety. They had all suffered at the hands of Darnant's people: and, fearful though they were, many eyes shone at the prospect of revenge.

The following day was spent in gathering branches and wands and stones, making bows, arrows, clubs, slings: and after dark, they left the Hold, leaving only the children, the infirm, and selected guards. Falyse and one of the forest women, Draenen, guided them; and by unseen paths and secret ways, they wound silently towards the Fountain – men and women, foresters and Venetic sailors, all armed, all determined, all ready.

Their progress was slow, but steady; but when the eastern sky began to glimmer grey through the trees, Penarddun whispered:

"Are we not near?"

"Very near," Draenen promised. "We will be there before the sun is seen."

It was not two hundred heartbeats later that they heard a shout – then more, and the clang of swords.

"A duel?" wondered Penarddun.

"A battle," said Falyse. "Some other enemy of Darnant has been before us."

"Then we shall aid them," Penarddun decided: and, turning to the winding column behind her, she at last raised her voice. "Advance!"

Drawing their weapons, they broke into a jog, no longer caring for noise – the tumult ahead all but drowned out their footfalls and the breaking of branches by now in any case – and came in seconds to the wide clearing around the Black Rock Fountain.

There were some three dozen armed men there, two thirds of them heavily bearded foresters in makeshift armour, a patchwork of pieces none of which went together; their enemies were far better armed and dressed, and wore the long moustaches of Eastern or Gaulish noblemen. Many already lay dead on the ground; the foresters had all but surrounded the nobles. Penarddun saw Lysenn, pale, dark-eyed, bruised, but defiant, standing alongside the beleaguered few, holding up a sword too big for her frame. Her wrists were red, scarred by a biting rope.

And then she saw Euroswydd.

He still wore the chain of the Speaker over his now worn and grimy tunic and cloak; he was thinner than when she had seen him last, his cheeks drawn, his eyes hollow. His face was sun-browned, and he had a wild beard with thick streaks of grey: the forest life had aged him half a lifetime. For a moment she felt a pang of pity. But he was there between Cangen and Taginos, beating on the upraised shield of one of the strangers, a fair-haired youth with a thin gold torque, with bloodlust in his eyes. The youth was pushed back upon the Black Rock itself, a great rough-hewn boulder with a sheen of water across its sable surface: his cloak was sodden and heavy from the spray of the Fountain, and was bearing him down so that he would soon be easy prey for Euroswydd.

She laid her sword across her buckler, and shouted his name as she charged.

He looked round with absolute surprise. She did not see it, but almost everyone in the clearing was reacting the same way, as the Gauls and the women of the Hold poured into the grove.

The foresters had hardly time to turn before they were on them: and now it was they who were caught, between the newcomers and the strangers. They were in utter disarray. Penarddun saw Cangen duck under Falyse's sword-swing and run for the trees; then suddenly she found a man twice her size looming before her – and cut him down before she had time to think, a single blow shearing through his thick jerkin and biting so deep into his collarbone that the blade was nearly wrenched from her hand when he fell.

He had come between her and Euroswydd. But her enemy had not fled – he was still there, turned now to face her, ignoring the Easterners, a malevolent scowl on his face.

They crossed swords.

Euroswydd was stronger than she, and desperate; neither was well armoured. But she had still the momentum of her charge behind her, and he was not yet over his surprise – and rage was on her side. He parried her first blow, but she gave him no time to riposte: she thrust again and again, now from this angle, now from that, like a wasp darting in to sting. Her lessons with Falyse had borne good fruit. Euroswydd blocked her time and again, but was too slow to come off his back foot: and he was tiring, and retreating. The forgotten young Easterner had straightened up, and was gazing in wonder at Penarddun: after a long moment, he raised his own sword.

"No!" exclaimed Penarddun. Euroswydd, seeing her look past his shoulder, instinctively half-turned – and she stabbed. Coming under his guard before he could even see to lower it, she drove her blade up into his chest. He gasped, and fell back: blood was dribbling from his mouth, and his eyes showed pure shock.

"But... we have children..." he said uncomprehendingly: and he fell to the ground.

She watched him gasp out his last. Around them, the battle was already almost over. There were few dead, nearly all Darnant's people – most of them had fled. Only two folk of the Hold had fallen, and not a single Gaul. At the foot of the Rock itself, she saw something she had not seen before: the body of a tall, broadly made man in black wool tunic and cloak, wearing a heavy shield. A long sword lay by him; his grey head had been hacked from his neck, and lay lolling in the pool at the base of the Fountain, eyes blankly open, blood swirling in the water.

She became aware that the young man she had rescued from Euroswydd's onslaught was still staring at her.

"Penarddun?" he said. "Is it truly you?"

She frowned, and peered into his face. There was a sunburst tattooed on his right cheekbone – the emblem of the Trinovantes. Suddenly, recognition flooded through her: she dropped her sword, and felt her eyes swim with tears.

"Imanuentius!" she exclaimed. "My dear, dear brother!"

Chapter 21: *In Cordelia's Camp*

> "We came to Britain with our royal camp to fight...
> The British kings were fain to yield our right."
>
> ~ Higgins, in *The Mirror for Magistrates*

Brother and sister clung together, weeping, there amid the field of blood. When at last they separated, the followers of both were gathering round, looking on with joy. Falyse, with Lysenn leaning on her shoulder, was smiling proudly; Perillus, bloodied and leaning heavily on a branch turned into a makeshift staff, nevertheless beamed. Imanuentius' comrades watched in wonder.

"My friends!" he exclaimed. "This is my sister, Penarddun ferch Belin, Queen of the Silures! I have not seen her these six years come autumn."

"But – how?" she managed to say. "What are you doing here? What has happened? The war..."

"The war is over," said Imanuentius. "Clarvorus is dead, and King Diviciacus has made peace. I am King now."

"King?" she said – then, realising what that meant, added falteringly: "Then, Cassamus...?"

"Fell," said Imanuentius gravely. "In the same action as Clarvorus. He has been given sacrifice and all funeral honours; I negotiated peace with the Belgae and friendship with King Diviciacus, and the chiefs named me King. We are all well – Vellaunos is at home in Dun Belin, and Nennius..." He paused. "The peace had to be sealed in marriage," he said.

"Fesonas to Clarvorus' son Pir, Nennius to Queen Lydore. And we have recognised Lydore as High Queen of the British Belgae – Pir and Fesonas are her subjects. I fear to face Father when I meet him in the Otherworld. But there was no other way – and they all consented. Consented truly, not as you were made to. I am not Father."

"I know," said Penarddun quietly. "But how do you come to be here?"

"We came west with Diviciacus," said Imanuentius, surprised. "Did his couriers not reach you? We arrived at Avalon weeks ago."

"We have had no couriers," said Penarddun, surprised. "What way did they come? If it was by this road... well, you've seen how safe it is."

"Was," Imanuentius corrected her. He stooped, and, curling his lip in distaste, picked up the head that lay by the black-clad man. The grey hair and beard were neatly kept, Penarddun noted; the staring cold eyes were icy blue. "This is the scourge of the Deepwood," he said. "This is Darnant. Father told me about him before he died – how his old enemy had become the bane of the West. When I heard of his sacral combats, I sought him out; I set up my own capture. I knew he would not be able to resist fighting a true king. I had men following to spring me free when it was done – but I hadn't reckoned that he would have so many more. If it hadn't been for you, we'd all be dead – but at least I'd have known I took Darnant down first."

"Darnant is dead," breathed Falyse. "Darnant is dead! The gods be praised!"

The word ran around the crowd, first a whisper and then a shout, a cry of joy and release in that forest that had lain so many years under the outlaw chief's dark shadow.

"Darnant is dead! Darnant is dead!"

"Yet Cangen and his mother live," muttered Penarddun; but few heeded her.

Imanuentius and two of his nobles – a bluff stout sandy-haired Cassian named Cloff, and a Bibrocian, Llyfn, who had a hunched back and one arm far longer than the other, but wore a hauberk adapted to his shape and a long, curved shield which protected him from many angles, and had fought as hard as any against Darnant's people – had come to the grove by chariot: now the dead of their side, the two forest folk and five Easterners, were laid in the chariots to be carried away for burial. All of the wounded were fit to walk save only Perillus, who grimaced and declared that he had ridden with worse than corpses. As for the dead of Darnant's clan, eleven in number, they were decapitated, and the grisly trophies tied to the chariot rims; then their bodies were piled before the Fountain, covered in brushwood, and set alight. Half a dozen women of the Hold were assigned to see that the fire did not spread to the trees; they would follow after the others when the burning was done. For now, they were headed out of the wood, to the east, the Dobunnic side – and to the camp of Diviciacus, High King of the Belgic peoples.

Penarddun and Imanuentius walked alongside the chariot in which Perillus lay. His breathing was laboured and he winced when the road was rough, but to begin with his eyes were clear and he had no difficulty in speaking. When he weakened, it seemed only that he was tired: they had seen his wound, and it was deep but not deadly, unless it had been allowed to bleed out. He slipped finally into sleep, and Penarddun smiled down at him – but moments later, he was awake, clawing at the sides of the chariot, struggling to sit up, and spitting bloody foam from his mouth.

Penarddun gasped: but Falyse was by her side, knife in hand. In one move, she slit the front of Perillus' tunic open, and tore off his bandage. The wound below was black, its edges spongy and oozing: it looked as if it had been rotting for a week, and smelt worse. Imanuentius gagged, and Penarddun covered her mouth.

"How could this happen?" she whispered.

"Poison," said Falyse. "It was Cangen who wounded him: it's always been said he treats his blade. The gods know what foulness went into the wound." She turned to Imanuentius. "Does King Diviciacus have healers?" she asked. "This is beyond my skill."

"Yes," he said. "The Lady Gweledydd is in our camp, and others from Avalon. There are no healers like them."

"Then there is hope," said Falyse, looking into Perillus' face. "There is hope, do you hear? Stay alive, and we will bring you to the wise women of Avalon."

The journey seemed desperatcly slow. At every jolt of the cart, Perillus shuddered and retched. They inched onwards, the sun seeming to move faster than they did towards day's end; but at last the trees grew thin, then failed altogether. The sun was low now: but at last, as their path wound through the hillocks, they were hailed from above.

"Who goes there?"

"Twr!" shouted Llyfn, waving his curved shield in the air. "By the gods, it's good to hear your voice!"

"Llyfn?"

The man called Twr stepped into the open, from where he had been standing in the shadow of a high rock face. He was tall, fair, broad-shouldered, and armed in Belgic style.

"How fares the King? And who are your new companions?"

"Friends unlooked for," said Llyfn with a grin. "The King has met his sister in the woods – Queen Penarddun! She saved our lives. But Darnant is dead, at King Imanuentius' hand!"

"Praise the gods!" exclaimed Twr. "You at least have good news, then."

"What has befallen here?" asked Imanuentius sharply.

"The High King was attacked while scouting out the edge of the forest," said Twr. "Queen Cordelia drove off the enemy, but he was hurt in the fighting. They say he will mend, but it was a sore fright to all of us."

A mutter ran back through the army: "Diviciacus is hurt!" Penarddun bit her lip.

"We have a friend here who is badly wounded," she said. "Can physicians be spared from the High King's side? Without aid, he will die."

Twr looked grave.

"I wish your friend well," he said, "but I can promise nothing. I will sound the horn to let them know that friends are coming, some hurt; the High King's camp is not far. It may be your friend will find succour there."

Perillus' face was dark, and he was scarcely breathing; the last short distance round the curve of the low hill and up to the quickly-erected palisade, built of pallets and withies, seemed to take as long as the journey from the Rock.

As they passed through the gates under the anxious eyes of sentries, a slender youth came running out from the largest tent. He was dressed in eastern style, with Trinovantic tattoos on his arms: he looked familiar –

"Where is the King?" he said. "Where is Imanuentius?"

And for the second time that day, Penarddun knew a brother.

"Nennius!" she cried.

Nennius' jaw dropped. He had been a fosterling among the Cantiaci when she went away to the West, only seven when last they met; of all her siblings she knew him least, but had missed him as desperately as Imanuentius and Fesonas.

"Penarddun?" he faltered. "Is it really you?"

"It is, oh, it is!"

She was weeping again as she embraced Nennius: but after a few moments she forced herself to stand back, and say:

"We must speak later of all that has passed – all five of us, if Vellaunos even remembers me. Is Fesonas here?"

"No," he said. "She's with Pir – her husband – in the East; I shouldn't be here either, but Lydore had a bad dream – she saw her uncle felled by a boar in the forest. Darnant must have been the boar; thank the Three Mothers the High King lives."

"Not Darnant," said Penarddun. "Darnant is dead; Imanuentius killed him. But how fares the High King? How many healers have you here – can any be spared?"

237

Nennius looked grave.

"Lady Gweledydd has not stirred from the High King's side since he was brought back," he said. "Her woman Llys and the dwarf Ardian attend her; other than they, our most skilled healer is Queen Cordelia – and she has gone in pursuit of the enemy. If Darnant is dead, that is good news indeed – she may have swift victory."

"She may," said Falyse grimly. "But Cangen and his mother live. The Battle of Deepwood is not over yet."

Diviciacus' pavilion, a large and elaborate tent of skins, stood out among the mostly makeshift huts of the camp; and Penarddun strode straight towards it. The guards, at a nod from Imanuentius, parted, and admitted her.

Inside, the tent was lit by braziers: the heat seemed to buffet Penarddun as she entered. Four more sentries stood guard; and on a pallet bed, erected in the centre to give the healers free movement to every side of it, lay Diviciacus.

Penarddun's immediate thought was that he should have been taller. Older, too – more like, not Llyr, but perhaps her father: more like a High King. The man on the pallet could not be much taller than she was, and was slight of build, with no beard and but a thin moustache, his sleeping face almost boyish at first glance. As her eyes became more accustomed to the light, she could see the lines around his eyes, the hardness of his muscles, the scars on his arms and face: but only when she peered closely. He was still round-cheeked, with no visible trace of grey in his blond hair; and though the sheen of fever was on his brow, his breathing was even, and he looked to be sleeping peacefully.

Gweledydd, sweating almost as badly as the fevered King although she wore only a light robe with the sleeves tied back above her elbows, stood by his side, her hand resting lightly on his arm.

"What do you want?" she rasped. Her voice was a harsh croak: she was exhausted and sounded thirsty with it. "Why do you disturb the High King in his sickness?"

"Your pardon, my lady," said Penarddun quietly, bowing her head. "But I have a dear friend who will die if you do not aid him."

"Can you not see that my lady is done?" exclaimed a woman who she guessed must be Llys. She stood a little way aside, next to a low table on which were arranged what looked to be Gweledydd's instruments and potions; Ardian was next to her, holding a mortar with some greenish paste in it.

"Peace," said Gweledydd. "I will have quiet in this tent. I am weary, it is true, and besides I must remain with Diviciacus; but you two can attend Queen Penarddun's friend. I am sorry I spoke sharply."

"Where is he?" asked Ardian.

"He lies in a chariot outside," said Penarddun. "He took a slash to the chest from a poisoned sword. The wound isn't deep; but it is black."

"That's very bad," said Ardian. "A rotting wound, so near the heart..."

"Bring him in," said Gweledydd.

"My lady?" wondered Llys.

"Bring him in," she repeated. "Put him on a pallet or a withy or whatever he can be carried on, and bring him here, lay him beside the High King. If he is so sore hurt, we are his only chance: we will heal him."

Penarddun bowed her head.

"Thank you," she said.

"Thank me when you know he's going to live," said Gweledydd shortly. "I wish my mother were here; the gods have blessed her, I swear she can heal with a touch. I am only mortal."

Penarddun stepped out into the camp.

"Bear Perillus into the High King's tent," she said. "Lady Gweledydd and her people will attend him."

She wanted to go in with him: but she knew she would only be in the way. She allowed Awel to go, but kept Falyse and Sicora with her: they sat by a camp fire with her brothers, and told their stories – all that had passed since she had left Dun Belin, more than six years ago. It was nigh dark before Llys and Ardian came out of the tent; their eyes were hollow and their faces grimed with the soot of the braziers, but Ardian was smiling.

"Your friend will live," said Llys.

"Can we see him?" asked Penarddun. "When will he wake? How long will it be -"

"He sleeps," Llys interrupted. "As does my lady, and as should we."

"He will be a while mending," said Ardian gently, "and maybe never as strong again. But the wound should have killed him. Gweledydd is too modest – she has her mother's touch. She has worked miracles today. Awel is with him – he hasn't left his side." For a moment Penarddun foolishly wondered how he knew who Awel was: but of course, they had just spent many tense and burning hours together.

"Thank you," said Penarddun quietly. "For everything."

Just then, they heard a clatter of hooves outside. The password was given, and two chariots admitted to the camp: in the foremost rode a tall sandy-haired woman in Gaulish armour, at the sight of whom Imanuentius leapt to his feet.

"Arante!" he exclaimed. "What has happened? Is all well with Queen Cordelia?"

Arante smiled, and nodded.

"The fortress of Darnant is taken," she said. "The enemy are scattered in the Deepwood; we are victorious."

Chapter 22: *Purification*

"The weight of this sad time we must obey,
Speak what we feel, not what we ought to say.
The oldest have borne most; we that are young
Shall never see so much, nor live so long."
~ Shakespeare, *King Lear*

It was a few days yet before they were able to join Cordelia at Darnant's fortress: Nennius and Imanuentius would not leave the camp until Diviciacus was well enough to ride in his chariot, at least when bound in place, so that Cordelia might receive him there; and Penarddun had little inclination to leave her brothers behind. But the High King mended quickly, and soon they were ready to go. Perillus was walking a little by then, and would have come too if Awel had let him; but he finally agreed to remain at the camp. Penarddun was glad to leave Awel with him, after Falyse pointed out that Cangen and the crow priestess would like nothing better than to burn the Merlin for their gods.

By this time, the joy of victory had been somewhat dampened. Mefus and Falyse had said when the news first came that they believed Darnant to have had more than one base camp: and it had quickly become apparent that the outlaws had regrouped somewhere. Two of Cordelia's patrols had been attacked, and five men killed. The Battle of the Deepwood, it seemed, must yet go on.

A clear path had been cut through the undergrowth to Darnant's once hidden fortress, and banners hung along the way bearing the viper of the Silures and the dragon of Avalon. Along this they processed, Diviciacus and Gweledydd – who accompanied the High King at his own insistence – riding in the first chariot; Penarddun and her brothers in the second. At last they passed through the stout turf-built gateway into the fort itself.

There, on a wooden platform facing the gate, flanked by guards armed in Gaulish style, stood Cordelia, with a Silurian banner at her back; Arante, Ardian, and Llys, who had gone ahead the day before to announce the High King's approach, attended her.

Before her, the Lady clasped a long-bladed sword, sheathed, point downwards, with a gilt-bronze hilt graven with dragons like Urganda's pendant; the scabbard was a stiff lattice of woven leather.

"Hail, Cordelia, Queen of the Silures, Lady of the Lake," the High King greeted her.

"Hail, Diviciacus, High King of the Belgic peoples," she replied. "Welcome to the second Forest Hold: for this fort is purged of the filth of Darnant, and is now ours." She looked at the others, and smiled. "And hail to you, my kinsfolk and my friends," she said. "You too are welcome." They bowed their heads.

"Is that what I think?" Draenen whispered to Falyse, not quite quietly enough, with a nod towards the sword.

"It is Excalibur," said Ardian softly. "The sword of the Penteyrnedd."

"The sword of the Lady," Llys corrected him. "The Penteyrnedd is only the bearer."

Diviciacus was looking quizzical; to Penarddun, too, the name was unfamiliar.

"It is one of the four treasures of the Children of Don," said Gweledydd. "They were made by her son, Gofannon the Smith, when the gods first came to these isles. To Brut was given the Stone of Kingship, to Lugh the Spear of Victory, to

243

the Dagda the Cauldron of Plenty, and to Nodens the Sword of Light. He bore it in the war against the Fomorians: but after he lost his hand, he gave up war and dedicated himself to healing: and he gave Excalibur into the care of Latis, who entrusted it to the priestesses of Avalon.

"When Llyr came to Avalon," she went on, "this sword was thrown into the mere to keep it from him. He was the first Penteyrnedd not to bear it. When the waters receded last summer, it was found again. The blade was rusted almost away, but the hilt was as good as new, and the scabbard had been kept hidden in the temple. Llyr wasn't interested in that – he never understood that the scabbard meant as much as the sword. My mother had the blade reforged: and she presented it to Queen Cordelia."

"So there is a true Lady of the Lake once more," said Llys.

After their formal welcome followed a loving greeting; they got down from their chariots, and Cordelia from her dais, and all embraced. But they could not long speak of pleasant things without turning to the matter of Cangen and his mother.

Cordelia's people had by now located the second fortress. When Diviciacus heard that, he was eager to go against it in arms: but Gweledydd declared him still too weak, and when the others agreed he let himself be persuaded to cede command to Nennius, who was eager to do some deed to match Imanuentius' slaying of Darnant.

Nennius selected four captains: broad-shouldered Twr, the strongest of Lydore's people; hunchbacked Llyfn, with his strange shield; Synnu, another Belgic, cross-eyed but smooth of tongue, and accounted among the bravest; and dark-eyed Dagon, the grandson of a Carthaginian merchant who had been trading on the south coast when his city fell to Rome, and had settled there. Taking half the soldiery, they set out with banners flying and carnyxes blaring: while the rest remained to await word of their success.

A day passed, then two, and they heard nothing. On the third morning, Penarddun went to Imanuentius.

"Nennius should have sent word by now," she said. "I am worried."

"I, too," he agreed. "We should seek the High King's permission to go after him. He won't like it, though – Nennius wanted this glory for himself."

"He's not fool enough to value it over his life," retorted Penarddun.

As it turned out, however, the word long sought came that morning: and it was not good. Llyfn and Dagon returned to Cordelia's fortress, dragging between their chariots a bloodied man, tall and bony, with a thick grey beard. Before the Queen's dais, they cut him loose, and threw him to the ground.

"Highness," said Llyfn, inclining his head – half sideways, the closest to a bow that his back would permit without making him wince – "Lord Twr beseeches your help."

"Twr?" exclaimed Penarddun, before Cordelia or Diviciacus could reply. "What has happened to Nennius?"

Dagon looked at the ground.

"Prince Nennius was taken captive," he said. "That is why we have come – he would not have sent us."

"The outlaws have greater numbers than we thought, and poisoned darts and knives," added Llyfn. "There is some secret way out of the fort; they have entered our very camp and slain men sleeping. We lost Peris, Blodyn, and many more."

"On the way we took this creature," said Dagon, giving the bearded man a kick. "He's one of Cangen's – whether he was spying or running away, he's not told us yet."

"I... only... wanted... to live," rasped the man. Imanuentius ran over, and seized him by the beard, brandishing a knife in his face.

"What will they do to my brother?" he exclaimed. "What are they doing to him now? Speak, or I'll open your throat!"

The man grimaced.

"Cangen... will hurt him," he said. "He... is not... Darnant. He leads men... to destruction. That... is why... I ran."

"As if Darnant was any better," spat Llyfn.

Imanuentius levelled the point of his dagger against the captive's eye: but Penarddun stood forth.

"Wait," she said. "Nennius is alive; and this man can get us into Cangen's fortress."

"How?" wondered Imanuentius.

"By capturing me," she said. "And Lord Twr."

Imanuentius took some persuading to agree to Penarddun's plan, as it did not involve him in the taking of the fortress: instead, he was to take half the remaining force and make as if to encircle it and come from the other side. If he was perceived, the outlaws would be distracted; if not, they would be trapped. Meanwhile, Penarddun and a few of her closest companions went with Dagon and Llyfn, and the captive, Griant, his bruises salved and wounds washed and bound.

They were welcomed at Nennius' camp by Twr, and an unexpected figure – the Druid Dardanon, who had arrived there but a few hours before. His beard was longer and streaked with grey, and he smelt of rotten leaves after so long living in the woods, but the gold chains still gleamed in his ears, and the fire of fanaticism in his eyes. Penarddun was glad to see him: he fitted perfectly into her plan. Griant, after all, would need accomplices.

So it was that Griant, Dardanon, and a few men chosen for being unknown to Cangen, presented themselves before the fort with Penarddun and Twr in tow, their hands looped together with loose ropes, and called on Cangen to admit them and their prisoners.

There was a long pause: then the gates swung open. They passed between hollow-eyed spearmen, and were brought to Cangen, who stood leaning on a staff, white-faced and obviously wounded, but smiling triumphantly.

When Twr saw that smile, something snapped. Forgetting the plan, he threw off his false bonds, whipped his dirk from his sleeve, and hurled it with all his strength. It flew true, and buried itself in Cangen's heart.

Penarddun bit her lip, and gripped her own knife, waiting for the inevitable assault – but none came. Cangen's men were staring uncomprehendingly. Every face was sunken, ravaged with hunger. Nobody moved – until, suddenly, with a high keening wail, the crow woman appeared as if from nowhere, arms upraised, sacrificial knife in hand, almost flying towards Twr. Penarddun reacted almost before she knew what she was doing, launching herself against the priestess, knocking her off her feet. The knife fell to the ground; Falyse kicked it aside; and as the priestess clawed at Penarddun's feet, she found herself seized and pinioned by Dagon. He dragged her to her feet, holding her up in front of Penarddun.

"Now," said Penarddun, composing herself as best she could, "where – is – my – brother?"

"Where is my son?" the priestess spat back. "Where is my lord Darnant?" Twr strode up and struck her across the face. Penarddun winced: but before she could say anything, a voice spoke up from the largest of the scattered huts.

"He lives, lady."

In the door there stood a girl, small and thin, with grimy hair and dark green eyes like forest shadows. She could be no more than twelve or thirteen, but seemed ancient, as if she bore the weight of an unhappy people's history. "So does Lysenn."

"You!" spat the crow-woman. "You traitor!"

"Who are you?" demanded Twr.

"I am Delyn," said the girl flatly. "Ferch Darnant."

"Darnant's daughter?" exclaimed Sicora.

"You are no daughter of his, or mine!" stormed the priestess.

"I wish that were true," Delyn threw back, angry for the first time. "You were monsters both, and your son the worst of all. I have known more kindness from Lysenn, a prisoner, than I ever saw from you in my life! At least I have kept her out of Cangen's clutches. I'm glad he's dead – I only wish he could die a thousand times!"

From the hut behind her, blinking, bleared, the two prisoners now emerged, leaning on one another. Lysenn was very thin, and had faded bruises on her arms and face, but looked to have taken no serious hurt; Nennius was pale, limping, and holding his belly. Penarddun started forward, but he held up his hand.

"You'll hurt me if you embrace me," he croaked. "But I'll live – Cangen's sword didn't touch me, and Delyn has kept us from the torturers."

"All throw down your arms," said Twr, "and gather before us, where we can see you." The outlaws did as they were bidden; meanwhile, Llyfn and Dagon, who had been waiting without, led their men into the fort, and filed around the walls so that they held all sides of it.

Most of the prisoners had their eyes cast down, or jutted their chins out and glowered in surly fashion. Only the wild-haired priestess stood straight-backed and defiant, eyes blazing.

"What should we do with them?" asked Llyfn doubtfully. It was to Nennius that he looked, but it was Dardanon who replied.

"This place must be cleansed," he said. "Their crimes have been horrible, an offence to the gods, the worse for being committed under a shroud of piety. Let them be given to Ogma's justice. Let there be built a wicker man."

Penarddun suppressed a gasp.

"They were taken in honest battle," she said.

"And hence would be meet for sacrifice, even were they innocent," replied Dardanon.

"I do not think it would please the Queen," she insisted. "Or the High King. To burn all, that is no justice. They cannot all be equally guilty."

"They are not," said Delyn.

Her face was clear and her eyes bright: she showed all the assurance of her mother. Some of Twr's men made scoffing noises, but Nennius gestured for quiet. All of the forest women who had come with Penarddun looked on her gravely and attentively.

"I will show you the guilty ones," she said. "Though my brother was the worst. May he meet justice in the Otherworld."

"My curse on you!" spat her mother. "Traitor! You give up your people to these, these Easterlings! You're not fit to lick your brother's shoe!"

"It didn't stop him making me, though," said Delyn calmly. She looked her mother full in the face. "I was wrong, though," she said. "He was not the worst. You were. Remember Eiddew? What he drove her to? You let that happen, you let her blame herself – when it was you who made him what he was! Everything, everyone, belonged to your precious Cangen to take and use, always. A thousand times you saw it, and you did nothing; you urged him on!"

Her mother hawked and spat in her face. Delyn did not flinch, but coolly wiped it off; then she turned, and walked along the line.

"These two stoned a baby once, and laughed," she said. "This one was my father's torturer; he could keep men alive in agony for days. This was another... like Cangen. An abuser of women and girls." She turned her back on them. "Those are the worst, that I know of," she said flatly. "None are innocent."

Twr looked to Penarddun.

"These shall burn, then," he said. She was not sure if it was a question, but she nodded. She felt the eyes of the forest women on her: neither thankful nor reproachful, but accepting. This was how Darnant's story ended; this was how it must be. "Dardanon, give the judgement."

Dardanon curled his lip. He looked disapproving at the idea of showing mercy to any: but though as a Druid he could have asserted his authority to judge them all, he did not.

"So be it," he said.

"This is no trial!" exclaimed one of the men. "You haven't let us speak!"

"No, it is no trial," said Dardanon. "The wicker man is not an execution: it is an honour you do not deserve. You have been chosen to be given to the gods; and the gods shall have their due."

"Bind them," said Twr. "We shall build the cage around them. It will have no legs, but we can paint a face and form on it. Gather shields, thatch, withies, beams from the palisade: whatever will burn."

"It will not be a true wicker man," said Dardanon doubtfully. "They should be brought to Portskewett and kept for the Queen's enthronement."

"No," said Lysenn hastily. "The reek of them would befoul the day, and cast an ill shadow over Queen Cordelia's reign. Let them die quickly, here in the forest they have so long defiled, before the forest people." Twr nodded.

"Are they to be slain before they burn?" asked Penarddun, keeping her voice as neutral as she could.

"No," said Dardanon. "Let life ascend in the smoke to the nostrils of Ogma."

The four men and the priestess were hauled from the line of prisoners, and bundled together like sticks, a rope run around the whole group of them, seven, eight, nine times. The one who had demanded a trial was weeping and shaking; the woman shouted as she was pushed against the others:

"May you all die as I do! I call on the Mor-Rigan to sow discord in your clans and hearths, and turn your children's hearts against you! May she set the daughter's knife in the mother's breast, the son's foot on his father's neck! May my

251

vengeance feed you to her battlecrows, and make them grow fat upon you!"

Materials were gathered as Twr had ordered, and piled around and over the five captives, until all noise within was muffled. There was no attempt to give shape to the cage, or even to bind it together with more than a perfunctory link of rope here and there to keep it from tumbling down. Dardanon was right, it was no true wicker man: but it would serve its purpose.

When the great heap of wood was done, the rough outline of a man was daubed on one side of it in mud, and handfuls of leaves stuck on to give him hair and a tendrilly beard. The face between the leaves was blank and featureless.

"It will serve," said Dardanon. "Strike a flame."

"There is a fire still smouldering," Falyse pointed out. Twr strode over to it, and snatched up a branch: he blew on it until it glowed bright red-orange, then hurled it onto the wicker man. It sat there, a feeble trickle of smoke struggling up from it. Nothing else seemed to have caught. He swore under his breath: then picked up a broken shield, hacked half in two and left on the ground, and dug it under the burning embers, scooping up ash and charcoal and black logs and still flickering flames all together, and tipped the whole fire onto the heap of wood and thatch. For a minute it seemed as if it would do no more damage than the first branch: but slowly, creepingly, the flames began to spread. Then, suddenly, they were leaping and growing, engulfing the whole structure – and the men inside began to scream.

The noise could not have lasted long, but seemed to go on for ever, and still to echo through the wood when at last they fell silent. Penarddun blinked, and reminded herself of what these five had done. Even through the muffling wood and the roar of the flames, she thought she could distinguish every voice – but none was female. The Mor-Rigan's priestess died in silence. Her curse was spoken, and she had no more to say.

"Ogma, Giver of Eloquence, Speaker of Justice, accept this our sacrifice," Dardanon intoned. The watchers shuffled their feet. Nobody seemed to know what to feel.

"We will not wait to see the end of the fire," said Twr shortly. "We have seen the end of the criminals; that is enough. Turn the man Griant loose and let him be gone. Bind the hands of the prisoners, and make stretchers for the wounded: we are for Portskewett, and the Queen-making."

They were turning to go when Penarddun noticed something on the ground, that had fallen from the priestess' sleeve when she attacked. Puzzled at the way it caught the light, she walked over, and picked it up.

It was blackened and chipped, but still whole: the glass cup that Glóir had given her at the Waters of Sulis six years before. She hugged it to her as if it had been a child; and she did not let it from her hand until they reached Portskewett.

Urganda's Story

When I was a child, King Bladud was my hero. It was inspiring to know that a man of learning, not of war, had become the greatest king of his time – and of course he was always a friend and patron of Avalon. And his travels abroad were mysterious, magical, fascinating. A great deal of nonsense has been talked about them, but I took pains to find out the truth.

He began training as a Druid when he was fifteen, leaving his brother Lludd to be heir to the Silures; who knows how different things would have been if Lludd had lived? Bladud went to the sacred isle of Mona, where his quick wits and capacious memory soon impressed his masters: and in less than a year he was chosen to accompany the British representatives to the great moot of Druids in the Carnutic Forest in central Gaul. He was not, of course, to speak in the debates or give judgments: he was there to listen and learn, and to act as servant to the older Druids: but it was still a very great honour.

The party sailed from Mona to Armorica with fair winds, and there joined with a number of Gaulish Druids for the journey inland. Though many of the tribes in their path were at war, they passed safely and without fear: for none would molest the holy ones on their way to the great gathering. There were gathered Druids from as far afield as Ulaid, Caledonia, Spain, and the Gallic lands south of the Alps: it is not often that so great a moot happens – I have seen only one.

The Carnutes at that time were already trading with the Greek settlers at Marseille, as the tribes further south had long done: and it chanced that there was a party of Greeks at their Queen's hall when the Druids gathered. Among them was one, a philosopher, who had studied in Athens, and had heard a legend that an ancient sage of Greece named Pythagoras had taught the Druidic Order their learning: and he had come with the merchants hoping to learn the truth of this in the Carnutic Forest.

Of course, for one outside the Order, let alone a worshipper of foreign gods, to attend the debates of the Druids at the sacred moot was unheard of. It was dismissed as the greatest of blasphemies: but the Greek was not daunted, and sneaked secretly into the sacred grove to hear the contentions. He was caught, and the Druids would have sentenced him to die: but the Queen and her chiefs argued on the side of mercy. The trade of Marseille was valuable to the Carnutes, and they did not wish to anger the merchants. So there was a heated argument: and then another thing unheard of happened. Bladud, a boy barely begun in his studies, under the strictest instructions to keep silent and leave matters to his elders, spoke up – and he spoke for the Greek. He declared that the learning of the Druids could never progress or grow greater if they isolated themselves from the wisdom of other peoples; that we should learn from the Greeks and teach them in turn.

At last the Druids agreed to forego the execution, on condition that the merchants were exiled from the Carnutic lands for one year, and the philosopher for life. But they decided to send one of their most learned men to Athens to determine whether the Greeks indeed had wisdom worth learning – and Bladud, because of his boldness in the Greek's cause, was chosen to accompany this envoy. They travelled first to Marseille, where Bladud looked first on the wonder of Greek building, and marvelled that men and not gods had made such things. There too he first heard the name of Rome. All talk was of the coming war with Carthage, and what part the Greeks would play. Of Carthage he had heard: their merchants had been buying tin and hides on the south coast of Britain for three hundred years.

From Marseille they shortly thereafter took ship to Athens: but on the way, they had to fight free of a pirate ambush, and the Druid with whom the young prince travelled was mortally wounded. Yet Bladud, rather than return to Gaul, chose to remain in the city, attend the Academy, and learn all he might. There he discussed everything from the transmigration of souls to the reality of the world itself, with men from all over the world – dark-skinned folk from utmost South and furthest East mingled with the Greeks, and shared their wisdom. There too he met Mago and Saron, and was drawn into the secret world of opposition to Rome; and so his studies ended by giving way to war. He fought in Macedonia, in Carthage, and in Lusitania beside the great Viriathos, returning to Britain only when that mighty man was traitorously slain by two of his own warriors. Most folk in Britain may never have heard of Athens, but the name of Viriathos is famous here, and songs are still sung of his defiance of Rome.

It is not true that Bladud returned in disguise, nor that he became an ordinary swineherd. Alaron's pigs were sacred, and the care of them was a ceremonial duty of high place –

worthy of a Druid prince. And when the goddess healed him, he and Alaron were married. They had no thought to kingship, until after his brother Lludd was murdered, and nobody but they could save the Silures from collapse and the whole of the West from bloody war. They named their first child Lludd in honour of the dead king: and not long thereafter King Bladud led a shipload of men back to Lusitania to aid in the war there, as he had sworn he would. But the Romans had at last mastered the terrain, and cut them off from their Celtiberian allies; they were defeated and harried, and only a miserable few returned to Britain, in an open boat. They survived storms that should have swamped them a hundred times: and in gratitude to the sea god, Bladud renamed his young son, in honour of the sea. So Lludd became Llyr. He had Alaron's fair colouring, as his daughters would: so striking among the black-haired Silures; and from what I hear he was a sweet child.

They brought Llyr to Avalon with them once, to receive the blessing of the Lady, my mother. He was then a child, Gogoniant an infant, and I not yet born. Did he think then of how he would return: Of seizing Gogoniant, carrying her off like a sack of corn so that he could call himself "Penteyrnedd": I hate the word. he has corrupted it beyond all meaning. Avalon is better without it.

The Belgic invaders never came this far: but they provided cover for Llyr nonetheless. After Bladud's death, Llyr had moved quickly to take power in Siluria and wipe out all who stood in his way: then, while my father and the war host of the Durotriges were massing to defend our southeastern front in case the Belgae should come there, he fell upon

257

Avalon. He did not burn us out or commit great slaughter – he had not come for that. He had come for Gogoniant and the name of Penteyrnedd – a title to impress the tribes beyond Severn, and a claim to the favour of a goddess whose home he had sacked. They came silently, by night, up the river, and around the hill from its shadowed side, away from the path: and they cut a rat-hole in the palisade and poured in through it. Yes, they smashed open houses, seized gold, slew those who resisted them – but from the beginning they were looking for Gogoniant. By the time I woke up, they had found her: and Llyr was standing in the moonlight before the hall, declaring himself, and informing us that nobody would take any more hurt if we allowed them to depart. Gogoniant was sobbing, and shivering; he had her by the wrist and was gripping as if he meant to twist her hand off.

My mother had her sword in her hand, but she dared not attack. The danger to Gogoniant was too great. Oh, he'd not have killed her if he could help it, but he could have cut off a hand or a foot before anyone could come nigh him, and none dared take the chance that he would not. So he hauled her out of Avalon, and went back to his ship, warning us not to follow. His chiefs, I believe, would have had him rape her on the ship that night to make good his title: but he played a slow game, eased her captivity bit by bit, and seduced her by small concessions – or so I guess, for she denied that he had ever been brutal. I know that she came to accept him, cleave to him, she might have said love him – but she would not be the first slave to love her chains because they have grown lighter. I judge neither her nor Penarddun. I have never been a captive, let alone endured what they had to.

Gogoniant never came to Avalon again. My mother hardly spoke of her, and when she did spoke as if she had died that night. She never said that I was to be the Lady, not in as many words, but I was sent as soon as might be to train as a Druid, and I often overheard mutterings about making me a suitable marriage – though whether they meant a man who would challenge Llyr for the title of Penteyrnedd, or one who would not, I do not know. I enjoyed my training: I spent time at many holy places, including the Waters of Sulis, where I was taken under the wing of Glóir. She spoke much of Alaron and Bladud, and how grievously Llyr was betraying their legacy of justice: and it was she who inspired me to follow in Bladud's footsteps, and go over the sea. I had some wild ideas of travelling to Athens like Bladud; but in the meantime Gaul was far enough – I wanted to see the Carnutic Forest, learn from the Gaulish Druids, perhaps meet Greeks as Bladud had and discourse of their philosophy – although Glóir warned me of a peculiarity the Greeks had, that they would not discuss such ideas with a woman. Bladud had shaken his head much over the fact that a people in other matters so wise should entertain so foolish a prejudice, but had found that the Academy not only excluded women, but taught that the female mind was entirely incapable of grasping the concepts they studied there. But I had a young girl's naive hope that I should be the one to enlighten them.

I chose the wrong year to travel.

I had barely arrived in the lands of the Carnutes when the great German tide swept into Gaul. The Cimbri and Teutons, their own lands in the far north hit with famine, had migrated south through Germany, picking up adherents from many other tribes along the way. They had invaded Roman Noricum and won great victories: if they had pressed on then to Italy, Gaul would have been spared and Rome might have fallen. But for whatever reason, they had turned west, and had crossed the Alps into Gaul. They wanted land – peacefully if it was to be had so, but they were prepared to fight for it. A massive council of the Gaulish tribes was called. Some were for fighting, others for accommodation: but it had occurred to many that the richest lands in Gaul were those in the warm south, ruled by the Romans and their allies. Many with a grudge against Rome or against Roman-aligned tribes urged that the Germans should be pointed southwards – and not a few Gauls were eager to join them. They had charismatic leaders, chief among them the gigantic warrior Teutobod, whose war-hammer could fell a charging aurochs: and both chiefs and Druids were divided. It was decided that a man of princely lineage should be sacrificed, to read the spatters of his blood. One was found who had lately been deposed for oppressive exactions upon his people, and was handed over to the justice of the Druids: and his blood foretold victory for the Germans. Therefore it was with as many Gauls as Germans and Alpine tribesfolk at their back that they invaded the Roman Narbonnais: and Druids joined with the German Wicca-women to read the will of the gods and determine their course. I was among them.

I shall not weary you with the course of that war – the great victories, the Roman Consuls slain, the long oppressed southern Gauls who rallied to us. It suffices to say that I saw in that time the best and worst of man; and that we enjoyed many years of victory, but the tide finally turned against us.

The Teutons separated from the rest: they were surprised and slaughtered, and Teutobod sent in chains to Rome, where they paraded him through the streets in triumph then strangled him with a cord. The Cimbri and their allies, ignoring the warnings of the Wicce, invaded Italy in search of vengeance: but what they met was annihilation. I was not with them. I had lost a lover when the Teutons fell – Gweledydd's father; his name does not matter now. When the portents foretold that the invasion would fail, I instead joined a riverboat heading down the Rhine, and from the Belgic coast took ship to Britain.

I did not know, when I left the Cimbrian army, that I was with child. I was sure enough by the time I had made landfall and was on the road home to Avalon, and I was glad – my firstborn would come into the world in that holy place, in the sight of Latis and Afallach, as Gogoniant's should have done. I wondered if she had children: I had heard of none before I had left Britain. Of course, the Silures were not anxious to let word of her miscarriages be spread around the West. But I came home to find my mother dying. In a few short years she had aged by decades; she wheezed when she breathed, and could barely walk. She wept for joy to see me again, to hold me, and to lay her hands on my belly: and at last she said what she had not in all those years when I was learning the ways of the Druids:

"Take up the rule of Avalon when I am gone. Serve the gods as Lady of the Lake."

I made no promise, but let her think that I would. But I never meant to. Gogoniant was the elder, and the first wed, and if she had no daughter yet, she still might. She had been the Lady since that terrible night, though my mother had

261

continued to exercise the Lady's authority in the Durotrigan lands: and only she had any right to relinquish that title. From her I might have accepted it; from my mother, I could not. It was not hers to give.

She lasted only a few more days. Gogoniant should have been there to see her laid in earth: instead, I conducted the ceremony, and thanked the gods for receiving her into the Otherworld which is the true Land of the Living. But when it was over, I knew what I had to do. I had to go to Portskewett, and soon, before I was too far gone to travel: and I had to ask the sister I had not seen in a lifetime to take up her duties, and be the Lady of the Lake.

I might not have been the Lady, but I travelled in all the Lady's state to Portskewett. The Deepwood was safe in those days – Darnant had not yet come out of the East to plague it – and my train passed through it unmolested. We had sent runners ahead to announce ourselves, though not our mission: and we expected to be welcomed in style. Welcomed we were – Llyr did not turn me away that time; he had some fear of the gods – but grudgingly, and with small ceremony. Goll was then a young Druid, not long admitted to the Order: he had barely a year's seniority over me: but he, rather than Llyr, oversaw our welcome. We had already seen our horses stabled and been allotted lodgings ourselves before we even saw the King; and even then the Queen was not with him.

It was with dark forebodings that I asked where my sister was – but the answer was joyous. She was with child, no more than a few days from her time, and was laid up in bed – indeed, both Llyr and Goll assumed that was why I had come. That was why they had been suspicious: they feared that, if the child should be a girl, I meant to spirit her away and raise her in Avalon. In the end, I had to do that because the child was born a boy.

Many tears were shed when I met Gogoniant again: and that very night, while I was with her, her pangs came on. It was a difficult birth, and she spoke to me in whispered sobs of the children she had lost, and her fears that it would happen again; but I gripped her hand and helped her through, and though I feared at one time to lose them both, both lived, and Ardian was born healthy, male – and a dwarf. Gogoniant cared nothing: she kissed the boy over and over, and praised the Three Mothers for giving him to her: but I knew that the King would not see it so. A halfling daughter Llyr might have accepted; but Ardian was his firstborn son.

When the King was told, he did not rage as I had feared; he trembled, and then wept. But when his eyes were dry again, he was adamant. He felt himself shamed by the boy's existence, and would not pass him through the oak or even give him a name. He commanded that he be taken to the Deepwood and there exposed to the weather and wild beasts. Gogoniant screamed, begged, even struck him, but he would not be moved. Then I spoke. I said that I would take the child, and that they would never hear of him again. Gogoniant was quieted: I think at first hearing my offer felled her, and before she could summon the strength to turn her rage on me, she had realised that I meant him no harm. I will allow that Llyr probably knew it too: he did not press me on what fate I meant for the child. He was content enough that he should disappear from Siluria and be given out as dead. No doubt he expected me to keep the secret of his true birth: well, let him expect *what he liked. But before I departed, I insisted on one thing: the boy must be named, and by his parents. So he became Ardian; it was Gogoniant who chose the name, but Llyr gave it to him. There was a strange tenderness in the High King's eyes when I departed with the child; he was a father, and nature will sometimes sway a brute heart.*

It was given out west of the Deepwood that Ardian had lived a few days and perished; and I brought the little bundle to Avalon, and there brought him up alongside Gweledydd, who was born a few months later. But I never deceived him about his birth. From the first he knew that he was my nephew, and a prince; and when he was old enough I told him the full story. It nigh broke his heart. He had always known how cruel the world could be to people like him, but had scarcely felt it, for he lived in Avalon, under my protection.

Had he been willing, I would have trained him as a Druid, as I did with Gweledydd. But though he was eager to read Ogham and to know the secrets of the stars, he had no desire to dedicate himself to the gods – nor had he any hope that kings or chiefs outside Avalon would take him seriously or abide by his judgement. Few of our secrets are open to those outside the Order, but I have bent my vows as far as possible to educate Ardian in the manner he desired. Though he is not likely to take up any chief's service, he is in name a bard: for they, at least, are permitted some Druidic privileges.

"It is fitting", he said once, "that I should be only half a Druid, when I'm only half the size of one." He can discourse as learnedly as any Druid I have known, though only with me or Gweledydd – he is wary of revealing his learning to outsiders.

He was taught also smithery, hunting skills, and such forms of combat as his condition would allow. It has always been both his wish and mine that he should be as well fitted as possible to survive outside Avalon, should he need to do so – though he has had little desire ever to leave since Llys took up with him. As a youth he was very shy with girls he liked: he found it difficult to believe that any could have an interest in him: but she pursued him, and won him, and made him hers – and she protects him as would a mother bear.

So good has come from the disordered reign of Llyr. Ardian is happier here than if he had grown up as Prince of the Silures; there is a Lady of the Lake once more, and she is a Queen honoured throughout the West; the Penteyrnedd has doffed that foolish title and all claim to rule over the free chiefs of the Durotriges, let alone other tribes. And the next Lady is here in Avalon, where she belongs – and she is the sweetest child I have known since Ardian and Gweledydd were small. There is peace now among all the tribes, and even the Belgae are bound by ties of alliance to old houses of Britain; and the Deepwood, so long contaminated by Darnant, is clean at last.

I am glad that I have lived to see this springtide; may it lead to a happy summer.

Chapter 23: *Spring*

"When that King Leir was dead, Cordeil his youngest daughter
held and had the land."

~ *The Prose Brut*

Avalon, 77 B.C.E.

The acclamation of Cordelia as Queen had been
unanimous: and she and Diviciacus made progress through
the West, visiting Maglor and the Demetian princes, and the
new King of the Ordovices – and praying for the shades of Llyr
and her sisters. Penarddun remained the while at Portskewett
with her children, before wintering with Cordelia at Gray Hill:
and when Imbolc came, they travelled together to Avalon, to a
gathering of princes from far and wide, called by Diviciacus
before he should return to Gaul, to acknowledge Cordelia as
the Lady, and little Urganda as her heir.

The elder Urganda, still strong and bright of eye, made
them welcome, and threw a feast which lasted many days, all
the chiefs of the Durotriges contributing hogs and calves.

Thither came Imanuentius and Ydorus, the Queen
whose low birth had turned so many chiefs against him;
Nennius and his Belgic warrior wife Lydore, with the four
captains; Fesonas, the sister Penarddun had not seen in so
many years, and Pir, her husband; even little Vellaunos, her
youngest brother. Delyn ferch Darnant, whom Nennius and
Lydore had taken under their protection, came with them: for
the first time Penarddun saw her smiling, a cracked, crooked
expression, as if she were desperately unpractised in it.
Aganippus and his shield-bearer Denapol, Picell with the new

Speaker of the Dobunni, Glóir from the Waters of Sulis, Gandales from far Scilly, envoys from the Dumnonii and from the tribes to the north, were all there. Perillus, walking with a stick but healthy again, Scaliger, forgiven for his betrayals and reconciled with all, Awel, openly proclaimed as the Merlin, were in as high honour as the princes; and Penarddun did not have to press hard to secure a promise that Falyse, Sicora, and Mefus would be treated as if they were her sisters.

The Demetic princes flaunted their fertility, Pwyll showing off the heavily pregnant Rhiannon, and Perion his sons: Elisena's wide-eyed, inquisitive boy Amadis, and Tungra's plump little blond lad, who had been given a Germanic name from his mother's people, Florestan. Perion seemed rather put out that Penarddun had four children to display, and dropped heavy hints that Elisena was pregnant again.

As for her four, who she had worried would be unequal to the pomp and attention after having lived such hidden lives, she was relieved to find that they took naturally to it, loving their fine clothes and the cooing of so many women; even the twins stopped fighting for a little while, under Mefus' benevolent influence.

A mock battle was fought, a dozen Belgic princes in green cloaks against a dozen Britons in white. The Britons were ultimately victorious, and all ended in jovial comradeship: although Perion of the Demetae had stormed off the field after being disarmed by Denapol, he was at last pacified.

At last came the moment when Urganda, holding Excalibur before her, asked if any knew of any reason why it should not be passed to Cordelia.

Dardanon cleared his throat.

"There is the matter of the Lady's marriage," he said. "King Aganippus has a realm to rule in Gaul, and the future

Lady Urganda is to live here while her mother rules in Portskewett: how can both Avalon and the Silures have an heir? All others of the House of Llyr are dead or princes of rival tribes."

Cordelia was unabashed, and her answer, when she gave it, sounded almost rehearsed: Penarddun was sure afterwards that she and Dardanon had planned this together.

"Is it not the law," she said evenly, "that, even as a king may have more than one wife, a reigning queen may take as many husbands as she please?"

"It is," agreed Dardanon: his voice was grave, but his arch expression, cocking his left eyebrow, belied it. "It is rarely practised: great princes prefer to know whose children they are raising."

"But there will be no question of that if I remain in Gaul," Aganippus pointed out. "Let it be known that, what Queen Cordelia does, she does with my blessing." He glanced sidelong at Denapoll, who smiled back at him.

"Who, then, is to be Penteyrnedd?" asked Dardanon.

"Nobody," replied Cordelia. "That title has wrought too much bloodshed. The 'prince of princes' was never meant to be a High King, only the Lady's co-justice and battle leader of the Durotriges, and his title should reflect that. He shall be named henceforth for the dragon, the symbol of Avalon, and shall be called Pendragon."

"And have you chosen a... Pendragon?" asked Dardanon.

"I have, by private consent of the chiefs of the Silures, my husband Aganippus, the priestesses of Avalon, and not least the man I have chosen," said Cordelia. "Stand forth."

Picell of the Dobunni stepped up, and took her hand. There was a brief silence: then Penarddun, smiling broadly, began to applaud – and soon all the gathering had joined in, and were shouting Picell's name. When the noise died down, Urganda signed to her priestesses, and they began to sing.

> "Thou art a shelter in heat and cold,
> Eyes to the blind, to the halt a staff,
> A rock at sea, a fort on land,
> Thou mak'st the sick rise and the sad to laugh.
>
> "Thine is the skill of the Fairy Queen,
> Thine is the beauty of Eithne fair,
> Thine the calm of Bride serene,
> Thine the courage of Macha rare.
>
> "Thou art the joy of all joyous things,
> Thou art the light of the beam of the sun,
> Thou art the kind host's open door,
> Thou art our lodestar, our all, our one.
>
> "Thou art the step of the hind on hill,
> Thou art the step of the steed on plain,
> Thou art the grace of the gliding swan,
> Fair as sunlight and soft as rain.
>
> "The best hour of the day be thine,
> The best day of the week be thine,
> The best week of the year be thine,
> The best year in the world be thine."

Cordelia took the sword from Urganda, and girded it onto Picell: then she signed to Awel to step up and join them. Taking his right hand in her left and Picell's left in her right, she raised both aloft: and Urganda declared:

"Hail to the Lady, the Pendragon, and the Merlin! The blessings of Latis and Afallach be upon them, now and for ever!"

Penarddun clutched Bran and Branwen to her. Her eyes were brimming with joyful tears; she felt for the first time as if all fear was banished from her heart.

Spring had come at last.

FINIS.

A note on Ardian

I hesitated in giving Ardian the royal heritage I have done, for fear of appearing derivative of *A Song of Ice and Fire*. I therefore feel the need to explain his origins.

My Ardian is a composite of two characters. Ardian in the Amadis romances is a dwarf of the mythical variety, originally a servant of Urganda's; while Puignet in *Perceforest* is, like my Ardian, a person of restricted growth. (I am aware of the sensitivities surrounding the word "dwarf" in this context, but any currently accepted phrase would have been too anachronistic to get away with.) Combining them was an obvious step, as two Avalon-associated little people in the same generation seemed too much for plausibility. When I first decided to do this, I had no thought to making him a son of Llyr: but then I noticed something.

Puignet is described as the first cousin of Sebile, the character from *Perceforest* on whom Gweledydd in this novel is partly based – and my Gweledydd is Llyr's niece by marriage. To preserve this relationship I needed either to invent new characters to be Ardian / Puignet's parents, or to make him the son of Llyr and Gogoniant. The former route would have further expanded an already sprawling cast and added new digressions to my plot; the latter was both neater, and far more interesting dramatically, adding extra facets to several characters and their relationships: and ultimately I could not resist it. So Ardian became a prince.

How I have used sources

The process of weaving together disparate romances and myths into a single whole within an historical framework has not been a simple one. A glance at my protagonist's own immediate family will show the complexity of the identifications I have undertaken. Penarddun has four surviving siblings: leaving aside her youngest brother Vellaunos, of whom more will be heard in later books, we have Imanuentius, Nennius, and Fesonas.

Imanuentius is an historical Trinovantic king, but his family is unknown. However, when I decided that the best way to reconcile the legendary genealogies with the sketchy known history of the British tribes was to make Belin (more commonly known as Beli, but I have gone with the more euphonious and probably older form) a ruler of the Trinovantes, Imanuentius naturally became his son. Nennius and Penarddun do both appear as Belin's children in Welsh tradition, though they are never mentioned together.

On top of this, I have identified them all with characters from *Perceforest* – Imanuentius with Perceforest himself, Nennius with his brother Gadifer, and Penarddun with the originally unrelated character Sarra. Thus, Fesonas – Perceforest's sister in the romance – enters the story. Many, if not most, other characters are similarly indebted to multiple sources.

Myths and the gods

Students of Celtic mythology may have noticed that I have played around somewhat with the mythological backstory here, if less than with the main story. There is a simple reason for this: the myths of the British Celts survive only in late, fragmentary, heavily Christianised forms. We can strip away the accretions of romance that overlay them, work in what little we know from archaeology and Greek and Roman sources, and (more usefully) search for parallels in the closely related and much better preserved mythology of Ireland: but ultimately we still see only glimpses of the tales the Britons told. For the purposes of fiction, I have had to undertake some reconstructive work, drawing on those later romantic additions as well as on ancient sources and Irish analogues, in order to give a sense of cohesive mythological belief to the society I have depicted.

www.ingramcontent.com/pod-product-compliance
Lightning Source LLC
Chambersburg PA
CBHW060532260626
47161CB00003B/872